The Borrowdale Body

By Rebecca Tope

The Borrowdale Body

REBECCA TOPE

Allison & Busby Limited
11 Wardour Mews
London W1F 8AN
allisonandbusby.com

First published in Great Britain by Allison & Busby in 2024.
This paperback edition published by Allison & Busby in 2024.

A CIP catalogue record for this book is available from
the British Library.

10 9 8 7 6 5 4 3 2 1

ISBN 978-0-7490-3171-8

Typeset in 10.5/15 pt Sabon LT Pro by
Allison & Busby Ltd.

By choosing this product, you help take care of the world's forests.
Learn more: www.fsc.org.

Printed and bound by
CPI Group (UK) Ltd, Croydon, CR0 4YY

For old friends Liz, Sally, Margot and Mary

And with thanks to Prue Harrison for such great friendship and help on the ground

Author's Note

As with other titles in this series, the story is set in real places, but High Gates House is an invention.

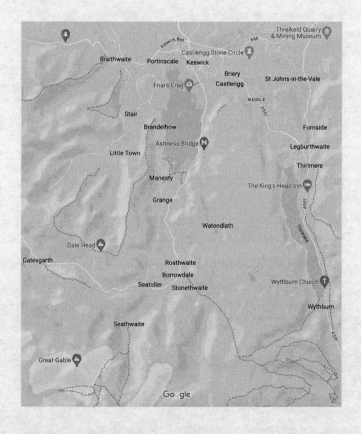

Prologue

'Superb!' breathed Christopher Henderson to himself as he stood alone on the bridge at Grange in Borrowdale and looked up and over to the right at the very handsome house he had come to inspect. He could only see half of it in the jumble of rock and wall and river that typified the landscape in this spot. The bridge itself was a thing of beauty. The road that crossed it veered around a succession of bends, bringing a three-dimensional slideshow of surprising views to the traveller. Christopher had never been here before.

High Gates House was built of dark Lakeland stone, and stood apart from the tiny village, as so many such proud mansions did across the whole region. Its history was a chequered one, with rises and falls and ultimate decline into shabbiness under the care of its latest resident. Christopher had done his homework and had a basic grasp of events leading to its unhappy current state.

Grange was barely five miles from Christopher's auction house in Keswick, and yet he had barely been conscious of its existence until now. The Borrowdale valley – some romantically called it a glen – was a world apart, reserved for walkers and birdwatchers. Great crags loomed above it, the steep sides unusually well adorned with properly indigenous trees, as opposed to the conifers that had been planted elsewhere. At the end of April, the different shades of delicate new leaves were a painter's delight.

The house had a grandeur that shouted money and influence, even through the shadows of its unhappy recent state. It was providing Christopher with the most exciting house clearance sale of his career so far. The contents of twenty rooms and more were to be transported to the auction house in Keswick and a special sale devoted to selling it all. His staff – two of them taken on specifically for this undertaking – would have to work overtime to catalogue everything, and extra drivers and vans employed to convey it all. People must be found who knew how to handle delicate porcelain, marble busts, tattered first editions and faded pictures behind fragile glass. Every rug, every aged teddy bear, every cup and plate and fork and spoon had to go. There would be issues of security, and reams of inventory.

He had left his car briefly on a patch of gravel beside a sign telling him not to park. It had seemed necessary to get a sense of the place before diving into business. Now he got back in and drove the short distance to High Gates, winding along a small road that led northwards towards Derwentwater. A motorbike came whizzing round a bend, missing him by a whisker. 'Shouldn't be allowed,' Christopher muttered to himself. A car was parked at one side of a wide entrance to the driveway to an invisible house, and another had squeezed itself onto a verge that was much too narrow for it. In another month, the traffic would be a source of rage on all sides, even in this remote valley.

Strictly speaking, he had left the real Borrowdale behind him, but the crags on his left were impressive enough to make him feel small. At the front of the house there was space for four or five cars. Later in the year, desperate tourists would venture to park there, ignoring signs and cones. Anyone could see the place was uninhabited.

Inside the house, his first impression was of a wholesale presence of dust. It covered every surface and even coated the walls. The furniture had not been covered with white sheets, as he had half expected, but sat as if asleep or frozen. All that was needed was a magic wand for it all to come alive again. Drawers and cupboards were filled with the paraphernalia of daily life, as well as the trappings of opulence. The rugs were best quality, the pictures genuine oils and watercolours. In the study, a wall of shelves contained books that someone had actually wanted to read. Novels, histories, reference works and a magnificent big atlas all attracted Christopher's interest. A lower shelf held stacks of very old magazines – *Punch* and *The Illustrated London News* going back well over a hundred years.

The last owner of the house – Sir John Hickory – had died in a room upstairs six months before, and from that time on, the house had been shut up and abandoned to the machinations of professionals who sent emails and made phone calls, but seldom went near the place itself. Sir John's heir – a remote relative who had been hard to locate – had instructed it to be advertised just as it was and had been quite content with the three million pounds that had been offered for it. Christopher was the last in a long chain of personnel engaged in the transfer of ownership of everything the childless Sir John had possessed, and still the whole procedure had some way to go.

Sir John had been a peer of the realm, last in a not-very-long line of mill-owners and engineers. They had made money easily in the decades preceding World War One and built the house almost absent-mindedly, because that was what you did. An only child, John had reluctantly married another only child, and between them they failed to produce an heir. Poor Ruth suffered five miscarriages before removing herself from the marital bed and dying before she was forty. 'I feel like Henry VIII,' Sir John had sighed.

Christopher mused on all this as he explored the rooms and their multifarious contents. Tomorrow the real work would begin, and all he had to do now was make a rough assessment of exactly what would be required. His thoughts turned to families and inheritance and his own situation. His wife, Simmy, had given him a son, for which he was suitably grateful. The child was altogether wonderful, and they were currently engaged on trying for another. It was so far not going well. Simmy was pessimistic about their chances and impatient with his reassurances.

'You know I'm really not very good at this,' she reminded him. Her first child had been stillborn, and she was now convinced she was too old to manage any more. They lived in a converted barn in Hartsop just south of Ullswater. The property had been almost magically given to them by a distressed woman who only wanted to escape the area quickly and sever all ties. It suited them very nicely, but there were moments when Christopher felt he might have preferred to choose a place for himself. Hartsop was a cul-de-sac in more ways than one.

And then there were days like this when he got to see the inside of a neglected mansion, which was every bit as thrilling as walking into Aladdin's cave would have been. It was more than he could absorb on his own, and instinctively he took his phone out and called his wife.

Chapter One

Just over a month later, Simmy was not having a very good day. An unexpected east wind forced her to go home again to collect a jumper, having set out for a brief walk with her child and dog. Robin was showing no signs of being chilly, but the dog was hunched up and reproachful.

It was not her turn to do the walk in the first place. Christopher had defaulted, thanks to the huge clearance sale he was embroiled in. Instead of taking his usual Tuesday off, he had worked every day that week, and into the evenings. Simmy felt abandoned and resentful. Robin was cutting a recalcitrant tooth and Cornelia was in the last few days of her first heat.

'I never imagined a dog could be hormonal,' Simmy grumbled, having found the whole thing much more trying than anyone had ever warned her. She was in much the same state herself, depressed at the confirmation that once again she wasn't pregnant.

It was the last day of May and the Lakeland gardens were displaying competitive levels of flamboyant azaleas, cherries and other flowering things. As a florist herself, Simmy felt intimidated by the unrestrained burgeoning of colour. Business at the shop was slow, after the excesses of Mother's Day and Easter. People were less eager to arrange flowers in their houses when everything was so exuberant outside.

The clearance sale had been all-consuming for the past two weeks. But the two-day event was finally upon them, starting in three days' time and Simmy was determined to be there. It was the event of a lifetime, after all. Sir John Hickory had captured her imagination and she envied her husband his involvement with so much fabulous treasure. She had wanted to go to Grange with him on one of the many trips to transport the house's content to the saleroom, but there had never been a good moment. After all, the Borrowdale valley itself merited a proper inspection – something her father had been saying for years, in vain until now.

'But you need to climb Castle Crag, see the Lodore Falls, visit the mill, look at the church at Grange,' he enthused. 'I spent three days there in a tent about thirteen years ago.'

'I'll do it properly one day,' Simmy had promised. 'But at this rate I'm only going to get a quick glimpse, if Christopher ever takes me with him. He talks about it all the time, but I've still never been.'

Russell Straw suppressed his frustration. There had been a time when his daughter had gone with him on his walks amongst the crags and fells, before she had a baby and got married and everything changed. His wife had never been as enthusiastic about wide open spaces, and her knees were not what they once were.

But Christopher belatedly had an idea that would go part of the way to satisfying both his wife and his father-in-law.

'Come with me tomorrow,' he invited Simmy. 'I've got to go through the house one last time, before we send the keys back. The lads can't promise that they went through absolutely every cupboard and there might yet be corners of the cellar to look at. Jack said he thought it might have been partitioned off at some point, with more areas to explore. I never got round to checking. Mind you, if we do find anything, it'll be too late to go in the sale. We printed the catalogue three days ago.'

Simmy hesitated. 'You don't want me to do any skivvying, do you? I'm not going to be there as an unpaid cleaner?'

He stared at her in mock horror. 'Perish the thought! What an idea! The place isn't our responsibility in any way. I was actually going to suggest we make a real little outing of it and have lunch at the cafe there. Besides, you keep saying you wish you could have seen the house – not to mention the whole area. Here's your chance. It'll make your dad happy too. He thinks it's an outrage that you've never been there.'

'Sorry,' she said. 'But it will be all bare and scruffy now, won't it? Faded patches where the pictures were, and everything sad. No carpets or curtains. Poor house.'

'Actually, a few of the curtains are still there. You're right about it being sad, though. I saw Fiona having a little cry over some of the lots, last week. It's the man's whole life, all laid out and catalogued. There is something horrible about it. People keep saying so. I doubt if it'll put them off buying the stuff, all the same.'

Simmy had heard a great deal about the chief items going under Christopher's hammer – a marble bust, paintings, collections of porcelain, rare books, Pacific Island carvings. Excitement had spread all around the world, enquiries and commission bids coming in great numbers. Two extra people had been shipped in to handle all the work.

'And yet he wasn't particularly rich,' Christopher mused. 'It was his grandfather who collected most of the good stuff a hundred years ago or more. He must have been in the right places at the right times and had a good eye. The things from the Far East are amazing. All Sir John did was give it house room. His main interest seems to have been local history, and that was only after he retired.'

'It's all amazing, according to Ben,' said Simmy. Ben Harkness was nineteen and a university dropout. The thrills of an auction house had provided ample consolation for the disappointments of academe.

'This could be the making of him. He's going to learn more this month than I did in two years.'

'So you'll come with me?' he prompted, a few moments later.

'Of course I will. Just try to stop me.'

She prepared for the excursion by phoning her father and asking for hints as to what to look out for in Borrowdale.

'I can't believe you've never been there,' he said, not for the first time. 'Pity I can't come with you, but I've got an eye test. I've got a pretty fair grasp of the Hickory history, though.'

'I should have gone before this, I know,' she replied readily. 'So now I'm making up for it.'

'It's a glen,' he began. 'With a hazy history. It was always regarded as inaccessible, until a century or so ago. Grange is lovely. It's at the northern end. There's a remarkably comprehensive display, all about it, in the Wesleyan chapel by the bridge. I saw it last year. Gives you an excellent overview, but it takes a while to read everything.'

'No time for that. I phoned you instead. Christopher wants to show me High Gates and then have lunch. We'll have the baby and the dog with us.'

Russell sighed loudly. 'So, what do you want me to tell you?'

'Just what's special about it, I suppose. All I know is that Grange is close to Derwentwater and has a good bridge.'

'Let me think, then. Sounds as if you're not going to be seeing much of the real Borrowdale. But Grange itself is interesting. The main thing I remember is the woodland on the north side. A brilliant tree cover, right to the top of the fell – shows you what it could all be like if they took the sheep away.'

'Christopher already mentioned the trees.'

'Oh. Well, there was a woman, Margaret Something, who built the church and the school and lived in that big hotel when it wasn't a hotel, and did all sorts of influential things.'

'Would Sir John have known her?'

'Don't be daft. She died in the 1880s. But he might have known people who remembered her, I suppose. Just.'

'Barely,' said Simmy sceptically. 'They'd have to be born in the 1870s.'

'So? They'd have still been alive in the 1950s, and your Sir John was born about 1935. That works, doesn't it?'

'Only if he lived there all his life.'

'He did, you idiot. That's the whole point. I thought you

knew all this. His great-grandfather built the house, and now there's nobody to follow on, which is why everything's being sold. End of the line. Tragic. There must have been a time when the house was full of family and servants. They lost three sons in the First World War, but still struggled on. Surely Christopher's explained the story to you?'

'Not really. Or if he did, I wasn't paying proper attention. I've always had trouble with ancient history, as you know.'

'This is *recent* history, Sim. Which you should probably bear in mind. There could be people around who hold strong views and passionate feelings about the whole business. The sale of a prominent property like that will rock quite a lot of boats.'

'Don't say that,' begged Simmy, aware of a throbbing premonition that the Borrowdale business might well prove all too memorable.

Chapter Two

The weather that day was unreliable, but Christopher insisted that it would improve. 'It won't stop the hikers,' he said. 'They don't like it too hot.'

They drove out of Keswick, and onto small roads that defied any attempt to maintain a sense of direction.

'I got lost the first time I came,' Christopher admitted. 'Went round in a big circle. Then I thought I was facing south when it was actually north.'

'I'm not surprised. Half the signs are hidden behind clumps of cow parsley. I would have turned right here.'

'This is the crucial one. Well spotted. Most people get the bus, apparently. There's nowhere to park in Grange.'

Three miles further on, they noticed a bus stop near a turning into Grange itself. Simmy duly admired the double-humped bridge and the lavish covering of trees.

'Where's Borrowdale, exactly?' she asked. 'If this is Grange.'

'It's no single spot. The real drama is to the south of here – Honister Pass and some sort of museum. If you go north along the side of Derwentwater, you don't see much of Borrowdale, I suppose. That's what we'll be doing. People keep talking about how remote and mysterious it is. Have you heard of Hugh Walpole?'

'I think not.'

'Nor had I until Jack started on about him. He wrote novels set here. It's a family saga, sort of thing, very popular in its day.'

'I never had Jack down as a reader.'

'I think it's more his wife, actually. But he's pretty clued up about the local area and the history.'

'When did the Walpole man write his books, then?'

'Must have been in the twenties, I guess. We can google him if you're interested.'

'I'll leave it to my dad – although he probably knows it all already. I'm surprised he hasn't got round to giving me a little lecture all about him.'

'Ta-da!' sang Christopher suddenly, bringing the car to a halt. On the back seat, the child and the dog both jerked into alert interest. 'How about that, then?'

The house was constructed of the dark local slate, the deep grey sometimes glowing blue in certain lights. Well proportioned, it had a timeless dignity and confidence that inspired a kind of awe. 'Gosh!' said Simmy.

'Isn't it superb! When I first saw it from the bridge, that's the word that came to me.'

'It looks as if it's always been here. It's better than the other one we passed, lower down.'

'Borrowdale Gates – yes. Mind you, that's a handsome building as well. The Heathcote woman had it built. I was reading about her the other day.'

'She must be the one my dad was talking about. He says she's crucial to the history of the place.'

'I think he's right. She must have come here quite often. She and Hugh Walpole and Arthur Ransome and Beatrix Potter. Except I have a feeling they weren't all alive at the same time. Your dad would know, I suppose.'

'Indubitably. It's lucky we've got at least one historian in the family. I get a headache as soon as I try to imagine how it must have been two centuries ago. It all goes blurry in my mind when he tries to explain it.'

'You need a sense of history when you work with antiques,' said Christopher pompously. 'But I have to admit I'm a slow learner.'

They drove through the gateway, where one gate was so askew that any attempt at closing it had long been abandoned. The other was upright, but its black paint was peeling badly. Simmy looked up at the great house in front of her. It seemed to have been built right into the rock face, looking east as far as she could tell. 'Derwentwater's that way, is it?' she asked, pointing vaguely.

'More or less. There's a good view of it from the top floor.'

'Poor house. It looks so neglected.'

'I know. It's a miracle it wasn't burgled while it still had all its contents. I suppose nobody really knew about it. Everything was handled very quietly until we'd shifted most of the stuff. It's been bedlam since then.'

'Tell me about it,' said Simmy with heartfelt resentment. 'I've hardly seen you this last fortnight.'

'Soon be over,' he assured her. Then he sighed. 'It's been a real roller-coaster ride. I'm going to be sorry when it stops.'

'Which is why we're making this sentimental journey for one last look,' she summarised. 'What'll happen to it now?'

'Almost certain to be turned into a hotel. New bathrooms everywhere, windows replaced, probably new floors as well. There's plenty of scope.'

'Not much space for cars, though. Where's everybody going to park?'

'They'll work something out. There's more space than you think.' He looked at the two youngsters on the back seat and said, 'We can leave Cornelia for a bit. It won't be too hot for her.'

They all – except for the dog – got out of the car and approached the front door. Simmy felt as if she was intruding where she had no right to be. Christopher took an old-fashioned key from his pocket and operated the single lock halfway down the door.

'Haven't seen a door like this for a while,' he said with a laugh. 'I'd almost forgotten they could be so simple.'

Their own front door in Hartsop had been installed in place of the wide opening it had possessed when a barn. It had a fancy system designed for maximum security that both Simmy and Christopher faintly disliked. For a start, it needed two hands to get the door open, which was never convenient.

'The past was a better country,' said Simmy, quoting her father. 'They did things more easily there.'

'Which is a lesson I've been learning ever since I took this job,' her husband agreed. 'It applies to almost everything. I often wish I'd been born a century earlier.'

She looked at him with interest. 'Do you?'

'Well, I have been lately. I think it might have something to do with Sir John and this place, actually. I've got foolishly fond of it.'

'Oh.' She stepped into the substantial hallway, with patterned stone floor tiles and a broad staircase at the far end, and left Christopher to bring the baby buggy in. Despite having heard little but stories about the place for weeks, nothing had prepared her for the reality. There was a strong sense of decay and despair. The thought of one man living here alone, into old age, with nothing but memories, was painful. 'Didn't he have some sort of servant? A cook or something?'

'A woman came in twice a week. He wasn't incapable. I suppose she washed his sheets and things, and ran a vacuum round. The carpets were phenomenal. All pure wool. The moths had found some of them, though. He cooked for himself, apparently. And made marmalade.'

'Pardon?'

'Marmalade. There were forty-one jars of it in the kitchen, all carefully labelled. The oldest went back to 1994. I think he was using the newest ones first, which was naughty of him.'

'Were there any old diaries or letters?'

Christopher shook his head. 'Nothing like that. He doesn't seem to have been very introspective. Plenty of books, though. Walter Scott, first editions. Lord Lytton. Lots of authors I'd never heard of. They won't fetch very much. The old newspapers and magazines are more interesting. Lovely bound copies of *Punch*. We've had to get an expert to look at them for us. Come and see the study.' He took his wife and son into a room at the back of the house, where there were two walls of empty shelves and pale patches on the other two where pictures had been. 'It didn't look as if he used it much. The dust went back much further than when he died. Except in a few places where there were gaps. We think he might have started selling some of the oldest stuff.' Christopher looked round at the emptiness. 'There was a fantastic old globe in that corner, and a nice hand-illustrated map hanging there.'

'You really got to know your way around, didn't you,' Simmy said.

'I came six times altogether. So did Hughie, Ben, Jack – and sometimes Kitty. And the really big stuff was moved by professionals. We all got to know it inside out.'

Robin was kicking his heels vigorously against the bar of his buggy, demanding attention. A few weeks earlier he had taken his first steps, and now wanted to walk everywhere – slowly and crookedly, clinging to a parental hand.

'No, you can't get out here,' Simmy told him. 'You'll get filthy.'

'I ought to go and have a look in the cellar,' said Christopher, without enthusiasm. 'I've avoided it up to now. They told me they'd cleared out some lamps and things that were down there, but it was dark and smelly, and they didn't like it. I suppose it's down to me to make sure one last time that we didn't leave anything.'

'Not me,' shuddered Simmy. 'Can I go into the living room?'

He smiled. 'Help yourself. But it's called a "drawing room", to be precise. Pity you missed seeing the kitchen in all its original glory. The copper pans alone will fetch hundreds. Pewter, silver, cast iron – all the stuff collectors go mad for. Honestly, Sim, the place was a gold mine. Lucky Jennifer is going to get a very nice sum at the end of all this.'

'The heiress, you mean?'

'Keep up, Sim. I must have told you at least three times.'

'Sorry. It still seems like a fairy tale. Surely she must have known it would all come to her?'

'She says not. Sir John's grandfather was her great-grandfather's cousin. That's pretty remote. She barely knew he existed, and obviously never met him, and thought there had to be people with better claims than her. Apparently, she argued about it with the lawyers when they told her she was the only one.'

'Are they absolutely sure she is?'

'Looks like it. Enough to satisfy me that she gets all the proceeds of the sale, anyway.'

'Seems a bit odd. All those generations and nobody to show for it.'

Christopher nodded. 'I know. As breeders, the Hickorys must have been abject failures. Most of them barely managed one child.'

'Like us,' murmured Simmy, wheeling her little son back and forth in the hope of keeping him entertained.

'At least ours has got some cousins,' said Christopher bracingly. 'And no great mansion to fight with them over.'

Simmy forced a laugh. 'I'm sure that's bad grammar,' she said.

'I'm going down to the cellar,' he repeated. 'Back in five minutes.'

Chapter Three

It was barely one minute before Christopher came up from the cellar, looking pale. 'Nothing down there, after all,' he said. 'I'd better go upstairs next.'

'Wait for me. I want to see the view.'

'What about Robin?'

'You can carry him. We can't leave him down here.'

Without another word, Christopher lifted the child out of his straps and went ahead, taking the stairs quickly. Simmy followed, trying to absorb every detail of the staircase, and the landing at the top.

'This must be five times the size of Beck View, and I thought that was big,' she remarked, thinking of her parents' former home in Windermere, which they ran as a B&B. 'Look at all these doors!' There was a broad passageway down the centre of the house, with bedrooms leading off it on both sides.

'A mere eight bedrooms,' said Christopher. 'So nowhere near five times the size. That's on this floor. There's three more above this, for the staff. Only one bathroom, though. Can you believe it? Plus a separate lavatory, and a privy downstairs.'

'So primitive,' laughed Simmy. 'However did they manage?'

'I don't think they bathed very much. It's a very modern obsession.'

Simmy had gone into one of the bedrooms and stood in the middle of the huge space. 'You could get six beds in here, easily. And a fireplace! But no view.' The window looked onto the stone face of the fell, only eight or ten feet away. 'Must get very cold and dark in the winter.'

'Hence the fireplace,' said Christopher. 'These back rooms weren't much used, I suspect.'

'But it's so *big*.'

'This one had two double beds, a cheval mirror, two wardrobes, a couch, plus writing desk, trouser press, bookcase and three very nice floor lamps. More than enough to amuse anyone without needing a view as well.'

'How's the wiring?' she asked, mindful of the endless regulations they'd been subjected to when they converted their barn to a house. 'Is it legal?'

'Very much not if it's to become a hotel. But it's only thirty years old, so it works perfectly well. Whoever did it then was extremely generous with sockets. Every room has at least four.'

'Electric was cheap then, I suppose,' said Simmy wistfully.

'Mm.'

Simmy was opening her mouth to ask him if he was all right when Robin interrupted with his habitual squawking, indicating that he was not being given his due attention, and was certainly displeased with the current situation. 'He's bored,' she said.

'He's a pest,' said Christopher affectionately. 'We should have left him behind.'

'Huh! And the dog's going to be feeling much the same, by now.'

'Well, we'll have to go, then. We'll leave the car here and walk down to the cafe. Maybe the brat'll be asleep when we get back here again, and we can have another look round.'

'Don't call him a brat,' Simmy protested. 'He might hear you. But it's a good plan. And can we drive home a different way? Isn't Honister Pass around here somewhere? I've never seen it. Is it like Kirkstone?'

'Worse. Steeper and goes on for longer. I've only done it once. There's a famous photo of it from the 1890s, with a poor horse pulling a buggy or something down it. It must have been terrifying. And we sold a painting not long ago, based on that photo.'

'Presumably it wouldn't have to *pull* to go down, if it's so steep. What stopped the coach running away and dragging the horse after it?'

'They had brakes, I guess,' he said vaguely.

Simmy had a vivid mental image of the scene, arousing strong sympathy for Victorian horses in general and a faint understanding of the harshness of life in this isolated spot not so long ago. 'It rains such a lot,' she remembered. 'The road must have been muddy most of the time.'

'Snowy. Icy. And then bumpy and hard in summer. I don't imagine the people of Borrowdale went out and about very much if they could help it.'

'So – are we going to risk it?'

'Not much of a risk these days. The car's just been

30

serviced, so the brakes should be okay. It'll be good to see it again.'

Again she found herself wondering if he was all right. His voice was flat and the tone oddly distracted. 'Did you—?' Again her child interrupted, even more insistently, drowning her words.

'Come on, then. This is hopeless,' said Christopher. 'But at least you get the general idea. I'm glad you've seen it, and we can have another go after lunch, if you like.'

They went back down the handsome staircase and out through the front door. Christopher carefully locked it, and they set off down the hill to Grange, having collected Cornelia from the car.

Simmy was still holding onto her question, and tried again as they reached the first bend in the winding little road. 'What did you see in the cellar? You came back as white as a sheet.'

'Did I?' He made a poor show of trying to laugh. 'Well, if you must know, it was rats. Two of them. Big ones. I didn't want to scare you and have you screaming in front of Robin.'

'Oh, God! Now I won't dare go back in there for another look. They might be all over the house.'

'At night they probably are.' He shuddered. 'It's irrational, I know. But they completely freak me out. Did I tell you about that time in David?'

'Guatemala, right? Yes, you did.'

'It's lucky you're the same about them. You don't just dismiss it as silly.'

'It would be better if one of us could cope with them. If we get one in our house, we'll both scream and run away, leaving Cornelia and Robin to deal with it.'

'Which they probably would.' This time his laugh was more successful.

The stroll down the gentle decline into the village and the river Derwent was easy and interesting. They passed the Borrowdale Gates Hotel, which felt like a kind of rival to High Gates. Christopher stopped suddenly for no apparent reason, and stared at something that Simmy assumed was a gatepost.

'Look at that!' he said.

She looked. 'What is it?'

'I don't know, but it was never designed to be part of a fence. It's from some kind of industrial machinery.'

The object was black, apparently made of iron, and about three feet high. It comprised cogs and bars that confirmed Christopher's observation that it was thoroughly out of place. 'I see what you mean,' she said.

'How on earth did it get here?' he wondered. 'Something dismantled, bits sold off, or left for anyone to just help themselves to. There's got to be a story.'

'Recycling,' she suggested. 'It's a nice sturdy thing, and someone's been clever enough to find a new use for it.'

'Right,' he agreed with a nod, clearly not quite satisfied. 'I suppose we'll never know.'

Ahead of them was a group of hikers, looking as if they were heading for the same cafe as the Hendersons. It was almost half past twelve and people would be feeling hungry.

'I hope it's not too crowded,' said Simmy.

'They probably sell food to take away. We can buy something and eat it near the bridge, if necessary.'

But it proved not to be necessary, and they all sat outside

on a modest-sized area with six or seven other people and two other dogs. Simmy was facing the river, although it was invisible behind buildings. The view was of an almost entirely tree-covered fell rising steeply not far beyond the river. Her eye was caught by a massive boulder sitting high up amongst the trees, appearing to hover ominously over the settlement that was Grange. One day it would work loose and crash down without warning. Gravity alone must make that inevitable. She drew Christopher's attention to it, and he turned to look.

'The tree roots are bound to dislodge it one day,' she said. 'Don't you think?'

He showed no concern. 'In about a million years, perhaps.'

'Or maybe next week.'

'It's attached to the mountainside. That's just one small part of it that you can see there. I don't think the trees will make much impression on it.'

'I don't believe you,' she said. 'But I won't worry about it now.'

'No, don't.' It was not Christopher who spoke, but a man at the next table. 'Your husband's right. We're safe for at least a thousand years, if not quite a million.'

The speaker was obviously a hiker, with sturdy boots and a rucksack. In his fifties, perhaps, which put him at the younger end of the general run of fellside walkers. Next to him was a woman of roughly the same age. Simmy became aware how different she and her little family were from everyone else in the place. The only similarity was in the possession of a dog.

'That's all right, then,' said Christopher with a laugh.

Their food arrived and both parents devoted some moments to ensuring their young son got some nutrition. Cornelia was under the table, whining to express her boredom. Their neighbour maintained his interest in them.

'Not here for the hiking, then?' he said.

'Hardly, with this young man,' said Christopher, sounding less friendly than he might have.

'Not really dressed for it, either,' said Simmy, who was wearing sandals and a fairly respectable pair of trousers. Christopher was even less suitably attired.

The man was clearly not satisfied. He kinked an eyebrow, and said, 'So . . . ?'

Christopher gave his wife a quick look, and said, 'We came to see the church, actually. It's a very unusual design.'

'Don't be so nosy, Steve,' said the woman who was with the questioner. 'Leave the poor people alone.'

Which Simmy felt was almost as annoying, in its way. It carried implications of superiority, and undue secrecy on the part of the Hendersons.

'How old's your little boy?' the woman went on to ask.

'Fourteen months. He's just starting to walk. And the dog's a bit younger and her name's Cornelia.'

'You're here for the hiking then?' said Christopher, turning the tables. 'Have you come far?'

'Got the bus from Keswick to Lodore, then we'll get over the Pass and home from Buttermere. We're here for another week or so. We're very fond of this place. Like to see it in all weathers.'

'Ambitious!' murmured Christopher.

'We've done it before,' said the woman. 'It's a thrilling walk.'

'Of course, the mining has left terrible scars up there,' said the man.

In spite of herself, Simmy's interest was caught. 'Has it? They mined for graphite, didn't they? And made pencils out of it.'

'Slate, actually. Graphite's somewhere else. The slate was for roofing. They had to take it down the Pass in horse-drawn carts. Apparently, the place was full of the noise of the squealing brakes. Can you imagine it?'

Simmy shook her head. 'Poor horses.'

'Indeed.'

'We should go,' said Mrs Steve, wiping her mouth with a paper napkin. 'Long way to go still.'

'Nice long evenings now,' said Simmy idly. 'You won't be caught out in the dark, anyway.'

'It's the last bus we need to worry about. It goes soon after six.'

'Not a problem,' said Steve. 'Even if we stop for an hour at the top.'

'Good luck, then,' said Christopher, making it very plain that he would be glad to see them go.

Ten minutes later, they too were ready to leave. Cornelia had made no attempt to hide her impatience, and Robin was showing signs of mutiny.

'This isn't really much fun for them, is it?' said Simmy. 'Isn't there somewhere we can let her off the lead?'

'Only if we head for the hilltops, and even then she might chase the sheep.'

Simmy was feeling lazy and bogged down with child and dog. Her mood of the previous day had only slightly lifted.

'I don't need to see the house again, really. Why don't

you go and fetch the car and we'll potter about down here? You can be back in ten minutes.'

His disappointment was unmistakeable. 'There's nothing to do down here. They'll drive you mad. Much better to keep moving.'

'We'll go into the church, then. Or that little chapel by the bridge. Or find somewhere to watch the river. Sorry, love, but it's not working very well. It was a nice idea, but you've had your chance to say goodbye to the house, if that's what you wanted. Let's call it a day and go somewhere else. What about Castlerigg? Cornelia can really run about up there. Better still, you take her with you now. She'll prefer that.'

Christopher and his dog set off at a brisk pace, having made no further demur. It was a short distance on a gentle upward trajectory, and they covered it in well under ten minutes. The car was where he had left it, and the house showed no sign of caring whether he bade it farewell or not. Next time he saw it, he supposed it would have changed drastically. *If* he ever saw it again, that was. There would be no reason to come here again – ever. In another week, with the auction lots all dispersed to their purchasers, and the finances settled, it would all be forgotten. Records might be broken in terms of the size of the sale. Bidders from around the world would flaunt their new possessions. Sir John Hickory would at best become a footnote in the history books, and his handsome house transformed into something quite different. Then a car came sweeping in through the crooked gates, stopping inches away from him, where he stood for a moment reflecting on it all. A woman jumped out, looking ready for a fight.

'Who are you? What are you doing here?' she demanded.

'I'm the auctioneer,' he said, rather daftly. 'Who are you?'

'I'm Jennifer Reade. I own this place – at least for a few more days.'

Christopher could not have abased himself any more if royalty had suddenly appeared before him. Here was the woman for whom he had effectively been working over the past month or more. It was her interests he was bound to serve and her disapprobation he would earn if he did it badly. The fact that she was young, tall, fair-haired and indignant all made him feel even weaker.

'Oh,' he said. 'Pleased to meet you.'

'What are you doing here? Is this your car? What happened to the gates? Have you got a key? And you've got a *dog*.'

The final observation seemed to cause her most irritation. It also stiffened Christopher's spine somewhat.

'I've got a wife and child down in the village, as well. I came for a final look round, to make sure we haven't forgotten anything. The gates have been like that for quite a while, I think.'

'Your vans and things didn't do it, then?' She was still in accusing mode. 'I saw it when I was here yesterday, and wanted to know what happened. You must have had to make a lot of journeys to shift everything.'

'Seventeen, with two vans each time,' he confirmed, with a hint of martyrdom. 'But we didn't hurt the gate.'

'Let's hope your substantial commission covers it, then. I gather, to my amazement, that you charge the *buyers* the same percentage as me. That's extortionate. You'll make thousands out of it.'

'We like to think we'll have earned it,' he said.

'Do you always take your whole family with you when you're working?'

'As a matter of fact, no. I was owed a day off, having worked overtime on this business for umpteen weeks. I thought we'd make a little outing of it, and I came here out of a sense of responsibility to the house.'

'That doesn't make any sense. Do you live near here?'

'Not really. I've come to like the place, I suppose.'

The woman turned from him and stared hard at the house.

'I'd never seen it before this week. I thought I should come for a look – make sure I'm doing the right thing. I wasn't going to, but Julian said I ought to. It took me ages to find it. I wasted most of yesterday driving all round the valley. Went south instead of north, I realised in the end.'

Christopher shook his head slightly. 'Anywhere's easy to find these days, surely? It's even got its own postcode.'

'I prefer to use a map. I belong to a movement – oh well, you don't want to hear about that. You'll think it's ridiculous.'

He let that pass, with difficulty.

She seemed eager to tell him about her experiences. She stared thoughtfully at the house, before producing a key from her pocket.

'I got this sent to me a week ago. I should use it now.'

'Do you want me to come in with you?'

'Like an estate agent? No thanks. Your dog's got muddy feet.'

'She hasn't, actually. There isn't any mud at the moment. And the house wouldn't notice anyway.'

38

'You mean it still hasn't been cleaned? But I *told* them.'

'It's a lot cleaner than it was, and there are bare floors everywhere, nothing left to get dirty.'

Jennifer Reade bit her lip and stared again at the house.

'It's awfully big, isn't it? It makes me feel like a person in a fairy tale. I never *dreamt* it would ever be mine. I hardly even knew it existed. And now here you are as well.' She brandished the key like a talisman. 'It's all been such a whirlwind, forcing so many decisions on me. Things I've never even had to think about before now. It's crazy. Now I'll be a millionaire overnight. Things like that just don't happen in real life. I feel as if I've turned into a whole different person.'

Christopher silently characterised her as a naturally competent person, currently somewhat out of her depth. She seemed to have a range of thoughts all nagging at her at the same time. Her words were almost random.

He tried to sound reassuring. 'You'll soon get used to it. You're not the first person I've met in this sort of position. Families can be very surprising.'

Cornelia was pulling at her lead, reminding Christopher that he was expected down at the bridge.

'I'll go, then,' he said. 'Will you be at the sale?'

'Pardon? Oh, probably. Julian says I shouldn't because it's going to be so sad, but I'm not sure I can resist.'

'Up to you. You can follow it online, if that suits you better.'

She shook her head tightly, quick jerky shakes that suggested considerable impatience. 'I don't do online,' she said.

'Gosh! I felt sure we'd had some emails from you.'

'You're wrong. I wrote you letters and phoned you a few

times. The lawyers emailed you, possibly.'

Christopher was standing beside his car, and now he opened the door and told the dog to get in. Cornelia did nothing of the sort but began to pull towards the house.

'No, you can't go in there,' her master told her. 'Just get in. We're late.'

He had realised that he and Simmy had only brought one phone between them, and it was in his pocket. She would be getting worried – or cross. Or both.

Jennifer Reade was walking towards the house door, the key in her hand. 'I'll go, then,' said Christopher. 'Wish us luck for Friday. Both of us.'

'What's the matter with your dog?'

The animal was resisting all attempts to get her into the car. Jennifer Reade took very few seconds to unlock the door and push it open. The dog tore its lead out of Christopher's hand and scampered after her, grinning triumphantly. Twenty seconds later, all three were in the hallway of High Gates House in various states of excitement.

'I suppose it's the rats she can smell,' said Christopher recklessly. 'They're in the cellar.'

The reaction was unexpected. 'Hey! Have you seen them? You didn't go down there, surely?'

'For about half a minute this morning. I'm not very good with rats.'

'I don't mind them at all. I might even go down and see what they're doing. Don't let your dog go, though.'

'I don't think she's that sort of dog. But don't worry. I have no intention of doing any such thing. Not her and not me. I don't mind telling you, I definitely do not like rats. One glimpse is more than enough for one day. They didn't seem very scared of me when I went down earlier on, either.' He shuddered. 'More the other way round.'

'It's bonkers to be scared of them. They're *completely* misunderstood, you know. I've got three pet ones at home. They're incredibly clever. I love them to bits.'

'These ones might not feel so friendly. Especially if they're hungry. They won't find much down there except for a few beetles.'

Jennifer made a sound indicating impatience. 'They won't hurt you, you idiot. Maybe one of your drivers left a pack of sandwiches down there.'

'Well, it's up to you, but I can't see any need to go down there, for either of us. If it's all the same to you, I really should be going now. It was nice to meet you.' He had grabbed his dog and was holding her tightly against his leg.

The woman simply ignored him and went to the cellar door, which was behind the main staircase. 'Don't be such a wimp. Wait one more minute, while I check it out.'

'All right, but be quick.' He was already at the front door. 'It's dark,' he called in a belated warning. He remembered that light from the ground floor only extended as far as the bottom of the steps.

In spite of the urgency to get back to Simmy, he could hardly resist a direct order to linger. Jennifer Reade carried a natural authority that ensured his obedience. He found himself wondering whether she'd been born with it, or acquired it along with her inheritance. He opened his mouth to call down that her minute had expired, when her voice floated up the steps.

'I hope you're still there, because I think there's a dead person down here,' she shouted.

Chapter Four

'Bring a torch if you can find one,' she ordered, her unnaturally calm voice coming loud and clear up the stone steps. 'I can hardly see a thing.'

'There might be one in the car.' He dithered, encumbered with the dog and consumed with a sense of chivalric duty, whereby he ought not to let a young woman remain unprotected in a dark cellar with a body. Somewhere deep in his mind was a fear that there could be a murderer lurking in the shadows. 'Are you all right?'

'Of course. Just hurry up, will you?'

There was a small feeble torch in the glove compartment, which he had never been able to work effectively. You had to twist the whole body of it, to the exact right position, and only Simmy could manage it. He shut Cornelia in the car and trotted back.

'We'd be better with a new light bulb,' said Jennifer, when he had finally scrambled down to her and offered the pathetic torch. 'I assume that's why nothing happens when I try the switch.'

'Probably. I don't expect Sir John came down here very much. There wasn't any wine or anything. So where is it, then?' He found himself nursing a growing hope that she was imagining the whole thing. Because otherwise, there could be quite a lot of trouble for everybody. His overactive brain was conjuring apocalyptic visions of the sale being cancelled, the police insisting everything be put on hold, the whole business causing massive loss and embarrassment.

'There, look. Under that filthy little window. There's just enough light coming in to see the outline. Actually, my eyes have adjusted quite well now. I can see much better.'

'Well, I can't. I can barely even see the window.'

'It's got weeds and stuff growing all across it outside. Come with me.' Taking a handful of his shirtsleeve, she led him across the murky stretch of gritty floor and he suddenly remembered the rats. Like a very small boy, he hung back. 'Come *on*,' she insisted. 'What's the matter with you?'

'Where did the rats go?'

'Where do you think? Into the walls. Under the floor. Where rats always go. Don't be so pathetic.'

'Are you sure it's a person? It might just be a heap of clothes. I still can't see anything.'

'Can't you *smell* it?'

'Actually, no. Thank goodness. I haven't got a very good sense of smell.'

'Well I can. It's not horrible, not decomposed or anything – just *there*. It must have happened quite recently, I should think.' They were inching towards the far wall, Jennifer not greatly more urgent than Christopher. He held his feeble torch in front of him, pointed at the floor. A dim circle of light showed them the way. 'We're both being silly,' she said. 'We've got to face it, whatever it is.'

Christopher's thoughts returned to the deeply

disconcerting implications. He imagined a loud procession of police vehicles disturbing the Borrowdale peace. Questions. Suspicions. Arguments. And the terrible likelihood that the sale of a lifetime would be disrupted as a result.

'I came down here this morning,' he said. 'That's going to look bad. Although I suppose . . . ' he tailed off, wondering why he felt guilty.

Suddenly they were there, looking down at a head and shoulders, the rest of the figure curled into itself, like someone innocently asleep. 'Shine it on the face,' Jennifer ordered.

The face was against the wall, but the little torch had just enough power, combined with the faint light from outside, to show ragged flesh where a nose and ears should have been. Teeth were visible where lips had gone missing. The smell Jennifer had referred to was of meat, raw and tainted but not yet gone bad.

'Oh, God!' choked Christopher, and promptly vomited, narrowly missing the corpse.

'Those bad rats,' said Jennifer, sounding unpleasantly normal. 'Are you all right? I expect it'll hit me in a minute, but all I can think is – how terribly inconvenient this is going to be.'

The way she was reading his mind made him feel worse. The implication that self-interest was coming to the fore was shameful. In a determined reaction, he said, 'I'd better call the police. Can we go back up? I need some air.'

'Come on, then. We need to talk about this.'

Somehow, they got up the steps and out of the front door, moving quickly, stumbling once or twice. Christopher went to his car, his thoughts incoherent. The dog would be getting hot. He wanted to get in and drive away, very fast.

'Hang on,' the woman instructed. 'What are you doing?'

'Letting the dog out. It's too hot for her now the sun's moved round.'

'Well, listen. I know we have to call the police. I mean – it's obvious, isn't it? That man might have been murdered – although I rather think he's just a vagrant or drug addict who crawled down there to die in peace. No foul play. Don't you think?' She stared at him, looking young and unsure, eyes wide, shoulders slightly forward in an attitude of submission.

Christopher shook his head, unable to think, standing by the open car door, holding his dog's lead. 'I don't know. It's too horrible.'

'I mean – what else could it be?'

'I don't know who he is.' He thought again of the mangled face and wondered if he would have recognised his oldest friend in that state.

'No, we don't. He's nobody we know. Nothing to do with anything. Just a random stranger.'

The *we* struck Christopher as odd. He and Jennifer Reade knew nobody in common. He still felt sick and increasingly scared. 'So what are we going to do?'

'We should try to think it all through logically. Pull ourselves together. The fact is, I suppose, that it affects you pretty much the same way it does me.' Again, the wide-eyed appeal to his maturity and maleness.

He knew what she meant, even as he wanted not to. His hand went to the phone in his pocket.

'We've got to call the police. It's against the law not to.' He gave her a pleading look. 'We've been here too long already. I'll have to explain what happened to my wife.'

Her eyes held a gleam of satisfaction. 'You're agreeing with me, aren't you? Listen,' she repeated. 'I have this awful feeling we might be sorry if we rushed into anything. Don't forget the sale starts in two days. We don't want anything to spoil that, do we? And, really, the thing is – the man's past caring, after all. We can leave it until the weekend, and not tell anybody now. You can easily tell your wife about me being here, and us having loads to talk about. You can say we sat out here and discussed the sale and I told you about the shock of inheriting this place. All that could take half an hour at least.'

He shook his head again, feeling as if Satan himself was tempting him.

She went on. 'Otherwise, you know what'll happen? They'll put a hold on the sale, for sure. There's no way they'll let me complete it now. I mean the sale of the house. But they won't want you dispersing the contents, either. If it *does* turn out to be murder, they'll think it has to do with the value of the estate. Somebody believing it's wrong, thinking they've got a claim, or trying to make off with something valuable that's been missed. They'll suspect you and the people who work for you. After all, you're the only ones who've had rightful access to the place. They'll be crawling all over you for weeks.' She subsided again, spreading her hands. 'Don't you think? I might have got it all wrong, but it's an awful risk, and what good would it do?'

'I can't see we have any choice.' Again, he fingered the phone. 'If we don't report it now, we can't ever do it, can we? How would that sound – *we forgot to say anything on Wednesday, but now the sale's over, it's come back to me, we found a dead body. Sorry about that.* Hardly.'

'Then we'll have to go away now and say nothing. The

rats will be doing us a favour, if you can bear to understand that. Don't forget you threw up down there. It'll have your DNA in it. But give it a day or two, and it'll all be gone. We can back each other up, tell the exact same story of how we never went down there, just hung about on the ground floor for a bit and then sat here chatting. As far as I know, the purchasers won't be coming here for another week or two. Even then, they probably won't go into the cellar. By the time they do, it'll just be bones, and the police'll have to do a whole lot of forensics and stuff.'

'They'll still question us. You, me, all my staff. The locals. Someone's sure to have seen our cars by now.'

'That won't matter. They won't have any idea when he died. Not to the nearest *month*, probably.'

'My people took stuff out of the cellar.'

'What was there?'

'A lot of empty wine racks. Nice wrought-iron ones. A tin trunk. Two old chandeliers, probably eighteenth century. Some bits of pewter. And a big picture frame that they could barely get up the steps.'

She looked at him, eyebrows raised in admiration. 'Wow! You rattled that off without even thinking.'

'It's my job.'

'The chandeliers sound nice. Perhaps I should have taken more notice of what I'd inherited, while I had the chance.'

Before he could answer, the phone in his pocket began to jingle. He took it out and saw an unknown name on its face. 'Answer it,' said Jennifer.

'Christopher? Where the hell *are* you?' came his wife's angry voice.

Christopher knew that anything he said over the next

47

thirty seconds would affect the foreseeable future for himself, his business and his family – and he was not ready. 'Whose phone are you using?' he blurted, playing for time.

'A kind lady let me use hers. It's a miracle I remembered the number. What's going on? You've been gone forty minutes. I thought you must be dead – or at the very least lost the dog.'

'No, we're both alive and well. The thing is, I met someone. It's Jennifer Reade.'

'Who?'

'You know. The person who inherited High Gates. She's here. We've been talking.' He met the woman's eye, which was full of encouragement and approval. Suddenly it was all much too easy. 'I just lost track of time. And I couldn't phone you, could I? I'm really sorry, love. I'm coming now. We can drive home over Honister. Is Robin okay?'

'He's gone to sleep. He walked all by himself halfway over the bridge, but then we didn't dare go far in case you couldn't find us. Honestly – I was really worried.'

'I know. I've got no excuse. But it was such a surprise when she turned up, and we had lots to talk about.'

'I'll give you three minutes – *max*.'

'Right.' He waited for Simmy to finish the call and turned to Jennifer. 'I have to go. But we need to speak. Put your number in here, will you?' He held out the mobile.

She took it. 'My home number,' she said. 'I don't own a mobile.'

'Of course you don't,' he said with a sigh. 'And you don't do email, or use a satnav, or have a website.'

He thought he was being sarcastic, but she replied in all seriousness.

48

'That's right. And yet I can still be tracked by the invisible powers, because I drive a car with a licence plate. Even so, I have a feeling I might be rather hard to pin down when it comes to it. Not too many cameras up here, that I can see.'

Christopher wondered whether he was in some weird reality where death didn't really matter, and young women never lost their self-control. Was this Jennifer some kind of heartless monster? Or was it him – had he swallowed her persuasion because he was a coward only interested in his own profits?

'I'm going now,' he said. 'I can't believe what a mess this is.' He took the phone back from her and got into the car.

'And you'll say nothing? I promise you it'll be for the best.'

'Looks like it. Until the sale's over, at least.'

'I'll see you there. We might be able to talk then. You won't regret this, Christopher Henderson. I promise you.'

'Time will tell,' he said. He drove down to Grange feeling as if he had made a bargain with the devil.

Simmy was reproachful but no longer angry. 'I realise you couldn't phone me,' she conceded. 'But really – it was a horribly long time.'

'I know. It was horrible of me. Get in now and we'll go the scenic route.'

Honister Pass did not disappoint, despite being busy with other sightseers. The car turned into a horse in Simmy's imagination, plodding up the gruelling gradient to the top with evident pain. The views were breathtaking, lending a sense of complete freedom to the adventure.

'Wow!' she breathed. 'Just look at it! Why haven't we been here before?'

'People don't drive up here too much, even now. It's officially difficult. Imagine it in winter.'

The whole experience left Simmy feeling uplifted.

'I'm going to love just knowing it's here,' she sighed. 'Even if they've made it a tourist attraction.' She had glimpsed the Infinity Bridge walkway high above the road, and shuddered. 'It's impossible to spoil something like this, isn't it.'

'Let's hope so,' said Christopher. 'Now we have to get down the other side.' He drove slowly in low gear, giving Simmy time to absorb the panorama in front of her, as well as to wonder just what had happened to her husband in those minutes spent at High Gates House.

Chapter Five

The next morning everyone was at the saleroom well before nine, the atmosphere buzzing with the imminent auction.

'Only one more day!' exulted Fiona. 'I can hardly believe it.' Her seemingly endless task of cataloguing all the lots, and then cross-referencing them so they could be easily located within the building, had demanded considerable overtime and a growing sense of importance. Viewers had been invited on this and the previous day, and so far everything had run smoothly. Three typos, one misplaced picture and a wrongly described piece of furniture was all that had so far been brought to her attention.

'We'll miss it when it stops,' said Ben Harkness. 'We're making history, you know that don't you?'

'You've told me seventeen times already, so yes, I do know.'

Ben's role had mostly involved sitting at the computer all day, researching hundreds of pieces of china, ivory, paintings, silver, books, rugs and much more. He, like Fiona, had swelled with importance as he made discoveries that would otherwise have gone unnoticed. The chandeliers from the cellar at High Gates had been traced to a German maker, whose immaculate records revealed that they dated to 1774. They had never been converted to electricity, and still had ancient candle wax sticking to them.

Viewers were admitted at nine and they came in droves. Ben recognised some from the previous day – people who could not satisfy themselves that they had properly looked at everything the first time. By ten he had heard the word *sad* at least twenty times.

'It's all so terribly *sad*,' the women kept saying. Some of them were quite pink around the eyes. 'The man's whole *life* is here.'

It was true. And it was awful to see. Too many uncomfortable verities were on display, on a number of levels. Ben was no sentimentalist, but even he could share in the sense of waste and futility, what had it all been *for*?

'There's just too much stuff in the world,' sighed one man as he fingered a canteen of bone-handled cutlery. 'Whoever's going to buy this?' *Good question*, thought Ben subversively. His job depended on all this stuff, after all. It changed hands in a never-ending dance that kept auctioneers in business. Even when a proportion of it got creamed off to charity shops, car boot sales and landfill there was still more than enough left for the collectors, investors and incorrigible magpies. But the man was right about the cutlery. Somebody would buy it, but for a small fraction of what it had originally cost in 1907.

Ben was learning new terms and discovering new objects by the hour. There was a *veilleuse* amongst the lots, which had taken him half an hour to correctly identify. The word itself had been drastically redefined since the object had been made. His researches took him to New Orleans, where one of the largest private collections could be found. He also stumbled upon Etsy and a nasty display of whimsical nightlights, which had the word shamefully applied to them. The real *veilleuse* was an object of wonder – and useful, too. It was designed to keep tea warm, with a concealed burner in the base under a lovely little teapot on a gilded stand. The things came in a host of different styles and patterns, painted with flowers, animals, faces, buildings. Sir John Hickory's mother-in-law had apparently contributed this one as a wedding present that was already an anachronism in 1958. Ben suspected that it had never been used.

But now someone would buy it and hide it away and Ben would probably never see another. Unless it went to a museum, he thought hopefully.

Christopher came in just before nine, looking tired. 'Not long now,' said Ben encouragingly. 'It's been a right old roller coaster, hasn't it.'

'Certainly has. I can hardly believe it's really going to happen at last.'

'I know.'

'No shortage of viewers, anyway. And commission bids flowing in, thick and fast. Poor old Kitty is going mad.'

Ben did not like Kitty. She had offered her services six months ago, having moved to Cumbria from London, trailing such impressive credentials that Christopher had little choice but to take her on. She was condescending, snobbish and short-tempered. Ben suspected that she had never been as important as she claimed. Her reference from Christie's left a lot unsaid – which Christopher had been too naive to notice. Handling commission bids was not difficult, but it did require total concentration. Mistakes caused real rage at times and protracted recriminations.

Commission bids were good news, all the same. They flagged up the items that were arousing most interest, and created a buzz around certain lots, especially if a buyer indicated a willingness to spend lavishly. Ben had noticed with delight that his beloved *veilleuse* had three bids on it already, making it highly likely that the eventual hammer price would run to an amazing four figures.

Christopher had gone again before Ben could respond to his remark. The viewers were crowding around the tables and shelves, peering at paintings hung on the walls and fingering the porcelain. Ben's role was to answer questions, watch out for clumsy handling of rare objects and direct people to the things they wanted to inspect. There was a separate room for books, and another for textiles, including rugs and carpets. None of the usual routine was in operation, and there had been a few bemused viewers who expected a normal fortnightly auction, having missed the news about the High Gates clearance sale. The book room had hitherto been the place for household goods and the rugs alone occupied a table that had always been used for tools and garden equipment.

Ben's girlfriend, Bonnie, had seen little of him over the past two weeks. She lived and worked in Windermere, while he was twenty miles away in Keswick. Even in normal times, the logistics were awkward and time spent together sadly limited. They regularly debated possible solutions but had yet to come up with anything workable.

'If only Simmy would relocate the shop to Keswick, everything would be fine,' they agreed.

Simmy's shop, Persimmon Petals, was doing perfectly well where it was, it seemed, even if its proprietor had to commute along a tortuous route from Hartsop, involving the Kirkstone Pass and the village of Troutbeck.

At lunchtime, Ben dashed out to the mobile sandwich van that toured the estate that included the auction house. He found himself jostling against Christopher in the queue. The man looked even tireder than before. His shoulders slumped and his eyes seemed sunken.

'It's all go,' said Ben, trying to sound sympathetic.

'Right.'

'Only a few more hours to go now. And I think the main rush was this morning. I can't imagine where they all parked.'

'No,' said Christopher.

'There'll be complaints from other units, I shouldn't wonder. The Screwfix people won't be pleased, for a start.' This was their neighbour on the industrial estate, who regularly objected to overflowing vehicles during an auction.

'Mm,' said Christopher.

Ben decided he was too busy to enquire as to his boss's state of health. There were plenty of women to do that, after all. And probably it was just exhaustion anyway, although he couldn't see that Christopher had been exerting himself any more than anyone else. Less, if anything. Maybe Simmy would sort him out at the end of the day and send him all fresh and bushy-tailed for the main event next morning.

It wasn't until four o'clock that he began to wonder if there was actually something genuinely wrong with the man. Fiona had said something about it to Jack, and Ben noticed several concerned looks flying around. The viewers had dwindled to a trickle, and everyone was going round straightening and checking, one last time. A small Japanese vase had gone missing, and Hughie, one of the temporary staff, was going slowly through all the CCTV footage trying to see who'd pinched it. It took him twenty minutes, but he found it.

'It was a woman with long black hair,' he announced. 'Does anyone recognise her?' One by one the entire staff inspected the film, taken from a height of ten feet, showing a foreshortened female snatching the vase and dropping it into her coat pocket.

'Can't see her face,' they all complained. So Hughie did another trawl until he found her arriving through the entrance lobby, her features clear and distinct.

They called Christopher, who was clearly making a big effort to listen and decree what should be done. 'She's not one of the regulars,' he said.

'Obviously,' muttered Kitty.

'We'll have to report it to the police. There's an estimate of three hundred quid on that vase,' said Ben.

'Right,' said Christopher. 'Thanks, Hughie – you did a great job.'

Christopher liked his temporary employee because he saw him as a younger version of himself. At twenty-five, Hughie had spent a year or two roaming Asia on a motorbike – which he still used for transport on his return. Having picked up some expertise in Chinese and Indian ceramics, as well as being highly competent with IT, he quickly made himself useful. He acknowledged the thanks with a small nod.

Christopher addressed the rest of his staff. 'Can one of you take it from here for me? I think I'll be getting off home now. I need to be on form for tomorrow.'

'Yes – go,' said Fiona. 'You look ghastly. Don't you dare get sick now. The whole thing depends on you.'

'I'll be fine,' he said, unconvincingly.

Ben phoned Bonnie that evening from his digs. 'How's it going?' she asked.

'It's okay. But Christopher's in a state. Fiona thinks he's ill. He's all droopy and quiet. Everyone else is absolutely buzzing. But if he goes to pieces, it's all going to be a complete fiasco. We haven't got anyone else capable of doing his job at this level. And some woman nicked a vase. We've reported it to the police, which we really don't like to do. Hughie's a brilliant detective. Very painstaking.'

'Who's Hughie?' asked Bonnie. 'That sounds funny, doesn't it.'

'He's here just for a few weeks. I'm not sure how Christopher found him, but he's been very useful. I think he's leaving next week, once the sale's over. Kitty likes him more than me, I think.'

'She's mad,' said Bonnie loyally.

'I thought at first he'd get in my way and interfere with my side of things, but he doesn't at all. He's addicted to the CCTV, but he's also good with the things. Yesterday he was arguing with Fiona about how to organise the rugs. There's a great big table of them, all rolled up, and people wanted to unroll them when they came to view, checking for moth and so forth. Well, Hughie had the sensible idea of turning them round so they can be laid *across* the table instead of along, if you follow. Clever things like that.'

'Mm,' said Bonnie, clearly losing interest. 'So, what's the matter with Christopher?'

'Just nervous, I guess. It's a big thing, after all. Career-changing, according to Kitty. Actually, I think it's partly her getting so fired up that's given him the jitters. The rest of us have been trying to pretend it's just another sale.'

'Simmy told me all about them going to Borrowdale yesterday. Christopher met the Reade woman, apparently, and was ages talking to her, leaving Sim and the kid to kick their heels with no car or phone or anything. She was really cross about it.'

'Yesterday?' he echoed. 'Wasn't he here yesterday?'

'Can't have been, because they went to see the house one last time. Funny you never missed him.'

'Not really. He doesn't have a lot to do these last few days – his turn comes tomorrow, and everyone's scared stiff he won't be up to it.'

'So did something happen yesterday to upset him? Simmy says he was funny all last night and would hardly speak to her. She assumed it was because he felt bad about abandoning her. But it was only about half an hour longer than he said. And he had a good excuse, after all. She was partly cross that she didn't get to meet the woman. I mean – fancy becoming a millionaire overnight like that.'

'She's coming tomorrow, so we'll all get to meet her. She'll be treated like royalty.'

'Oh – I forgot to tell you. Simmy says I can have Saturday off, and Corinne thinks it's all quite exciting, so she's bringing me up first thing. Can you save us a couple of seats?'

'You'll be lucky. Standing room only for gawpers. Because there's no way you're buying anything, is there?'

'Spoilsport,' she said.

Simmy had quite forgiven her husband by the time he arrived home on Thursday evening. She had been down to the shop, chatted to Bonnie, created three bouquets and a wreath, leaving her child with his perfectly willing grandparents, and had stopped to buy herself a new shirt before going back to Threlkeld to collect him. Bonnie had been delighted to have permission to attend the epic auction on its second day.

'I should have thought sooner to tell you it was fine,' said Simmy. 'I'll go to the auction tomorrow, and then come down to man the shop on Saturday.'

They had talked about Jennifer Reade, speculating on how she must be feeling. 'I suspect she regrets it all a bit, now it's too late,' said Simmy.

'How do you mean?'

'Why else would she have gone to see the house, right at the very last minute? Why didn't she just stay down in Swindon or wherever it is, and let it go without ever seeing it?'

'She must have been curious, I suppose.' Bonnie herself harboured scant sentiment for old buildings. 'Or maybe she wanted to keep an eye on Christopher. Didn't he say? Did he tell you what she's *like*?'

'He hardly said a thing. Just that they had a lot to talk about and lost track of time. I wasn't in a very receptive mood, anyway. He left me high and dry for *ages* – or it felt like that, anyway. Actually, if I'm being really honest, I was cross because he missed seeing Robin walk halfway across the bridge at Grange, without even holding on. It was amazing – he just kept taking one step after another. Lucky there weren't any cars, or I'd have had to pick him up. He wouldn't have liked that. As it was, there were three or four people all laughing and clapping. He did look funny, all drunken and determined. One of the people lent me her phone so I could call Christopher.'

'She's going to the sale, then? The Jennifer person? Both days?'

'No idea,' said Simmy.

Now they were all back in Hartsop, Simmy making a cottage pie and Christopher taking a shower, which was unusual. Robin and Cornelia were in a heap on the sofa watching CBeebies.

'Have you got dirty somehow?' Simmy asked her husband when he came back downstairs.

'A bit dusty. I wanted to wash my hair and pep myself up a bit.'

'Big day tomorrow.'

'Right.'

'Are you nervous?'

'What? Oh – a bit, maybe. Don't want to lose my voice, that's for sure. But Fiona's going to be right beside me, keeping me on track.' He smiled. 'It'll all be over before I know it.'

'You'll be glad when it is, by the sound of you.'

'I will. I'm ready to get back to normal.'

'All that money!' she sighed. 'I still can't believe it. And the house on top of it! She must be completely . . . what's

60

the word? . . . *boondoggled*! Is that it?'

'I suspect not, but I know what you mean.'

'But *is* she? You talked to her yesterday. How was she?'

'She was fine. Businesslike. Brisk. Seemed to be taking it all in her stride. Asked me some questions. Oh – and she's against anything to do with the digital age. Doesn't even use a mobile.'

'What? How is that possible?'

'It isn't, really. But she's very serious about it. Now she'll have so much money, she can probably get some sort of political party going, trying to take us back to former times, or something. She did say something about a movement.'

'Gosh!' said Simmy. 'I bet they'd win by a landslide if it came to it. We all hate computers running everything, if we're honest about it. I can just imagine what the manifesto would be like.' She laughed. 'All a dream, I suppose.'

'It's twenty years too late, at least. Probably more like fifty. We're stuck with it all now.'

Cheered by this exchange, Simmy went back to her cooking. Everything was all right again. Christopher was just jittery about the sale, which was completely understandable. The meal was consumed with everything apparently normal, Robin working his own spoon with comical results. Afterwards, Simmy reverted to the earlier topic.

'When does Jennifer actually get the money – from you, I mean?'

'Not right away. There'll have to be an outside auditor person to verify it all, since it's going to be so much. Ben reckons it could reach half a million.' He grimaced. 'I shouldn't have said that. It feels like tempting fate. It might only be half that when it comes to the point. Or less.'

Simmy did sums in her head. 'Eight hundred lots – right? If they average five hundred pounds each, as you said they might, that's close, isn't it? And think of your commission! You'll be able to build a whole new saleroom and branch out somewhere.'

'Stop it,' he begged. 'The average is sure to be way less than five hundred. There's a lot of rubbish – bent spoons and cracked vases. This is just Ben being Ben. He doesn't get the nuances. It's unlucky to speculate like this. Can we change the subject? Please.'

But there really were no other subjects. 'The commission's going to make quite a hole in the money she gets,' mused Simmy. 'And the buyers have to pay as well. It seems a bit . . . excessive, when it's such a big sale.'

'Don't you start. She said that to me yesterday, rather accusingly, in fact. It's just the way it works. It's always been the same. We have costs, you know. Extra staff, overtime, security. It all has to be paid for. And we make it very easy for all concerned. How else could she sell it all, without somebody like me?'

Simmy put her hands up in surrender. 'Sorry, sorry. I didn't mean to be annoying. It's the same as income tax, in a way. You just have to resign yourself to not keeping everything. I'm sure the woman's perfectly okay with it.'

'Well, she's not entirely, because she brought it up right at the start. But it must all be new to her, so she's going to have to suck it up, as they say.'

Simmy reverted to the most burning questions that she and Bonnie had dwelt on in the shop. 'What do we know about her? Is she married? Has she got siblings? Or kids?'

She looked at him, eyes wide. 'If there are siblings and she's the eldest, isn't that an awful example of primogeniture? She gets millions and they get nothing. Can that be right?'

'It's not right. Anyone with the same degree of relationship counts and they have to share it. She did mention a chap called Julian. Sounded like a boyfriend. She's quite young. If there are kids, they'll be little ones.' His tone was flat, as if he could hardly bring himself to answer; as if the whole thing was too boring to continue.

But Simmy was undaunted. 'I hope she's there tomorrow. I want to meet her.'

'Don't you dare!' he flashed at her.

She flinched. 'Why? Why ever not? What's wrong with that?'

'Mixing business and . . . idle curiosity. It would be bad protocol. She won't want people knowing who she is – she'll act like just another bidder.' He was flushed and stammering. 'That's the only way to do it.'

'Is that what she told you? She'll sneak in at the back wearing dark glasses and nobody's allowed to speak to her? Sounds bonkers to me.'

Christopher said nothing.

Chapter Six

At nine o'clock that evening Robin was sound asleep, and the light was slowly fading. A blackbird was singing exuberantly in the garden, its music coming through the open windows at full volume. A house nearby had a huge wisteria in bloom, sending waves of sweet scent across the tiny village. No traffic went past. The Hendersons sat quietly for a minute or two, each aware of dark feelings and something going wrong. Simmy could not remember a time when her husband had been so scratchy and unpredictable. They had known each other since the day they were both born in the same hospital, albeit with very long interludes in which they never met. He had always been easy-going, patient, ready to listen. He was not given to strong opinions or soaring ambition. The eldest of five, he was comfortable amongst people, with a knack of socialising without becoming too engaged. The sudden change was alarming, and she could find no way of addressing it beyond what she had already tried.

'One of us could go for a walk and watch the stars come out,' she said wistfully.

'Feel free. Take the dog,' he invited. 'You'll appreciate it more than I would.'

It was a relief to escape the atmosphere he was generating in the house, the truth of which she admitted to herself. She was half inclined to phone Ben and ask him if he had noticed anything of the sort during the day. But the explanation was so obvious that it seemed pointless. Christopher had stage fright. What else could it be? If there had been some wrongdoing over Sir John's possessions, he would have been happy to tell her about it. As it was, it only made him worse to have to explain himself or answer questions. She had done the right thing in leaving him alone and giving his precious dog some exercise.

She walked the short distance to the little car park that people used for Hartsop Dodd. Cornelia ran ahead and started up the path to the top of the fell. Simmy did not call her back, but followed until she was able to look back towards Brothers Water from a modest elevation. The sun had set, but there was a band of crimson still visible. And sure enough, the first few stars had begun to appear. A burst of early summer heat was predicted for the weekend, which was something to look forward to.

By Sunday, the sale would all be over. Either there would be stupendous sums of money generated, leading to rejoicing and congratulations, or else there wouldn't, in which case Christopher and his staff could reassure each other that they had done their best. Jennifer Reade would pocket her proceeds and never be thought of again.

But meanwhile, Simmy could not help thinking about her. She knew enough about men and marriage and affairs of the heart to recognise that her husband's abrupt change of behaviour had coincided with meeting a young woman who was about to become very rich. It would be the height of self-deception to overlook that.

Left on his own, Christopher could not prevent his thoughts from becoming overwhelming. Obsessively he went over every second of the time spent in Jennifer Reade's company. From there he moved to the implications and the panic they elicited. He had never been so frightened – even in Costa Rica on a precarious bridge over a rushing river, or Guatemala when he was convinced a panther was watching him. That had been a visceral physical terror. This was more of a dread of humiliation, loss of respect and status, and irreversible scorn from his wife. Desperately he groped for an answer, something that would take the course of events into unthreatening waters, where his own actions carried no shame. Until now he had not questioned Jennifer's assertion that discovery of the dead man would necessarily entail suspension of the auction. She had been so certain that he had bowed to her knowledge. Of course that mattered as much to her as it did to him – perhaps more.

The worst thing was the effort involved in keeping the whole story back from Simmy. He had never deliberately lied to her in over forty years. It involved a violence against his own instincts that he had never imagined could be so hard. How did other men do it? Men who conducted two totally separate lives for decades, almost every utterance a barefaced lie. Men who concealed the fact that they were compulsive gamblers, or homosexuals or international spies. The levels of self-control and constant caution that such situations must demand were unthinkable to the transparent

Christopher Henderson. He didn't think he had the brains for such obfuscation. Besides, without Simmy's input, her sensible questions and understanding, he had no idea what might be the best thing to do.

Once the truth came out, as it eventually must, Simmy would be appalled at his behaviour. She would feel betrayed and might never trust him again. It would blight their marriage for ever. She might even think he had done it out of a sudden stupid passion for Jennifer Reade.

It was this last awful thought that clinched it. Regardless of the consequences, he would tell his wife everything, the moment she came back from her walk with the dog.

It was nine forty-five when Simmy and Cornelia came back.

'It's lovely out there,' she said, the moment she was inside the door. 'We should make the most of these long evenings. I was thinking we ought to get more garden furniture so we can sit out in comfort.'

'Simmy,' said Christopher, in a tone she could not remember ever having heard before. 'Can I talk to you?'

'Oh. All right.'

He patted the sofa beside him, and she went obediently to sit down.

Her heart thumped. Was he going to say he was leaving her? 'Have I done something?'

'Of course not. Don't be ridiculous.'

It was not a good start, and she could see him wishing he had not said it. 'Sorry,' he added. 'I didn't mean that.'

'So what is it? What on earth's the matter with you?' The thought that he might be ill flashed through her mind and just as quickly disappeared. Illness didn't come on as suddenly as this had done, whatever it was.

'Something happened yesterday – at the house.'

'I thought that must be it. While you were with Jennifer Reade, right?'

He nodded. 'We found a body in the cellar,' he said starkly. 'And she wouldn't let me call the police in case it meant suspending the auction tomorrow.'

She sat very still and took a deep breath. 'I see,' she said, because she did, up to a point. 'But why should it? How could that even be possible?'

'What?'

She said it again, and added, 'Whatever made her think they'd do that?'

'Well – the *timing*, Sim. The police would be sure to think the man's death had something to do with the sale of all the effects, and the house itself, of course. They'd want to stop everything while they investigated. It was my first thought as well.'

'They wouldn't, though. They'd never be able to act that fast, for one thing. Unless . . .'

'What?'

'She must have known who he was – the dead man, I mean. She must have a reason to think he was something to do with the house or Sir John.' Her mind was working gloriously, as she gazed out of the window onto the darkness outside. 'She must need everything to go ahead, for her own purposes, and she made you think it was in your interest as well.'

'Well, it *is*. I couldn't begin to contemplate postponing the sale. It would be total and utter chaos. And what if it was *cancelled*? All that stuff. The money . . . the *work*.' He rubbed his face hard with both hands. 'I couldn't risk that. And I'm definitely going to call the cops first thing on Sunday, once the sale's finished. Saturday evening, in fact.'

'You're colluding,' she said flatly. 'And that's against the law. Was the man murdered? If so, you're in deep trouble already.'

'I don't know. It was too dark to see, and he . . . well, it was rather a mess.'

'So he might have been?'

'I don't know,' he said again. 'On balance, I would guess he'd just crawled down there and died of a drug overdose or something like that. I think Jennifer thought that.' He looked at her, turning sideways on the sofa. 'You're wrong about her. You make it sound as if it was all part of a plan, with me caught up in it, all innocent and unsuspecting.'

'And you're sure it wasn't, are you? You took everything she said for gospel. People do tell lies, you know.'

'I can't see how it could have been planned at all. She didn't know I'd be there. She had no idea we'd already looked round the house. I'd even been in the cellar before. She didn't know about that.'

'You didn't tell her?'

He frowned. 'I don't think so. I might have done. She probably thinks I went down there while the place was being cleared. It doesn't matter anyway.'

'How do you think the man got in there? It was all locked up. How long had he been there? Did Jennifer have a key? It's not making very much sense, the way you're telling it.'

His face crumpled and he flung himself back against the cushions. 'I don't *know*, Simmy. All I can tell you is that Jennifer made me agree not to say anything until after the sale. We had a bargain. She made me see it was in both our interests. I thought it would be easy – or fairly. I thought

I could just put it to one side for a couple of days. But it's driving me mad. I can't stop thinking about it. I didn't sleep a wink last night and I can hardly focus on anything at work. I feel as if I killed the wretched man.'

'Well, I'm glad you've told me,' she said, still just as calm. 'That's the main thing. We can sort it out together. I'm going to phone Moxon about it first thing in the morning.'

'No!' The word emerged as a strangled scream. 'You can't do that. It's not your story to tell. Talk to Jennifer first. She'll be furious that I've told you, but that's her problem. See what you think of her. Try to persuade her if you like. Once the sale starts, I'll feel much better about it.'

She rubbed her own leg abstractedly, hard enough to hurt. 'They would never have made you postpone it, anyway,' she said. 'Jennifer conned you about that. You should have known better than to believe her.'

His gullibility irritated her, while at the same time arousing her pity. 'She must be ever so persuasive,' she added.

'I told you. Businesslike. She knows her own mind. All that stuff about not using a phone or anything – that's like some sort of cult. She's like that. Everything she says comes over as definite. I don't think anyone could have argued with her.'

His words came in short bursts, as new thoughts struck him. 'What are we going to do, Sim?' he finished. 'Because we really can't go to the police tomorrow. I haven't got time and you're not going to.'

'You can't actually stop me, you know. Wasn't it obvious that that's what I'd want to do?'

'I don't know. I didn't think it through. I just couldn't carry on keeping it all a secret.'

Simmy had understood for a while now that she was the

strong one in this relationship. It had not been apparent until Robin was born, and she was still working out whether or not it mattered. Her first husband had been domineering, insecure and ultimately impossible. As a wife, she herself was not entirely confident, with her mother's example not very useful. Christopher was easy to love and easy to understand. Even now, having got himself into this awful pickle, she could perfectly well see how it had happened. Or so she thought.

'All right, I won't. At least not till after tomorrow's sale. But you realise that I'm colluding now, as well? If we tell them the whole story from the start, we really are going to be in serious trouble.'

'What's the worst that can happen? They're not going to send us to jail, are they?'

'I guess not. But it won't do your reputation any good. Concealing evidence. Putting your own interests before the requirements of the law.'

Again he rubbed his face, but this time there was a faint grin on his lips. 'I think I could live with that better than if they'd made us stop the sale. Every time I think about it, I go cold. All that stuff, all those people . . . all that *money* involved. Just getting the things insured for another few weeks would cost a small fortune.'

'Well there's one thing I'm going to insist on.'

'What?'

'You're not going to stop me talking to Jennifer Reade tomorrow. I'm taking Robin to Threlkeld first thing, and then spending all day watching you sell precious porcelain and priceless pictures and adding up the proceeds. With any luck, I'll get a seat next to Ms Reade while I do it. If you try to stop me, I'll report you to DI Moxon.'

'You drive a hard bargain,' he groaned. 'But I know better than to try to stop you.' He sighed. 'But please don't tell your parents anything about it.'

'As if I would,' she scoffed.

In the night, Simmy dreamt about the Grange bridge and the Honister Pass, all jumbled together with Robin crawling up a vertiginously steep hill with a large horse following him. She woke up in a panic and lay staring at darkness while she slowly sifted dream from reality. Beside her Christopher was sound asleep; the relief of unburdening himself, she supposed, combined with sheer weariness from the previous sleepless night. Now she was the one with the moral dilemma, which did not seem very fair. She had a strong suspicion that Christopher hoped they would never have to be involved with the police at all. Somebody would find the dead man and it would all proceed without any Henderson involvement. The fact of the auction would be irrelevant. And why should Simmy think otherwise? What would be wrong with that? Since she knew for absolute certain that her husband had not killed anybody, it would be perfectly ethical for his minor role to be concealed.

The trouble was, it felt wrong. It would be a betrayal of DI Moxon's trust. The slightly inept detective, based in Windermere, had become a close friend over the past few years. Local murders, in which Simmy had become embroiled, thanks – to her great surprise – to her work as a florist, had seen the two of them combining forces, along with Ben and Bonnie. Moxon had benefited considerably from Ben's intelligence and Simmy's naive willingness to help. People liked her and confided in her. Now and then they had disclosed more than was good for them, which sometimes led to the resolution of the investigation. Far from regarding herself as any sort of amateur detective, Simmy's sheer natural decency took her into murky realms at times. Since marrying Christopher, and moving to Hartsop, she had found that Moxon had become a more distant figure. At first, she had expected their ties to be permanently severed – but she had reckoned without the opportunism of the Cumbrian police. They had become aware that the florist had some sort of special, if accidental, female power, and in combination with the man from Windermere, things could often turn out in a remarkably successful fashion – which prompted them to summon him to their aid at times in areas beyond Windermere.

Borrowdale was considerably distant from Moxon's usual area of concern, although Simmy was hazy as to precisely where any demarcation lines might fall. If she called him and told him the story, he would be very likely to respond with some sort of action. The body would quickly be found, and the whole police machinery would grind into life, with all its unpredictable consequences. She knew she could not do that to Christopher. However unlikely it might be that his auction would be halted, even the slimmest risk was unacceptable. Her suspicion that Jennifer Reade might be using the auctioneer for her own purposes was growing stronger. The whole thing was too unlikely, otherwise. The woman could have killed the man herself, after all, and staged the discovery of his body purely for Christopher's benefit. Numerous questions as to *Why?* and *When?* were brushed aside as impossible to answer – yet.

She lay awake for two hours or more churning all these thoughts around and around. Feeling little personal anxiety over it, she nonetheless accepted that it mattered a great deal to her husband. He had been very slow to settle into a career, but now, in his early forties, he had found his rightful niche and was thoroughly committed to it. The showmanship of auctioneering gave an outlet to a side of his character that had been undeveloped until now. He enjoyed being the centre of attention, getting to know his bidders, learning the subtle tricks that would encourage them to raise a hand one more time and spend just that bit more than they intended. He relished the endless learning opportunities that lay ahead, freely admitting that he knew almost nothing about pewter, textiles or antiquarian books. China and porcelain were easy, furniture almost as much so. With Ben Harkness always at hand to fill in the gaps, there had been impressive progress over the past year. The rich variety of objects that passed through his saleroom never failed to excite them both.

And now they were on the very brink of the biggest sale in the area for fifty years. Not only would it produce a very handsome boost in income, but the kudos would be highly gratifying. Whilst publicity had been limited to the world of antique auctions, with nothing at all reaching the awareness of the general public, that might change after the event. If Ben's *veilleuse*, or one or two of the first editions, made noteworthy sums, the papers might well take it up.

All of which was vividly apparent to Simmy. She finally drifted back to sleep with the conclusion that in the great scheme of things, it would perhaps not matter very much if a dead man lay undisturbed for another forty-eight hours.

Chapter Seven

Russell Straw gave his daughter a surprise next morning when she delivered her child to Threlkeld. 'I'm coming with you,' he announced. 'You might have to drop me back before the end of the day if I get bored.'

'Oh!' Complications arose like bluebottles in her mind. 'Okay. I probably won't stay all day, either.' She addressed her mother. 'Will you and Robin be all right? I won't bring Cornelia. I've booked the local girl to take her out.' The dog had eventually won the affection of the Straws, once the irritations of puppyhood had passed, but Angie would have enough on her hands with Robin.

'Perfectly all right,' smiled Angie. 'Now he's starting to talk, we can't get enough of each other. I don't believe you've taught him half the nursery rhymes that you should. And he said "squirrel" last time he was here.'

'Of course he did. He lives in the Lake District. They'd exile him otherwise.'

Russell opened his mouth to speak.

'Don't start!' warned wife and daughter in unison. They all laughed, including Robin.

'He walked about twelve steps on Wednesday,' boasted

Simmy. 'When we were at Borrowdale. Or Grange, to be exact.'

'Did you go over Honister?' asked Russell eagerly. 'Isn't it something?'

'We did. It's incredible. Like something in the Rocky Mountains. I felt sorry for the car, but there were no glitches. Not then, anyway.' She stopped abruptly, fearing to reveal too much of the story of what had happened on Wednesday. Christopher had not outrightly banned her from telling it all to her parents, but she knew he assumed that she would not. Already less of a secret than Jennifer Reade surely hoped, it would cease to be one at all if two more people knew of it. Russell might start talking loudly about it at the auction. Angie might carelessly drop a comment in the village shop. Even without those leaks, they would be sure to urge Simmy to go to the police, because that was the right thing to do.

Although it had to be admitted that her parents often had unconventional ideas as to what was right. They might instead go charging off to Grange – only six or seven miles away – and have a look for themselves. Anything was possible.

'Come on, then,' said Russell. 'We'll never park if we don't go now. And I want a seat at the front.'

'Too late. We'll be lucky to find anywhere to sit at all, apparently.' They were on the doorstep, watching Angie as she held Robin up to wave.

'Don't go buying anything,' she ordered her husband. 'You're only there as an observer.'

'I'll phone you when we're leaving,' said Simmy. 'I've no idea what time it'll be.'

'Just don't come back at one o'clock wanting lunch. Robin and I are going down to the pub.'

'Lucky you,' said Russell. 'Fortunately, I have made other arrangements.' He brandished a small rucksack. 'Paté sandwiches, two bottles of cider and some brownies. No danger of starving.'

Simmy felt young and incompetent, relying on her parents for all of life's basics. The seven minutes it took to drive to the auction house and find a parking space passed mostly in silence. Russell sat with the rucksack on his lap and hummed nursery rhymes to himself. Simmy debated with herself as to whether or not she was going to be glad of her father's company throughout the coming day.

The first familiar face she saw was that of Ben Harkness. He was hovering in the main saleroom, looking like a cinema usher. Seating was haphazard, using chairs and sofas that were part of the sale lots. Numbered stickers were fixed to wooden arms, or backrests, or upper cushions. People sitting there were expected to be careful not to dislodge them. All the most obviously comfortable pieces were taken.

Ben cocked his head at a row of four upright dining chairs halfway down the room, and said, 'Better grab two of them.'

Russell grumbled quietly, to the effect that auctions he'd seen on television had proper rows of comfortable chairs for the bidders.

'They don't, Dad. Only at Sotheby's or Christie's. Nearly all of the ordinary ones have the same arrangement as this.'

'Well, after this, maybe they'll invest in something better. They'll be well able to afford it.'

'There wouldn't be enough space,' said Simmy, looking round and not really concentrating. The raised rostrum where Christopher would sit had been extended to accommodate two extra seats and a third laptop. Online bids would significantly outnumber those in the room, slowing down the proceedings, but boosting the profits. There was jade and amber that would attract buyers from the Far East, and interest had been coming from Australia, Argentina and many other far-flung spots. Kitty, the recent employee, was being trusted with handling the telephone bids that were expected, and which would also interrupt the flow of the auction, while the bidder tried to keep up with what was happening.

'Ten more minutes to go,' said Russell. 'Where's the main player, then?'

They had not seen Christopher at all since they arrived. Simmy knew better than to try to attract his attention. Even Ben had given her scant acknowledgement, once he'd shown her where to sit.

'Busy,' she said. Her insides had been growing tighter and heavier over the last few minutes, with a dread that she could not entirely explain. It felt like the moment at a wedding when the vicar said '. . . or forever hold thy peace'. Someone was going to step forward with hand upheld and cry 'Stop! This must not go on'. Someone would stage a dramatic entrance and the buyers would manifest alarm, indignation and disgust.

Instead, there was an atmosphere of muted expectation and an odd suggestion of melancholy. Listening to snatches of conversation from other potential bidders, Simmy heard the words 'heartless' and 'so sad' and 'did you see that poor old teddy bear?' Flipping through the catalogue, she understood the feelings. The early lots were of little value – the contents of the garden shed and garage, followed by the attic. She tried in vain to remember seeing a shed on the Wednesday visit, and she had never got as far as the attic, but the items listed were enough to conjure vivid images. Russell put out a hand for the shared catalogue and she gave it to him.

'Most of this is rubbish,' he observed. 'Listen to this: "Black frock coat, some moth damage".' He flipped a few pages. 'And this, "Scrapbook of newspaper cuttings from *The Times* 1947 to 1954". Who's going to want stuff like that?'

'We might be surprised,' was all she said.

Five minutes before the appointed start, Christopher, Fiona, Ben and a woman Simmy didn't recognise filed onto the platform and took their seats. Four screens positioned on the walls around the room came alive, and announced SPECIAL TWO-DAY HOUSE CLEARANCE SALE. Once the auction started, the lots would be displayed as they were being auctioned. Everybody settled down, whispering slowly subsided and Simmy remembered that she had wanted to speak to Jennifer Reade. She turned round on her upright chair and scanned the row behind her. 'What's the matter?' asked her father in a normal voice.

'Nothing.' She turned back.

'Young Ben's been promoted, I see. Looks as if he's got to keep track of all the bids. Not easy, I imagine.'

'He'll be fine,' said Simmy. 'They all will. It matters too much to make a mess of it.'

'Are the press here? Won't they want to make it into a story? What if something goes for a million quid?'

'It won't. But if it does, they'll be told at the end of the sale. People like it to be kept quiet, you know. It's all very confidential.'

'Sshh,' said a woman behind them and Christopher started to speak.

The sale went smoothly throughout the first half of the

morning, in that there were no delays or mistakes. Nor were there any startling bids, the lots fetching very modest sums. A few attracted no bids at all. The atmosphere subsided into something rather dreary, a few people getting up to leave, and Ben casting furtive glances at Christopher. Simmy had an idea that a more sparkling performance from the auctioneer might well have earned a few more raised hands or online clicks.

'This isn't very exciting, is it?' muttered Russell.

Simmy was trying to do some mental arithmetic, calculating the average hammer price for the first hundred lots. It came to somewhere around fifteen pounds. She looked round the room, studying the faces, but gleaned very little. People at auctions made a point of showing no emotion, like poker players. She nodded at her father in agreement and made a little pout.

'This stuff is rubbish,' he went on. 'That's the trouble. They can't expect to make much out of old flowerpots and rusty secateurs, can they?'

'It was part of the deal – they had to take everything,' she told him. 'It'll get better after lunch.'

Russell wriggled on the hard chair. 'If we can stick it that long.'

Simmy riffled through the catalogue. 'Pictures, curtains, clocks. It gets much more interesting after Lot 300. That'll be before lunch. He's on 147 at the moment, look, and it's not eleven yet.'

'He's very slow,' said Russell. 'Somebody told me they usually manage two hundred lots an hour.'

She didn't answer, but silently agreed with him. Christopher seemed to be running out of energy, just when he needed to be on top form. Behind her somebody said, 'This is not going well,' and someone else said, 'They're doing the boring stuff first, that's all.' Simmy turned round to flash a grateful smile, but could not work out which of the women in the row had spoken.

'I'm going to bid,' said Russell suddenly. 'There's a watering can I could use.'

'You can't. You haven't got a number.' This suddenly felt like a serious oversight, as if they had gatecrashed without a ticket. 'We should have got you one.'

'That's all right. He knows me, after all.'

'No, Dad. It doesn't work like that. You've been before. You know the routine.'

'Exactly. I've been before. So I'll be in the system. Ben probably remembers my number in his head.'

She gave in. He could even be right. And the pace of the auction was so slow already that any little hiccup caused by a numberless bidder would hardly cause any annoyance. 'Go on, then,' she invited.

Her father adopted a serious demeanour, waiting for the picture of the watering can to appear on the screens and then calmly raising his hand to bid five pounds for it. Nobody contested it and the hammer fell.

'Number?' barked Fiona, sitting at Christopher's elbow.

'Sorry. The name's Straw. I forget what the number is.'

Christopher whispered to her, and Ben waved a finger to indicate that he had successfully logged the transaction and they could go ahead. 'Told you!' said Russell to Simmy.

'What else are you going to buy, then?'

'I'm tempted by those first edition Walpoles, but I doubt I can afford them.'

'Books are the last thing of the day. We'll have gone home

by then. And of course you can't afford them.'

'He's terribly out of fashion, you know. I bet they'll go for peanuts.'

'Don't say that,' sighed Simmy.

'Cheer up,' he urged, suddenly a lot more animated. 'Aren't you glad you came?'

Talking was not exactly forbidden, but anything above a murmur was frowned upon. Christopher had a microphone and his words were in no danger of being drowned out, but there was an expectation that everyone would pay attention and not provide distractions from the serious business at hand.

'Oh yes,' Simmy said softly. 'Now, stop talking.'

'Sorry.' Russell mimed remorse and stared raptly at the auctioneer and his screens for the next five minutes. Simmy smiled to herself and took a turn at perusing the catalogue.

There were several things she felt she ought to be thinking about. Jennifer Reade primarily, and whether Christopher was all right. How much did any of it matter anyway, she found herself asking. It was an obscure dispersal sale, if that was what they called it, in a corner of England that put almost all its energies into catering for tourists. Those tourists were not present today. The people around her were locals – dealers, collectors and idle observers. Sir John Hickory had never been a household name or anything approaching it. The hype and excitement of the previous weeks had been misplaced, out of all proportion. And the fact of an unreported dead man in Sir John's house was surely of much greater significance.

Or was it? Her musings became confused and very murky. A life balanced against the acquisition of old objects of varying value. The interests of the living clashing with the duty due to the dead. Any civilised society would piously ordain that there was no dilemma. In honouring the dead, we give a mirroring respect to life. If it doesn't matter how you die, then perhaps it doesn't matter how you live, either. She floated into a succession of implications that had a shaky logical thread to them. How much weight could you give any individual life, anyway? And when did a life lose any genuine significance? If you thought abortion was perfectly acceptable, then you had to favour euthanasia as well – didn't you? Life became cheap and disposable in either case. Personally, she would rather there was never a need for either. Just a few rare instances, she decided, were all she could find to approve of. But Christopher's dead man had been a real person, not a barely formed foetus or an aged wreck. To conceal the fact of his death was to deny him the respect he was due. Every civilised society accepted this as an essential element in the system of law and practice. His body should be given protection and a proper disposal. Simmy shifted her weight on the hard chair and forced herself to stay seated – because she wanted to stand up and shout to her husband that he was terribly wrong. Looking at him, she could see that he knew it too. His performance had been fatally affected by the knowledge of his transgression, which was a kind of justice, Simmy supposed. The low hammer prices were his punishment. And Jennifer Reade's – which made Simmy feel very slightly better.

She switched her focus to the other members of the team. Fiona was looking worried, as was Ben. They both kept glancing at Christopher. A young man was standing below the platform, scanning the bidders, his manner alert and self-important.

'That must be Hughie,' she murmured to herself. She had heard his name mentioned a few times, but never met him.

Christopher had compared him to Ben, rather too favourably for Simmy's liking. Finally, the second woman, next to Fiona, had to be the briskly efficient Kitty. She was staring intently at her monitor, tapping the keyboard smartly and evidently of the opinion that things would be going a lot more quickly in a better-organised outfit.

And where was Jennifer Reade? Could she be one of the people standing at the back, squashed in amongst wardrobes and shelves and a rack of old fur coats? It felt rude to keep turning round to look, but Simmy did it a few times, unable to pinpoint anyone who remotely fitted her image of Ms Reade.

Christopher had reached Lot 165 and seemed to be more confident, speeding up and adding a few quips about the items going under the hammer. A very large wrought-iron plant stand in the shape of an eagle elicited a sudden flurry of competing bids. The auctioneer cocked his head at the image on the screen and remarked, 'Might look good with some spider plants for feathers,' which raised a few laughs.

Before he could move to Lot 166, Simmy's fantasy of an hour or two ago was suddenly made real. The door at the back opened with needless violence, attracting fifty turned heads, including Simmy's. Two uniformed policemen stood there, scanning the gathering. In unison they focused on the auctioneer, and one raised a hand as if bidding.

'This sale must be stopped!' he said loudly. 'Please cease the proceedings immediately.'

Chapter Eight

Ben didn't know where to look. First, he caught Simmy's eye, in the split second that she stopped staring at her husband. Then he too turned to Christopher, who was barely recognisable. His face was grey, his eyes bulging. His mouth was a rigid rectangle. It was painful to see, and Ben urgently wanted to do something about it. He stood up and faced the policemen. 'Why?' he shouted. 'By what right do you make such a demand?'

The officers ignored him, making him feel foolishly young, and instead made their way to the rostrum to address Christopher.

'Sir, information has come to light that requires us to suspend this sale. Nothing else will be auctioned here today. We ask you and everyone here to remain calm, and everything will be explained.'

'Huh!' snorted Ben. 'When did *that* ever happen?'

'Ben!' muttered Christopher.

Then Ben had an idea.

'Oh – it must be about that vase. I think Fiona reported it last thing yesterday. They said they'd send somebody over, but she told them it had better wait until Monday, with all this going on today and tomorrow. Fancy making such a fuss, silly fools.' He laughed and looked round in search of agreement, and perhaps even admiration at his clever deduction.

'It's not about the vase,' said Christopher tightly.

People were getting to their feet, hardly speaking, but watching the main players with great intensity. This was exciting, something new and unpredictable. The suspension of the sale did not greatly bother them, but Fiona was blinking at her computer screen and waving a hand to indicate agitation. The online bidders were clamouring, Ben realised. They would not understand anything of what was happening, and most of them had much more commitment to making purchases than those in the room. They might have heard the policeman's words but would find them even less comprehensible than the people there in the flesh did.

'Perhaps you could come with us, sir,' continued the officer. 'You and one or two of your colleagues.'

'But *why*?' Ben asked again, aware that his boss wanted him to remain quiet, but unable to comply. He could think of no conceivable explanation, other than some sort of fraud. Were Sir John's possessions stolen? A thought struck him. 'There's no ivory that you need worry about,' he added. 'Nor mother of pearl or pangolin skins.'

That must be it, he thought with a surge of relief. Being raided for banned animal products. And he had been immensely careful to ensure that every item they were selling complied with the law. He almost smiled. 'If that's all it is, we'll pass examination, no problem.'

'Ben!' said Christopher again. 'It's not about that.'

'Oh?' He gave his boss a long speculative look and took

86

the point. 'You know what's going on then, do you?'

'Just wait. Go and stay with Simmy. She can tell you some of it.'

Ben was caught in a dilemma. He wanted to follow Christopher into the office and hear what the police had to say. But he equally wanted to join Simmy and her father. Except, he realised, it wasn't for him to choose. He had to do what he was told.

'Okay,' he said. 'Take Kitty, then.'

He didn't know why, but the spiky female, with her superiority and know-it-all ways, seemed to him a more appropriate witness and support than the loyal but slightly drippy Fiona. There was Hughie, too, of course, but he had already melted away somewhere. Not surprising, thought Ben – he'd never been a proper part of the team, and would naturally not want any involvement with police matters.

Kitty flashed him a grateful look and moved closer to Christopher's side. Everyone on the platform but Fiona had stood up instinctively as the policemen approached. There was some shuffling, but no real movement. Fiona spoke first. 'Chris – what shall I tell the bidders? Everything's on hold.'

'Tell them that's it for today,' said Ben. 'Obviously.'

'But then what? When . . . ? I mean . . .' She floundered helplessly.

The policeman cleared his throat, and said, 'Come on, then,' to Christopher and Kitty. With slumped shoulders, Christopher put down the gavel he had been clutching, negotiated his way from behind the table and down two steps off the rostrum, sent one despairing glance at his wife, and meekly led the way.

Ben wove between bidders and furniture to find Hughie

and Jack both standing close to the doorway at the back of the room. People were bunching together to clear a gangway for Christopher's little group.

'This is *ludicrous*,' said Hughie loudly. 'What do you think you're doing?'

Ben, Jack and Fiona all gave him startled and disapproving looks. Kitty gave him a more friendly glance, seeming to agree with him.

Hughie didn't stop. 'You can't suspend an auction like this. Look at all these people! It can't be legal.'

'Be quiet,' Christopher told him. 'Don't make everything worse.'

'Sir,' said the policeman ominously. 'If you could just . . .' He made an ushering gesture. 'We don't have a lot of time.'

Christopher went out of the saleroom. Kitty followed closely. Jack left a moment later, shaking his head and looking pale. Fiona, Hughie and Ben were left to face the crowd, which Ben did bravely.

'All right, people,' he called. 'You heard the man. I don't know any more than you do about what's going on, or what happens next, but I can't imagine the delay will be very long. We'll put it all up on the website, as soon as we know ourselves – all right?'

Nobody moved to leave right away, but Ben could see that they were coming to the conclusion that there was no sense in staying put. As soon as one or two began the exodus, everyone else would follow. They would mill about outside for a bit and then start driving away if there looked to be no prospect of learning anything. All kinds of speculations would fly around, rumours would take root and before long there would be a full-blown story. Meanwhile, he had to join Simmy and Russell and extract whatever information he could from them. Somehow they got themselves outside and away from the loitering would-be bidders.

'So?' Ben challenged Simmy.

'Poor Christopher!' she moaned. 'Did you see his face? I thought he was going to collapse. And he hasn't really done anything. Not enough to warrant stopping the sale. It's what he'd been dreading. It was exactly like a nightmare.'

She was not making very much sense, but Ben did at least glean that she knew a great deal more than anybody else did. Even Russell was looking blankly bemused, holding his rucksack against his chest and shaking his head.

'Explain,' ordered Ben.

'Not here. I don't want anybody to hear us. We can go and sit in the car.'

Which they did, and within a very few minutes, Ben was in command of the whole business. 'We'd better call Moxon, then,' he said. 'And possibly a lawyer. Because it looks to me as if our Christopher's in pretty deep water.'

Russell had paid fierce attention to Simmy's account of Wednesday's events, and he as well as Ben quickly grasped the salient points.

'Something else must have happened,' he said. 'They'd never stop the sale on the basis of what you've just told us. Why would they?'

'It's that Jennifer woman,' said Ben, in instant agreement. 'She's playing some game, with Christopher as the patsy. She's dropped him in it, for some reason.'

Simmy heaved a profound sigh. 'I wonder. And where *is* she? She was supposed to be here today.'

'Busy causing trouble,' said Ben. 'She could have been

monitoring the auction online, don't forget. She'll know it wasn't going very well. She might have opted to put a stop to it for that reason.'

'Don't be daft,' said Russell. 'She wouldn't have had time, apart from anything else.'

Ben nodded submissively. 'You're right. It wouldn't make much sense, would it? It's got to be about this man in the cellar. But how could the cops have found out about him, if the woman and Christopher were the only people who knew he was there? That's right, isn't it?' he asked Simmy.

She made a little cough of helpless agreement. 'I suppose we can't know that for sure. The place is pretty thick with hikers and so forth. Anyone could start snooping about. But they wouldn't be able to get inside the house. It sounded as if he hadn't been dead very long – so there wouldn't be much of a smell yet.'

Ben made a knowing face. 'Ah, well – height of summer, flies and other things. Two days is a long time when it comes to decomposition. But up on the fells anyone would just assume it was a sheep. In fact, there very likely are a few scattered about. They fall into becks and get stuck between rocks all the time.' Ben had embarked on a degree course in forensic archaeology and knew a lot about such topics, learnt before abandoning his studies.

'I bet you the woman's gone and double-crossed poor old Chris,' said Russell. 'Not the way you said,' he told Ben, 'but something that's been planned all along. Some deep game to do with inheritance or . . .'

'Or what?' demanded Ben. 'We're both having wild ideas that can't possibly work in practice. Or have any remotely credible reason behind them.'

'I wish I'd forced Christopher to go to the police last night,' moaned Simmy. 'Just lay it all out straight and take the consequences.'

'He'll be wishing the same thing now,' said Russell tartly. 'He should know that honesty is the best policy.'

'He had his reasons,' Simmy defended weakly.

The three of them continued to sit in the car for another fifteen minutes, saying much the same things over and over. Ben was restless, aware that he should be in the saleroom finding ways to be useful, but much more interested in hearing what Simmy and her father had to say. The revelation of the dead man in the cellar thrilled him and gave rise to a host of theories.

'I agree with you,' he told Russell. 'That on its own wouldn't make them stop the sale.'

'It might, though,' Simmy argued. 'If they identified the body and worked out that he had some claim on the things in the house. Or the house itself. Christopher seemed to think there might have been a hint of that behind what the Reade woman was saying. At least, I think that's right. He was really scared that the sale would be stopped.'

'With good reason, as it turned out,' said Russell.

'He's in trouble, whatever happens,' said Ben darkly. 'Which is going to rebound on the whole business. Why didn't he have the sense to just report it in the normal way?'

Simmy was losing patience. 'I *told* you about five times. He promised her he wouldn't. They made a deal.'

Ben was not deterred. 'Funny sort of deal – more like she threatened him and he was scared into doing what she asked. What was her side of the bargain, anyway?'

Simmy gathered her thoughts. 'Well, letting it all go ahead,

I suppose. She'd want everything sold and the money handed over to her. She knew Christopher and her both had a lot to lose if that didn't happen as arranged. Reputation as well as money. She made him believe it was in both their interests.'

'We said all this,' Russell complained.

'I'll have to go back in,' sighed Ben.

Almost all the cars had gone, leaving a near-empty area between the road and the assembled auction lots that could withstand being left outside.

'That's my watering can!' Russell said suddenly. 'Look – sitting on top of that rainwater butt. Why would they bring that here?' he wondered irrelevantly. 'I'd have thought it was a fixture.'

'There was a bit of an argument about that,' Ben reported, never able to resist answering a question, however mundane or inappropriate. 'It wasn't connected at all – just sitting by the corner of the house, catching any overspill. It's a nice old one. You can't take the watering can until you've paid for it.'

'So maybe I'll go and see if I can do that, then.'

'You can't. It's all in limbo. Nobody's taken anything, look. All these outside lots have been sold, and they're all still sitting here.'

'You'd think people would hang around, then, until they could have them.'

'I suppose Kitty or Fiona told them not to. They might all come back this afternoon to see if we've got our act together.'

'Oh – there's Christopher!' said Simmy suddenly. 'They must be arresting him.' She made a soft moaning sound and threw open the car door.

The two policemen were walking on either side of Christopher, heading towards their car, which stood outside the big gate that opened onto the road. It was parked on double yellow lines. Simmy ran after them. Christopher threw her a quick look but seemed anxious for her not to say anything. He was every bit as pale as the last time she'd seen him, his eyes strangely hollow.

'Please wait,' she said. 'I'm his wife. Where are you taking him?'

'It's okay, Sim,' said Christopher, with an obvious effort. 'I'm not being accused of anything – nothing too serious, anyway. You don't need to worry.'

One of the policemen took a sharp inward breath of disapproval. 'Sir!' he said.

'All right,' Christopher threw at him, before facing Simmy with a look of blank bewilderment. 'It's Jennifer Reade, you see. She's dead. Somebody killed her.'

Before he could say any more, he was bundled into the back of the police car and driven away. It was crystal clear that he was not supposed to have said what he did, and Simmy felt a flash of satisfaction that he had managed at least that small act of defiance. She also had a piece of extremely significant information to convey to Ben and her father. She hurried back to them and repeated her husband's words.

'Blimey!' said Ben. 'So much for all our dim-witted guesses, then.'

'They don't think Christopher did it, do they?' said Russell.

Simmy was able to answer that with confidence. 'No. He said he wasn't being accused of anything serious. Not reporting a dead body must be all they can find.'

'That's fairly serious,' said Ben. 'Especially if they get the idea that he killed the bloke.'

'No, no,' Simmy insisted. 'He told me just now – he worded it deliberately, so we wouldn't worry about anything like that. I expect they've worked out that the man died of natural causes.'

'But *when?*' wailed Ben. 'When did Ms Reade get killed? Who found her? Where was she?'

'And why stop the auction?' said Russell, returning the whole discussion back to square one.

'That's obvious, at least,' said Ben witheringly. 'If she's the owner of everything we're selling, and she's died in the middle of it all, then nobody knows where the proceeds should go.'

Russell ducked his head in a gesture of forbearance. 'I can't see how it would be different if everything was sold. Easier, surely, to handle a lump sum of money, rather than all this *stuff.*' He waved an expressive hand to include the entire saleroom and its yard. 'What's the thinking – that's what I don't get.'

'Stop it,' said Simmy. 'Did you see his *face?* He was in total shock. He could hardly speak.'

'You just said he gave you a deliberate careful message,' Ben reminded her.

'With a tremendous effort, yes. He didn't want me to worry. But they've obviously arrested him.'

'We don't know how much he's told them already. Or what they'll make of it. These are just two uniformed plods, so they won't have got far. Why did they take such a long time over it, I wonder?'

'He probably had to see to the staff and decide what happens about the auction.'

Russell was sitting quietly in the back of the car, which was getting uncomfortably warm. 'We should go home,' he said. 'Maybe they'll let me go and pay for my watering can first. That'll be one thing out of their way.'

'Come on, then,' said Ben. 'You've already broken one rule by not having your number. I dare say we can wangle something, if it's that important.'

'Thanks, Ben,' said Simmy, on her father's behalf. 'Then we'll go. No point in hanging around here.'

She realised that she had not given her little son a single thought for about two hours. Nor was she anxious to be reunited with him – he was better off with his grandma, the way Simmy was feeling. All her thoughts were on Christopher, who had admittedly been in somewhat similar situations before, but this time felt much worse. For a start, his conscience was not entirely clear. He had done wrong, and was therefore not going to be able to maintain a steadfast response to whatever might happen to him. By admitting one crime, he laid himself open to accusations of others. This, she understood, was what he had been trying to convey in his few words to her before being driven away. *Yes, I did one bad thing, but they can't find me guilty of anything else.* It was small comfort.

Russell secured his watering can, which was made of a rustproof zinc and probably dated back a hundred years. The seam where the spout joined the main body was showing considerable wear, however, and he worried that it had little useful life remaining to it.

'You can grow a fern in it, then,' said Simmy.

'Good idea,' he said cheerfully, sitting in the front passenger seat and cradling it on his lap. 'Your mother's going to say I'm mad.'

'Probably,' Simmy agreed.

The short drive back to Threlkeld was not proving to be enough to change any of her thoughts or feelings. Leaving the auction house felt like abandoning her husband, which she knew was irrational. There was no place for her amidst the Kittys and Fionas and frustrated bidders. None of it was anything to do with her. It was surprising, really, that she'd even known about the Borrowdale body. Christopher had not intended to tell her about it. How much less sense would the events of the morning have made if she had remained in ignorance! As it was, she assumed she understood at least as much as anybody else did. And now she and her father would have to explain it all to Angie.

'Goodness knows what your mother's going to say,' Russell sighed, reading her thoughts.

'She'll be annoyed with us for wanting some lunch,' Simmy tried to joke.

'No she won't, because we've still got the sandwiches.' He looked over at his rucksack on the back seat. 'They might have got a bit warm, but they'll still be perfectly edible.'

'Lovely,' she said.

'Hard to work out what's going to happen now,' he went on. 'Technically, I would think the auction could be resumed tomorrow. They'd need a proper injunction to stop it. Actually, they probably didn't have the legal right to stop it today, come to think of it. I still don't understand what they thought that would achieve. Just a lot of confused and indignant people to deal with.'

'Being on the safe side, I suppose,' said Simmy vaguely. 'Do you think I should phone Moxon and see what he knows?'

'Couldn't hurt,' said Russell judiciously.

Which exactly summed up the position, she decided.

But first there were explanations to be given to Simmy's mother, who had not yet left for the pub. It took her a lot longer than Russell to grasp the salient points of the morning's events.

'Wait!' she begged, every few seconds. 'Do you mean that Christopher *knew* somebody was dead in the house and never said anything?' Then, 'But do we think the Jennifer person killed the man in the cellar?' And, 'How can an auction just *stop* like that? Where did everybody go?'

'We don't know, Mum,' Simmy replied patiently to most of the questions. 'I should phone Moxon and see what he's heard.'

'Poor man,' was Angie's surprising response to that. 'Hasn't he had enough of divided loyalties since he met you?'

Simmy hesitated. The accusation was exaggerated – until now the division between right and wrong, guilty and innocent had never been seriously in question. But perhaps this time it was different.

'You mean because Christopher should have reported the body?'

'Obviously. He put himself in the wrong. You said so yourself.'

'Did I?' Perhaps she had, in effect, if not in so many words. 'But he *knows* us. He won't take it the wrong way. He'll be upset if we don't keep him in the loop. He's probably not directly involved.'

Angie had little Robin on her lap, clearly not ready to relinquish him to his mother. 'Why *did* they stop the auction, though?' She frowned from husband to daughter and back. 'I never heard of anything like that happening before.'

'We don't know,' said Simmy yet again. 'Just guesses. Now we're wondering if they had the legal right to do it.'

'Somebody must have given the order for a reason.'

'Presumably.'

Russell was unpacking his rucksack, and handed Simmy a sandwich, clumsily wrapped in clingfilm. Robin leant over and deftly intercepted it. The resulting hilarity came as a big relief – for about two minutes. Angie ruefully accepted that her trip to the pub with Robin was not going to happen. She found cheese, apples and yoghurt for them instead.

'And you say Christopher *met* this woman, at the house in Borrowdale?' Angie said. 'When?'

'The day before yesterday,' Simmy answered patiently. 'We went there for a day out, and Christopher had the key, so we had a quick look round. He even went down the steps to the cellar but came rushing back because he saw a rat.'

'What?' It was Russell staring at her in alarm. 'You mean he went into the cellar by himself, when there was a body there?'

'He didn't see it. He didn't get further than the steps. Jennifer Reade took him down there again after lunch. That was when he kept me and Robin hanging about for ages by the bridge.'

'Bodd-ee,' said Robin, very distinctly, looking to his mother for approval.

'Clever boy,' she said, with a grimace.

'Well, I think it all sounds extremely messy,' said Angie decisively. 'Two dead people, an auction in limbo, your husband under arrest, and goodness knows what else.'

'I bought a nice antique watering can,' said Russell, after a pause. 'So it's not all bad.'

* * *

Back in Hartsop with her child and dog, Simmy released the dog into the garden and wondered what to do next. She had to consider her young charges before anything else. Cornelia, like Robin, was a little over a year old, and a great responsibility. After numerous occasions when she had been left for much too long alone in the house, a local girl had been found who would come and take the animal out for half an hour when required. She was called Lily and at the age of sixteen had abandoned school in favour of making wall hangings, bags and bedcovers out of raw Lakeland fleece and selling them online for impressive profits. She could do weaving, crochet and something called needle felting, which produced three-dimensional figures that Simmy found deeply appealing. As far as she could see, Lily had a great career ahead of her. She lived three doors away, with middle-aged parents who regarded her as something akin to a cuckoo chick. Cornelia adored her. Bonnie Lawson, however, for some reason had taken against her.

'She doesn't know she's born,' she said, more than once. 'Wait till she has to deal with the real world.'

Simmy could not see in what respect Lily was not already engaged in a substantial section of reality.

'She's making quite a lot of money, you know,' she protested. 'She's even got a contract with DHL to deliver to all her customers. Saves having to struggle all the way to the post office with a bagful of parcels.'

'Huh!' was all Bonnie would say to that.

It was nearly three o'clock, and the sensation of being suspended over a gulf of unknowable proportions was acute. Simmy had not heard from Christopher, or Ben or Moxon and she urgently wanted to speak to them all. Between those three men, the story must surely emerge more clearly. Ben would carry on with his theorising, asking questions and following up sudden guesses on the computer. Moxon would know how the police were thinking. And Christopher would need her for support. But she had a child and a dog to consider, as well as a shop with employees and uncertain plans for the weekend. The kitchen was untidy and it was high time she put another load of washing on.

She was struck by her own absence of real concern for her husband. His reassuring words still rang in her head, and she fancied she already knew what the worst-case scenario was, where he was concerned. He would be chastised for failing to report a body, and he would be bullied in various ways with regard to continuing the auction. Bad, but not terrible. Embarrassing, even perhaps mildly humiliating, but he would soon recover. Nobody thought there was any malice or criminality in him. The auction business operated in areas that were decidedly grey at times, but the Henderson operation was not known for shady dealings. Involved in a number of violent deaths, mostly through his wife and her work as a florist, Christopher was basically on the side of the angels.

He ought to have been released by now, all the same, and therefore sending at least a brief text to his wife. Would he have simply gone back to work, issuing information and instructions, and leaving his family for later? Was he perhaps still too stunned at the death of Jennifer Reade to function effectively? Were Kitty and Fiona and others so solicitous towards him that he hadn't a moment to himself?

Kitchen, washing and child were all swiftly dealt with, and she sat down in the living room with her phone. She had no doubt that Ben would have sent Bonnie a summary of the day's events, ahead of some sort of news story emerging in the media. Jennifer Reade had earned minimal coverage thus far, despite such a large and sudden inheritance being likely to arouse interest. The unusual two-day auction must surely have crossed the radar of at least the local paper, too. Christopher had placed his usual display advertisement in the preceding weeks, making the point that this was no ordinary sale. Wouldn't a reporter routinely call afterwards to find out how much the High Gates contents had fetched? And then they would have to be told at least some of the truth about the postponement. Except, of course, a murdered woman trumped everything and there would very probably be items on TV, radio and social media already.

So who should she phone first? The obvious claim to priority lay with her husband. A lot of wives would be feeling resentful at the extended silence and Simmy had to swallow down any such reaction. He would call if he could – of that she was confident. And that meant it would be futile to try phoning him. She might interrupt something delicate; more likely it would go to voicemail. Instead, she opted for a brief text.

'Am home now, being patient. Sending best possible vibes.'

She felt rather pleased with herself at this choice of words. Reassuring, undemanding, the pinnacle of wifely forbearance. She thought she ought to show it to her mother sometime, in a small piece of boastfulness.

The phone lay passive in her hand, an object imbued with an impossible array of emotions. It enabled as much as it frustrated. It was self-evidently *useful* – a word Simmy must have heard applied to it many hundreds of times. Although to judge by the many anecdotes she had encountered, the thing was essentially neutral when it came to its contribution to the sum of human happiness. It took away as much as it gave, and the only rational approach was to keep it firmly in its place.

She keyed the shortcut to phone Ben Harkness. When it came to the crunch, Ben was the pivot, the heart of every line of investigation and the source of every clever theory. He attracted information like a magnet, processed it like a computer and remembered every detail. 'What's happening?' she asked when he responded.

'Nothing. Literally nothing. Nobody knows anything, and we have no clue what we ought to be doing.'

'Where's Christopher?'

'No hard information, but we surmise that he's been taken off to Borrowdale to explain himself and re-enact everything that happened on Wednesday. Oh – one thing does stand out. Did you know that Ms Reade was technophobic? Literally, I think. She wouldn't use a mobile or a satnav or Facebook or online banking. None of it. Kitty knew because she's had to make special arrangements with the woman's solicitors about the clearance money. Although they're really not that special, when it comes to it, oddly enough. We still write cheques to some of the vendors and post them. It was just that some girl at the solicitor's office thought it was amazing and ranted on to Kitty about it, and she's just been telling it all to us.'

'Is it relevant?'

'Only that it must make it more difficult for the police to work out where she was at any given time. Her car will be on some CCTV footage and that's about it. She probably didn't use bank cards, either.'

'How old is she?'

'Was,' he corrected her automatically. 'Somewhere around thirty, we think. If we were in America, we'd assume she was Amish, but that doesn't work here. It's obviously some sort of personality disorder.'

'Maybe it killed her. I mean – if she'd had a phone she might have called for help.'

'Yeah,' said Ben. Then he yelped, 'Hey! Christopher's back. He's just walked in. Do you want to speak to him?'

'How does he look? He might have more important things to do.'

She heard muffled conversation coming from three or four voices before Ben came back.

'He says he's fine, and thanks for the text and he's coming home soon. Okay?'

'Great. Thanks, Ben.' And she finished the call.

Chapter Nine

'I hardly know where to start,' sighed Christopher when he got home. It was half past four, and they were both aware that this was at least three hours earlier than the plan had been. The sale would have ended sometime after six, followed by administrative work, mutual debriefing and arrangements for Saturday.

'What's happening tomorrow?' Simmy asked, remembering that Bonnie was expecting to attend a full day's auction.

'Nothing. We've sent out emails and Facebookery and phoned some people. It's all on hold.'

'But *why*?' The question was definitely getting stale.

'I'll come to that. Let me tell you about today first.' Which he proceeded to do, holding their biggest mug of coffee and picking at some cold chicken that Simmy had brought him where he sat on the sofa.

'She died at seven o'clock this morning. They know that for certain, because there were two people with her at the time.' He raised a finger to prevent questions. 'Two hikers found her on the road between Borrowdale and Honister. They assumed she'd been run over, but she was conscious and managed to convey to them that she had been beaten by someone while she was in High Gates House. They think she never saw who it was because she mumbled that she'd been asleep when attacked. Her skull was broken and she died there on the road, where she must have staggered or crawled, looking for help.'

Simmy could not hold back any longer. 'The poor thing!' She could visualise it all much too vividly. 'But lucky somebody found her. They must have been out early.'

'You know what they're like, especially this time of year. Anyway, she died right there in front of them, after only saying a few words. The main ones were "Stop the sale". She said that three times. The hikers were very definite about it. Then she lost consciousness and died before an ambulance got there.'

Simmy sat back. 'Well that answers one big question, then. Those poor people who found her. They must be traumatised.'

He blinked. 'I guess so. That didn't occur to me. It sounds as if they still thought it more likely she'd been run over. The police say there's no sign at all that a vehicle hit her. Either way, it must have been ghastly for them. I should have thought.'

'Well, you must have had a lot else on your mind. It's good that the police told you the whole story. It shows they don't suspect you of anything.' She tried to gather her thoughts. 'But how weird that she was sleeping in the house! There aren't any beds, and there was that *body* in the cellar.'

'They think she couldn't find anywhere else. Lakeland in June is hardly awash with empty rooms. And somebody

105

noticed one of the tyres was flat on her car.'

'Chris – the woman was a millionaire. She could have found somewhere. There are three hotels at least within walking distance. And a flat tyre isn't difficult to fix. She could have got a hiker to help.'

'Nobody knows what she was doing there, Sim. They can only guess. She might have *wanted* to sleep in the house, for some sentimental reason. It had been hers for just a few months – and she told me she'd only decided to go and see it at the last minute. She might have felt she should make up for lost time – something like that. I got the impression on Wednesday that she'd belatedly come to realise what she was losing. Until then she'd shown no interest at all in the house or its contents.'

Simmy gave him a close inspection, relieved to find few signs of lasting distress. The stunned look had gone, and he was obviously marshalling his thoughts quite effectively.

'So they stopped the sale because she said what she did. Without knowing why.'

'Not much choice, I suppose. They took their time, when you think about it. By half past seven they were into a murder investigation, based on her injuries. They clearly indicated a violent attack, and they soon worked out who she was.'

'Did they? How?'

'The clue was the house itself as well as the car. She'd barely got beyond the gate when the hikers found her. The fact that she owned it was soon established. Police went in and found blood. A quick bit of googling threw up our sale, which fitted with Jennifer's last words. It was a matter of moments, probably. They nearly took me back there, you

106

know, but then decided there was no need. I told them all about the dead man in the cellar.'

'Ben said they would take you back there. So . . . ?'

'The body wasn't there,' he said starkly. 'They trooped down into the cellar as soon as I told them about it and it had gone.' His face crumpled. 'That was the worst part of it all. They'd kept me at the station while they searched the house, and when they couldn't find anything, they didn't know what to believe, and I wondered if I'd gone crazy. But in the end, they grudgingly realised they had to take my word for it. Why would I make it up? They let me go soon after that.'

'That's . . .' She couldn't find a word for it. 'Like something out of a story.'

Christopher nodded helplessly. 'Nobody can make sense of it. I had to tell Ben, of course. He's beside himself with excitement.'

'Have you told all of them? Did the police say you could? Was it Penrith they took you to? Who did you see?'

'Some detective superintendent for a few minutes. I don't remember his name. Then they passed me over to a woman who seems to be new. Scottish accent. Wears Doc Martens. Gives the impression she'd enjoy a hearty game of rugby. I don't think she liked me.'

Simmy laughed.

'Anyway, everything's still on hold. I'm past caring about the sale, to be honest. At least I understand why it was stopped. It isn't really my mystery any more. I'm just going to sit back and wait for permission to carry on. The whole calendar for the summer's going to be thrown into chaos, but I expect we'll cope. Ben did say that the publicity might do us some good. When we do get started again, there'll probably be a whole new lot of bidders, because of the story.'

He was obviously trying to convince himself and Simmy did not have the heart to disabuse him too quickly. She responded cautiously with, 'Except we still don't know what the story *is*, do we?' She felt a surge of foreboding. 'I don't think we ought to speak too soon.'

'Let's forget about it for now. Is it too late for a little walk?' It was almost half past five.

Robin's afternoon nap was over and he had been brought downstairs to greet his father as soon as Christopher got home. The ensuing conversation had taken place over his head, where he snuggled next to Christopher on the sofa, thumb in his mouth.

'It is, really,' said Simmy. 'It's almost supper time. Robin would find it very confusing.'

'Nonsense. It'll train him up to be adaptable. I never did like routines myself. And it's a lovely evening. You said yourself we shouldn't waste them by sitting indoors.'

She gave in without further protest, despite a suspicion that small children depended on routine for their well-being and the coming night might well demonstrate the truth of this.

The walk was short but therapeutic. Scents of honeysuckle and roses bathed the little village in flowery well-being and Robin kicked his heels on the bar of his buggy with enthusiasm. No mobile phones went with them, and Cornelia was allowed to run loose all the way along the road to where it terminated in a car park. On all sides were views of fells and woodlands and handsome Lakeland houses. Sounds of lawnmowers mingled with occasional voices, but almost no car engines. A few of the Hartsop properties were holiday lets, which were generally occupied all the year round. Gardens were tended carelessly, with none of the competition experienced further south.

'There's Lily,' said Simmy, spotting Cornelia's walker. 'I think we owe her some money.'

'I haven't got any on me, have you?'

'No. She won't mind waiting a few more days. We might need her again soon, anyway.' Simmy waved at the girl who was standing in the street, looking up into a tree.

'Swallows,' she said, pointing at a group of swooping birds. 'The babies have fledged.' Cornelia had run up to her, and loving hugs were exchanged. The dog jumped up and wrapped its forelegs around the girl's knees. 'Hello, poochie,' Lily added. Her wholesale indifference to Robin was obvious, but not desperately offensive.

'She was okay today, was she?' asked Simmy.

'Fine. We went all the way to Crookaback, because I wasn't busy. It took more than an hour.'

'Gosh! We must owe you extra cash, then.'

Lily laughed. 'No – I would have gone anyway. I don't like to take any payment, really.'

'Well you must.'

'Oh – and a man came today. He was a bit weird, actually. He was waiting outside your house when I got back, and I didn't know what to do, so I pretended Cornelia was mine and I was just walking past. I didn't want him to see that I had a key.'

'Did you talk to him?'

'I wasn't going to, but he followed me. It was Cornelia's

109

fault – she didn't understand what was going on, and went up to your door, obviously going home. So he knew I was pretending. I wasn't *scared* exactly, because he was actually rather nice, but you never know, do you?'

Couldn't have been Moxon, thought Simmy. Nor any of Christopher's relations. 'Do you think he could have been selling something?' she said.

'Not really. He wanted you, Mr Henderson. He said you'd know what he meant if he said he knew you were trying to find a body. I mean – that was weird, wasn't it?'

'Very,' said Simmy. 'What did you say to him?'

'Nothing. I couldn't think of anything. I just walked up here and went in. My mum was home, luckily. I waited until he'd gone and then took Corny home.'

'Did he tell you his name?' asked Christopher.

Lily shook her head.

'Well, we're sorry you were bothered. If we find out who he was, we'll have a strong word about it and make sure it doesn't happen again. Did you tell your mum?'

Lily nodded.

'Good. So you're still up for some dog walking?'

'Oh yes! I *love* her. She's a *darling*. And I need the exercise. I'd spend twelve hours a day at the felting otherwise.'

Christopher was hesitating, staring up at the Dodd and apparently debating with himself. 'Sorry, Lily,' he said eventually. 'But I think I'm going to have to tell the police about that man. And they'll probably come and ask you to describe him. Would that be all right?'

The girl's reaction was endearingly childlike. 'Oh, that'd be fun! Is he a criminal, do you think? I hope I can help them catch him, if he is.'

Simmy managed a laugh. 'Steady on!' she cautioned. 'I'm not sure your parents will see it like that. There's been some trouble at Christopher's work. Somebody died. It's all rather a muddle at the moment. And it sounds as if this man's got something to do with it. He's not going to bother you again, I'm sure. Why would he? But . . . well, don't go off up the fells by yourself for a bit, okay? Just to be on the safe side.'

Lily was a bright girl. 'You mean because he'll guess that I've described him to the police and want to get even with me, or something? But then it would be too late, wouldn't it? It already is, in fact. There'd be no sense in shutting me up now. But I don't expect he's really a baddie. He seemed worried and maybe a bit *desperate*, but that's all. I didn't think he was dangerous at all, really.'

'He won't come back here,' said Christopher with an unconvincing certainty. 'If he wants me, he'll come and find me at work.'

Both females gave him sceptical looks but said nothing.

The Hendersons went home in silence, each trying to explain to themselves who the mysterious man had been. If anything, Simmy thought they were probably both more frightened than young Lily had been.

'Missed a call from Bonnie,' Simmy realised, some time later, after she had put a sleepy baby to bed. She listened to the message, which was long and anxious. 'She wants to know what's happening tomorrow. She's promised that we'll make two deliveries, because she thought I'd be there to do them. That means I'm going to have to go down there as planned. Can you take Robin to Threlkeld? It'd save

111

me masses of time and it's on your way if you're going to Keswick.'

Christopher had no reason to refuse, but she could see he felt it was an imposition. 'I don't know if I am going to Keswick, do I? The police might want to question me in Penrith again. Or even Borrowdale. And I need to tell them about the man who accosted Lily.'

She bit back all the traditional responses. *Well, don't bother if it's a nuisance. Okay, I'll do it, then.* Such remarks would convey martyrdom, impatience, and a lurking sense of imbalance that put the self-important father in the wrong. It had to be acknowledged that transporting a toddler was not high priority in a man's world, even in these enlightened times. Higher than it used to be, admittedly, but still readily avoided if deemed inconvenient. 'I think you'll fit it in without too much hassle,' she told him sweetly.

'I expect I will,' he agreed ruefully. 'But what about reporting this business with Lily?'

'You can do it in the morning. I can't see that it'll help them much. Lily can probably look after herself, although I dare say we'll have her mother after us.'

'Once the news about Jennifer Reade gets out, they'll draw conclusions and we'll be seen as dangerous to know. Mixing with shady characters and scaring young girls.'

'Worse, probably. The man – whoever he was – talked about a *body*. That's not acceptable by any standards, is it?'

'Not if he meant a dead person. I've been trying to think of something else it might mean.'

She gave this a moment's consideration before admitting defeat. 'What else *could* it mean?'

'Body of work. Corporate body. Body of water.' He

112

spread his hands helplessly. 'None of them fit, do they?'

She shook her head. 'Although body of work might just have possibilities. He might have said another word or two that Lily missed.'

'No, Sim. He meant the dead man in the High Gates cellar, who has now disappeared. He knows that I know it was there on Wednesday.'

'So who *is* he?'

'Not the foggiest. It can't be anybody I've ever met. Somebody who knew Jennifer, or Sir John, perhaps. Somebody with a hand in the whole disposal of the house.'

'You mean like an estate agent? Or a solicitor?'

'I wish I did mean that – but it would be terribly odd behaviour for either of them, wouldn't it.'

They both laughed at the images this conjured. 'He sounds more like an escaped convict,' said Simmy.

'Or a ghost.' In his younger days, Christopher had exhibited a rather fey side to his character, roaming through ancient ruins at dusk and constructing imaginative dramas around their mysterious past. Simmy had gone with him once or twice and been deliciously frightened by his fantasies. At some point he seemed to have dropped that sort of thing completely. Now she glimpsed a flicker of the earlier version and was inordinately pleased.

'The ghost of the dead man? Looking for his corporeal body? Oh – we forgot "celestial body". But that can't be right, either.'

'We're getting silly,' he said, with no sign that this was a bad thing. 'I'm even wondering whether Wednesday was all a dream. Did we ever really go to Borrowdale?'

'I'm afraid we did. But with Jennifer dead, you and this

mystery man might be the only ones left who know for sure there was a body in the cellar. If he died of natural causes, that is. Otherwise, whoever killed him can be added to the list.'

'I was hoping I might have imagined it.' He closed his eyes and rubbed his forehead. 'Nope. I saw the mess of his face. I saw at least two rats. And I was sick.'

'Pardon?'

'I might not have told you that bit. He looked so gruesome that I threw up. More or less on top of him, actually. Jennifer said there'd be my DNA in the vomit, but the rats would soon clear it up.'

'This is very horrible,' she said queasily. 'I wonder if there really is DNA in vomit.'

'We'll have to ask Ben. I believed her at the time.'

Simmy frowned and suppressed her moment of weakness. 'I don't think there can be, you know. Not unless there's blood in it. Although I suppose quite a bit of saliva comes with sick, and that's good for DNA.'

'Stop it,' he begged. 'I knew I shouldn't have told you.'

'Don't be daft, it was just when you first said it . . . it's nothing so horrible, really, is it? And when have I ever been squeamish about this sort of thing? Certainly not since having a baby and dealing with so much bodily fluid. But seriously, the point has to be that Jennifer convinced you, and used it to scare you. Right? Is that how she persuaded you to keep it all secret?'

'Partly. More that she said the police would stop the sale.'

'Which they did, because she wanted them to, in her dying breath. Which seems a bit inconsistent. Something

114

must have changed between Wednesday and this morning.'

'Right! And it has to do with the man who spoke to Lily. Somebody killed Jennifer in the night between Thursday and Friday, while she was in the house. That's pretty odd as well, because I'm sure she said she wouldn't be going back there again. It doesn't fit with anything she told me. I'm not sure the house would have been hers by then, anyway, unless something delayed the final completion of the sale.'

'We need Ben,' said Simmy for the second time.

Christopher moaned. 'I dream of the day when we stop saying that. Meanwhile, I know you're right. Although I'm not sure he's completely au fait with the complexities of selling a house.'

'He'll have all he needs on the computer. Yours at work, I mean.'

'How come?'

She hesitated. 'Well, maybe now Jennifer Reade is dead, that isn't true. Gosh, it's a mess, isn't it. Who's going to get the house and money and all the things now?'

'It's tempting to think the answer to that question is also the answer to who killed her. It's a pretty strong motive, after all.'

'Well, we can't even begin to try to work it out, because we've got no idea who that might be.'

'She mentioned somebody called Julian. Sounded as if he might be a boyfriend. I'm still in shock, you know, after hearing she's dead. It doesn't seem possible. I *liked* her.'

'Did you?' This came as a surprise. 'I thought she sounded bossy and untrustworthy.'

'Nobody's perfect,' he said with a brave attempt at a grin.

'Ben can probably find the Julian person. Are they on Facebook or something?'

He blinked at her. 'Simmy, I *told* you. She's off the grid, or whatever they say. Wouldn't have any truck with anything digital, apart from the landline phone. Wrote letters, used cheques, maps, proper books, like something fifty years ago. Definitely no Facebook.'

Simmy sighed. 'I forgot. Or rather, I hadn't thought through all the implications. It sounds rather refreshing.'

'You suggested that's what killed her, one way or another. You might be right.'

Simmy was following a whole mass of thoughts, trying to visualise the woman's life. 'Must be lovely not to even have a mobile.'

'It's absolutely not. It's perverse.'

Simmy was still going over the same ground they'd covered an hour or two ago. 'Well, she only has herself to blame, then – having to crawl out to the road instead of calling 999.'

Christopher shook his head. 'We can't know what happened, for sure. But I'm thinking it's Moxon we need now, more than Ben. We need him to tell us whether anybody really believes me about the body in the cellar, for a start. And whether anybody's gone missing, and who Julian is. And we have to report this sinister man who accosted poor Lily.'

'Not necessarily to Moxon, though.' She found herself wanting to excuse the Windermere detective who had always been such a friend to her. He did not relish having to work with the people at Penrith, who made little secret of their feelings towards him. He had enjoyed rather a quiet

116

life until the spate of murders began a few years earlier. They had involved Simmy, Ben, Bonnie and Christopher in varying combinations, and managed to highlight the detective's own somewhat inadequate contributions to the investigations. In Askham a few months ago he had redeemed himself to some extent, largely because Simmy herself had been under suspicion. 'Better to get back to the one who interviewed you this morning, I should think.'

He eyed her carefully. 'Not Moxon, then?'

She tried to explain, with scant success. Her husband had never quite understood her relationship with the detective, alternating between a vague jealousy and a profound gratitude as one adventure followed another. 'Anyway, I've got to get back to Bonnie,' she remembered, glad to change the subject. 'And we haven't had any supper. What a very peculiar day it's been.'

Chapter Ten

Saturday morning brought no improvement to the peculiarities of the situation. Nobody knew what they should be doing. Ben, Bonnie, Christopher – even Russell and Angie – all demanded to know what happened next and where they ought to be. And Simmy was the person to whom they addressed their demands, which she felt was very unfair.

'How should *I* know?' she almost shouted at her mother, who phoned at ten to nine. 'I'm supposed to be halfway to Windermere by now, but people keep stopping me.'

'You're going to the shop, then?' said Angie calmly. 'So who's having Robin? And where's Bonnie going to be?'

The answers to these questions were just as obscure to Simmy as they were to her mother. 'I think I'll have to take Robin with me. Nobody else seems able to guarantee they can have him. Christopher was supposed to bring him to you, but he says he has to go to Penrith right now because of something that happened yesterday.' Much of this, she knew, was grossly unfair, and was entirely Christopher's fault.

'I thought I was having him,' said Angie, somewhat less calmly.

'I know. I'm sorry. But I haven't got time to bring him

118

over. I'm hopelessly late already. Bonnie's getting a bus to Keswick. Tanya's got an exam on Monday and wants to spend all day revising. There's a big delivery of roses coming at eleven and I really have to be there for that. And Bonnie's signed me up for two deliveries.'

'And where did you say the boy's father was in all this? Oh – going to Penrith. Can't he come here on the way?'

'It's really not on the way, Mum.'

'So why don't I drive over to Rheged, meet Christopher there and collect Robin – and the dog, if you like. That is precisely on his way and much shorter for me than coming all the way down to you would be. You can't have them with you in the shop, and in the van making deliveries. That's ridiculous.'

For the thousandth time Simmy regretted her parents' move from Windermere to Threlkeld. Most of her plans for the shop over the coming years had been predicated on the grandparents being available close by to take charge of the child. As time went on, the complications and frustrations only seemed to grow larger.

'Would you really? That would be great,' she said, with a noticeable fall in stress levels. 'I didn't like to ask you.'

'You think it'd set a precedent,' said Angie shrewdly. 'Well, it won't. But you are going to have to figure something out before next spring, if not sooner. None of us can go on like this.'

Maybe Christopher will be out of a job and can stay at home all day, came the outrageous thought. Such a thing could not possibly be allowed to happen. And anyway, it wasn't so much a job as a way of life. The auction house was now under her husband's personal management. He was

119

the boss and it was up to him to ensure its survival. Besides, there was no real basis for thinking the current debacle would seriously jeopardise its future. They had all elevated the High Gates auction to unrealistic proportions, when it was really only a sudden boost to the normal routine. Nice, but not crucial, when it came to the crunch. Or so she hoped.

'You're right, I know,' she told her mother. 'The sensible thing would be to find a shop in Keswick or Penrith. That would make everything a lot simpler.'

'Up to a point,' said Angie cautiously. 'You're still a fair way from either of those, stuck out there in the middle of nowhere. You should probably aim for Pooley Bridge, if you're thinking of relocating. And what about Bonnie?'

'Not now, Mum. I'm seriously late now. I'll leave the little 'uns with Christopher, then, and he can hand them over at Rheged. I'll make sure he's got nappies and everything. I'm eternally grateful. Forever in your debt.'

'Go, then. I'll see you at some point today, I expect.'

'I expect you will,' said Simmy.

The shop was all-consuming, when she finally got there. With no assistance, she was hard-pressed to juggle customers, deliveries and new orders. Normally on a Saturday there would be the two girls, Bonnie Lawson and Tanya Harkness, both in their teens, serving customers and keeping track of online activity. They could not make deliveries, which was a slight disadvantage, especially when it came to weddings, but Verity, the woman who worked there on weekdays, would drive around on a Friday afternoon doing her best to satisfy everybody. Bonnie had stuck to her plan of going to Keswick, despite the postponement of the auction. Simmy couldn't blame her. She had not seen Ben since the previous Sunday, and justifiably felt that she was missing out. Quite what the two youngsters intended to do with their sudden leisure remained unclear. Simmy hoped that they would address the mystery of events in Borrowdale, and make some kind of discovery or breakthrough, because the complexities of the case were going to drive the Hendersons mad otherwise.

As for Christopher, Simmy's feelings were growing more uncomfortable every time she thought about him. He had behaved badly – or at the very least been gullible and too easily influenced by his client, or whatever he called her. The police would understandably be regarding him with suspicion, unable to credit his story of the body in the cellar, and yet aware that no sane person would invent such a tale. Borrowdale was not a place they would associate with organised crime, violence or anything of that sort. It might have an aura of mystery, though. Simmy visualised the winding lanes, the river and the looming fells. That massive boulder that seemed to hang over Grange had left her with a sense of foreboding. The famous Honister Pass added to the atmosphere of ageless self-sufficiency, too. The place was difficult to access, even now. If you took a car, there was nowhere to park it. If you caught a bus, you lost all independence and might be left to fend for yourself. And there was all that *history*. Farmers and miners, rich female benefactor and handsome mansions. Even more than Hartsop or Askham or Dacre, Borrowdale was decidedly isolated. Except this was the twenty-first century and everyone had a phone to connect them to the rest of the world, and the notion of danger and adventure was largely an illusion. Hikers took water, maps, sandwiches, rain capes

121

and the ubiquitous mobile and were risking almost nothing by striding up the steep sides of the numerous crags and being stunned by the fabulous views.

But Jennifer Reade did not fit that picture. She was from Swindon, had apparently never been to Cumbria in her life and did not carry a phone. Early reports of her, when Christopher Henderson had been asked to clear her suddenly-inherited house, did not chime with the woman of the last few days. She had been almost casual at first, not interested in seeing High Gates or its contents. It had taken Sir John's solicitors six weeks of intense research to locate her, and to assure themselves that she was the sole member of that generation with any claim to inherit. Christopher had explained the process, somewhat uncertainly.

'If there's anyone else in that same generation, they'll get an equal share with her – I think. But there isn't.'

'They've probably stopped looking, now they've found her,' said Simmy.

As far as Christopher could ascertain, Jennifer Reade had absolutely no sense of history or continuity.

'Just sell all of it,' she told her solicitor, ignoring dark warnings about probate and inheritance tax and an infinity of complication. 'I can't see I've got much choice,' she told the auctioneer, when he finally got through to her on her landline in her two-bedroomed Swindon home. 'What else am I going to do with it all?'

'She could at least come up and see it,' he had complained to Simmy, back at the end of April.

They had agreed about that, and the miserable end to three acquisitive Hickory generations. 'She says she barely even knew he existed,' sighed Christopher.

And then, apparently, the woman changed her mind at the very last minute and drove herself the length of England to have one quick look at the place before her very brief ownership passed out of her hands. Or so Christopher had understood on Wednesday. Even on his first garbled telling of his experience, Simmy could see that there was more to it than that. What had brought about the sudden decision? Who else was involved? What murky business had been going on unseen, in Swindon or elsewhere?

And who was the body in the cellar that Jennifer so urgently wanted to remain undiscovered until after the auction?

Customers arrived in a slow but steady stream. Having the two deliveries to make was weighing on her mind, and she resolved to close up at twelve-thirty, dash down to Newby Bridge and Bowness to the two addresses where the bouquets were to be presented, and then back all the way up to Threlkeld to retrieve her child and dog. She would be lucky to get there by two, with no thought for lunch or shopping or murders or auctions.

At eleven, the promised order of mixed scented roses arrived. Simmy had always deplored the way florists' roses had no scent, and had made it her business to acquire some that did. They were hard to find and expensive, but Bonnie had fashioned a sign for the corner of the street window, saying OUR ROSES HAVE GENUINE SCENT, which had been very effective. Demand had grown and supply was a challenge. People came from long distances to buy them – especially those who had no gardens of their own. One of the most eager customers drove all the way from Whitehaven. For some people it seemed almost like an addiction.

At ten past twelve, a familiar figure came through the door, causing Simmy a jolt of surprise that was itself surprising.

'I never expected to see you,' she said daftly. 'But I don't know why I didn't.'

'You look busy.' A stout customer had passed him in the doorway and a woman was browsing amongst the ferns and succulents. Simmy was keying something into the computer on the little counter.

'On my own today,' she nodded. 'Bonnie's gone to Keswick and Tanya's got exams.'

'You know why I'm here, I assume.'

'Sort of. We've been talking about you, but we weren't sure whether you'd be involved in this Borrowdale mess.'

'Inevitably,' said DI Moxon with a grimace. 'Seeing as how I'm such good mates with the wife of the key witness.'

'Is that what he is?'

'By default. He's the *only* witness, apart from the poor hikers who had to watch the Reade woman die. They're in rather a state, as you might imagine.'

'I'd have thought their testimony was quite a lot more useful than Christopher's.'

The woman by the ferns cleared her throat, reminding them of her presence. 'Sorry!' called Simmy. 'Can I help you to choose something?'

'Possibly.'

There followed five minutes of dithering, during which Moxon stood placidly by the counter and watched people passing in the street outside. At last, the woman departed with a small cheap fern that Simmy feared would quickly die under her ministrations. She had learnt to recognise incompetent gardeners, forcing herself to part with healthy plants that deserved much better.

'Christopher's testimony is . . . unusual, as I understand it,' said Moxon, as if there had been no interruption. 'A disappearing body. Never come across that before.'

'Are you part of the investigation? I mean – Jennifer Reade *was* murdered, I suppose?'

'It's getting to be a habit – shipping me in to the Penrith outfit, because I have some sort of inside knowledge of the characters involved.'

'Meaning me and Christopher? That's awful. Poor old you.'

'The worst part is the driving. Speaking of which, I've just been all the way down to Manchester airport and back. I had to collect someone – he's in the car.'

Simmy blinked at him. 'Who is he?' Evidently not a suspect, or he would not have been left unsupervised for so long, she presumed.

'That's rather a long story. The thing is, we're both gasping for some coffee and some cake. It's intensely unorthodox, but I did wonder whether you'd like to join us at the Italia or somewhere.'

She smiled at his admission of unorthodoxy, which was not at all unusual.

'Are you sure? I'm not remotely involved in this, you know. It's all about Christopher and the saleroom.'

'It wouldn't hurt,' he said. 'The man's called Warwick Bennett and he's related to the victim. I think he might talk to you. He's pretty shell-shocked, and he's just flown here from India.'

'You want me to be a nursemaid – or what?'

'Nothing of the sort. Just be sociable. I'm only his

chauffeur, basically. He wants to know the whole story about Ms Reade, and the people in Penrith are obviously interested in seeing what he has to say. Meanwhile, he just needs a bit of normality.'

'Well – it won't hurt, I suppose, as you say. But listen – I've got to make some deliveries after I've closed up. I can do them now, if I close early. Give me twenty minutes – they're very local. Luckily, I got them made up between customers. I thought it'd be bedlam here on my own, but it's been quieter than usual since about ten o'clock. I should worry about that, by rights, but it's been a relief.'

'Come and find us there, then. We'll wait for you.'

The lack of urgency was typical of the man. His old-fashioned style of policing was increasingly irritating to his colleagues, but given his record of 'cleaning up' the string of murders in the area, nobody dared criticise him too loudly. None of the other police officers knew the extent to which he had relied on Simmy, Ben and Bonnie, although they had their suspicions. *If it ain't broke, don't fix it* was the motto at the Cumbrian police stations, despite a growing awareness that very little was conducted according to proper protocol where DI Moxon was concerned.

'Let me get on, then,' she chivvied him.

The plan worked neatly, and the three of them were enjoying a light lunch by twelve fifty-five. Moxon introduced Simmy to his companion with some delicacy.

'Mrs Henderson's husband met your – cousin? – a few days ago. He's handling the sale of the house contents.'

'Yes,' said the man. 'You told me.' He was tall and thin, with very straight black hair falling over his eyes. His clothes looked rumpled and he carried a leather bag over one arm like a housewife doing her shopping.

'You've come from India, just now?' Simmy asked him. 'You must be exhausted.'

Warwick Bennett shrugged. 'That's right. Bangalore. I've got a business there. All this family drama has come as a big shock.' He glanced at Moxon, eyebrows raised. 'I'm not sure how much I should say,' he admitted.

The detective waved a relaxed hand. 'I don't think you need worry about that. Mrs Henderson will understand that it's complicated. Nothing you say will go any further.'

'Oh,' said the man uncertainly.

'He only heard a week ago that Sir John had died, and he was in line for part of the inheritance,' Moxon explained. 'So he came as quickly as he could, to stake his claim, so to speak. The death of Ms Reade has thrown everything into complete chaos, as you might imagine.'

Simmy addressed Mr Bennett. 'Did she know about you? I mean – didn't she think she was the sole heir to the whole estate? That's what my husband understood when the sale was being arranged.'

He paused, looking into her eyes, composing his reply. 'We really aren't cousins in any normal sense. My grandparents were connected to Sir John's mother. Jennifer Reade links to his father's line. It's a miracle that I've been traced. But if I've understood it correctly, she and I had identical claims to the property. The solicitors told me we would split it equally between us.'

'Still a very nice inheritance,' said Simmy, thinking *And now you'll get all of it*.

'Indeed,' he said, with an air of reproachful melancholy.

'And you had no idea Sir John existed?' she went on.

'Ah – I never said that.' The man glanced at Moxon. 'I've always been aware of my forebears. I can give you a detailed breakdown of the descent through the generations, if you're interested. But perhaps it's enough to explain that my grandfather married a Hindu woman, hence my appearance. He was a tea-planter, which I know is a cliché. His mother was Sir John's grandmother's sister. I remember him talking about the family in England which had made good money from slate mining, and romanticising about all meeting up one day.'

Simmy had not drawn any conclusions from his appearance, but she could see his dark hair and eyes might fit with his explanation.

'And there's only you who qualifies as a descendant?' She was still viewing the whole matter through the eyes of her husband. If this was an authentic beneficiary, he would have no more difficulty proceeding with the auction. Questions were, as usual, swirling insistently through her head. 'How did you make the connection with Jennifer, then?'

He paused again. 'Actually, I didn't. And it wasn't as much as a week ago that I heard the news. It was Sir John's solicitors, who must have decided to follow one last branch of the family tree and managed to identify me. It must have taken quite a lot of detective work. Then, of course, it was chaos for a day or two, emails and phone calls, trying to get my head round it all. I contacted just about everybody I knew here in the UK, looking for more of the picture.'

'But nobody told Christopher? Or Jennifer? It must have made a huge difference to all her assumptions.' Light was beginning to dawn, very slowly and patchily. The sudden last-minute discovery of this man could only have shaken Jennifer Reade rather badly.

'Jennifer Reade was not an easy person to communicate with, according to the solicitors. Sir John's people talked to her people, they organised everything with estate agents and the auctioneers—'

'That's my husband,' Simmy reminded him.

'Right. Yes. Anyway, after a couple of days I realised I'd have to come in person. And here I am.' He concluded with a watery smile. 'And I've obviously walked right into an almighty mess, with poor Jennifer bumped off at the crucial moment.' He looked again at Moxon. 'And the British police are kindly looking after me until I find out where I stand.'

Moxon nodded and said, 'There are things we hope you can help us with.'

'Of course. I'll do my best. Although . . .' He tailed off and made a helpless gesture, tilting his head like a little boy.

An innocent abroad, thought Simmy foolishly. The story was one of surprise and confusion, and some of it was hard to believe, but the man was real enough.

It was clearly time to go. They had eaten toasties and drunk hot drinks, and were all focused on driving northwards through the Lake District on a Saturday afternoon. 'The traffic's going to be awful,' said Simmy.

Moxon stood up, eyebrows slightly raised. 'It would have been nice to catch up a bit,' he said mildly. 'How's the little one? And is that dog learning any sense?'

Cornelia had never been especially lacking in sense, but her puppy days had been undeniably trying at times.

'They're both coming along nicely,' Simmy said. She could feel him deliberately not inspecting her middle for signs of another pregnancy but said nothing on that subject.

Warwick Bennett also got up and hovered beside the table. He really was tall, Simmy noted. And perhaps five years older than her original guess. His hands were clasped together, the little bag still hanging from his left arm.

'It was nice to meet you,' said Simmy, wondering whether she would ever see him again. 'I hope everything gets sorted out quickly. There must be a lot of anxious people wondering what happens to the house now.' That point had only just occurred to her. 'Will the hotel people still be able to have it?'

'Probably,' said Bennett.

Moxon led the way. Simmy walked behind the two men, trying to construct a coherent account of all she had just learnt, so she could convey it to Ben and Christopher. She wondered about Moxon's intentions in deliberately introducing her to Warwick Bennett. Did he want a second opinion on the man? Or had he simply snatched at the chance of seeing her? She knew he was fond of her, that he sought her out on flimsy pretexts now and then. And she also knew full well that the only reason he was involved in the Borrowdale investigation was because he knew her and Christopher.

She had no cause for complaint at any of this. She liked him and was glad to have been included. They spent a final few seconds on the pavement outside before going to their respective cars.

'I'll speak to you soon,' Moxon told Simmy. 'It's going to be a busy weekend.'

Chapter Eleven

Simmy phoned Ben before she left Windermere, thinking her best move would be to sit down with him and try to construct some sort of logical hypothesis about what had happened in Borrowdale, given the new information about Warwick Bennett.

'Bonnie and I thought we'd go to Carlisle, actually,' was the response. 'We were just leaving.'

'What? Why?'

'It's nice there. We've only been once and Bonnie wants to explore.'

This was a startling break with tradition. Whenever there had been a murder, Ben and Bonnie had always pushed themselves into the heart of the investigation and relentlessly ferreted out clues, connections and theories until the thing was resolved. Ben had been witness to the suspension of the auction and the effect on Christopher. And the details this time were surely sufficiently bizarre to get him working overtime on it.

'But . . . what about Borrowdale and Jennifer Reade and everything? Have you spoken to Christopher today? Did he tell you about the man who came to Hartsop yesterday?'

'No and no. What man?'

'He said something to Lily about the disappearing body in the cellar. Come on, Ben. There's never been anything like this before. It's completely bewildering.'

'Hang on. Have I missed something? Nobody's told me anything since the middle of yesterday. I thought it was probably all in hand, and we just have to sit tight and wait for the go-ahead to carry on with the sale.'

'I told you there was a dead man in the cellar of the house. That's what started the whole thing off. And now the body's gone missing. Disappeared. And a man left a cryptic message for Christopher yesterday saying he knows about it. He spoke to Lily – the girl who walks the dog.'

'Oh.'

'Never mind "Oh". Why are you being so unhelpful? This isn't like you.'

'Um . . .'

'And now this distant cousin's shown up, and gets all Sir John's stuff now Jennifer's dead – probably. But he can't be the killer because he only landed at Manchester airport ten minutes after she died, or something. Although . . . maybe it was him who spoke to Lily. And he's not actually a cousin.'

'Please stop.' The boy's voice was strained. 'The thing is, it's Bonnie . . .'

'What? What's Bonnie? Is she there now?'

'Yes – she's gone to the loo. And she's not very happy. Don't forget last time. You can't expect her to throw herself into all this, after what happened. Think about it,' he finished on a note of exasperation.

Now it was Simmy's turn to say, 'Oh.' How could she have been such a fool? 'I see. Oh dear.'

'It's awkward.'

'Can she hear you?'

'No. She's going out to the car now flapping at me to hurry up.'

'Okay. So go to Carlisle, then. But we do need you, Ben. I must have said that five times yesterday and today. Moxon's out of his depth, as usual, but at least they're letting him be part of the team. There's somebody called Julian in Swindon – where Jennifer lived, apparently—'

'Please *stop*,' said Ben again. 'Look – Bonnie's staying over tonight, but I'm taking her back to Corinne's tomorrow morning. They're doing a boot sale somewhere. I can be at your disposal for the rest of the day. That's soon enough, isn't it?'

Tomorrow morning felt a long way off to Simmy, as she wrestled with all the facts and guesses and frustrations around events in Borrowdale. Anything might happen in the meantime.

'All right,' she sighed. 'So now I'd better retrieve my baby and see if I can find my husband. Have a nice afternoon.'

'I'll come to Hartsop tomorrow after I've dropped Bonnie. It'll be about eleven, I expect.'

'Thanks.'

She had not been fair to Ben, she admitted to herself as she drove out of Windermere. His involvement in the whole affair had been limited to what had happened at the auction house, and although Simmy had told him much of what she knew when the sale had been suspended, she had not updated him since then. She had taken for granted that he would be making himself available for whenever she got around to catching up and picking his brains.

So now she felt very much on her own. Moxon had been sweet as well as informative but had left her to her own devices after that. Christopher was apparently back in Keswick, ensuring that the unsold contents of the saleroom were all secure, as well as handling the constant stream of enquiries from people who had missed the emails and other announcements. Several would undoubtedly show up expecting an auction and demanding an explanation. That was in addition to his visit to the Penrith police station – when Simmy could not help thinking a phone call would have been quite enough.

Angie and Russell had to be relieved of their child- and dog-minding duties before much longer. While they were usually more than happy to take over, they did have their own lives, and it was a weekend – when the Hendersons might be expected to take charge of their own dependents. Russell might, she hoped, be receptive to some brainstorming about the murder, but that too was unpredictable.

Her own brain was whirling with elusive connections and suspicions. Faceless men – one of them almost literally so – came in and out of consideration. Antiques, family history, deserted old houses – they all combined to form a shadowy picture that she felt might well come into focus if only she could talk it through with somebody. Had Christopher been told about the cousin, Warwick Bennett? It could not be possible that he was the same man who had spoken to Lily, given his movements, which left a worrying impression of a network of malefactors lurking around. So how many of these people knew each other? And where in the world had the dead man gone?

She felt suddenly lonely. Where was everybody when she needed them? Why did she not have a close female friend to share everything with? This lack had become more acute since having Robin. Days spent at home with baby and dog only had meaning if she could report the details to someone. Christopher would listen if pressed, but the domestic trivia was hardly gripping. Bonnie's former foster mother, Corinne, was satisfying to chat to, but opportunities were rare. Bonnie herself usually plunged into anything to do with murder and mystery, but as Ben had just pointed out, recent events in Askham had changed that. For a while it had all become too real – as it had for Christopher a few years earlier when his father had been killed. It had taken him a long time to share in Simmy and Ben's determination to discover the truth of each case as it came along. Ironically, it had been Askham that had shown him that there could often be very little choice in the matter.

She arrived at Threlkeld soon after two o'clock, to find Robin and Cornelia curled up together on the sofa half asleep. Russell was sitting on a chair in the same room, and Angie was outside tinkering with some honeysuckle that had become unacceptably rampant. Simmy joined her child and dog, leaning over them for a collective cuddle.

'Mum-mum,' said Robin with a lazy smile.

'We've been doing nursery rhymes all morning,' said Russell. 'Amazing how they come back so easily, after forty years. I counted twenty-four and could probably dredge up that many again if I tried.'

Simmy could see that he was tempted to list them all and headed him off.

'Moxon came to see me this morning,' she said.

'Oh? Was that nice?'

'It was, actually. He's officially part of the investigation.'

'People away on holiday, I presume. Has he had any brilliant insights yet?'

'Don't be like that. He does his best.'

'Perfectly fine chap – you don't have to convince me. That time in Hawkshead . . . well, he went well beyond, as they say.'

'He did,' said Simmy with feeling.

'So where do we stand now? What happens with the auction? Where's Christopher? And the boy Ben?'

'I don't know. Christopher's probably in Keswick, but I haven't heard from him. Ben and Bonnie have gone to Carlisle. Bonnie's having a bit of a wobble, apparently. She hasn't been altogether right for a while now, although I didn't properly realise until today. The business in Askham really shook her up.'

'Hm,' said Russell, and Simmy knew he was thinking of Angie and how she believed that people were entirely too easily 'shaken up' these days. 'Let's hope Ben settles her down again, then. What's in Carlisle?'

'Nothing in particular. Just somewhere to look round, I think.'

'Are you taking these two home now?'

'I suppose I should. You'll be wanting to get on. I don't suppose you've walked the dog.'

'You suppose right.'

She did not stir from the sofa, but watched her mother through the open side window, as she clipped away some of the twisting strands of vegetation.

'I can smell that honeysuckle from here.'

'It's a good year for it, apparently. I told her not to trim it until it stops flowering. The bees love it.'

'It's nice to have a proper garden,' said Simmy vaguely. 'And time to devote to it.'

In the Windermere B&B, the small garden had mostly been covered in stone chippings and the surviving shrubs left to their own devices. Angie had dodged the traditional competitive practices of Lakeland gardens, aware that she could never hope to keep up. She managed some aubretia on the wall, and a slightly sad Mermaid rose over the front door, and claimed to be satisfied.

'She won't let me touch it, except for my special little patch at the end,' sighed Russell.

'You should take a stand. It's yours as much as it's hers.'

'Not worth the bother,' said the man who typically liked a quiet life. Then he gave himself a little shake. 'We could go to Borrowdale,' he said suddenly. 'I'd like to see the house that all the fuss is about.'

'It'll be heaving with people,' she objected. 'And what about these two?'

'They can stay here. Or we could take the dog.' He flopped back in his chair. 'But we probably won't even get out of the car – just drive the loop over Honister and back past Derwentwater.'

'I don't see much point, Dad.'

'It's glorious up there, you know. It lifts the spirit just to get a glimpse of the views from the top of the Pass. And I've never even been to the slate mine at Honister. I should rectify that.'

'Dad – it's all adventure sports and expensive stuff to buy in the shop. Ben was talking about it a little while ago. You wouldn't like it.'

'Oh well.'

It struck her that her father was feeling a similar set of emotions to her own. A sense of time passing without enough social contact, too many thoughts unshared and minor disappointments. The non-appearance of a second child affected them both in the same way. Something badly wanted, but beyond their control to achieve. Did Christopher also feel the same, she wondered? Or was Robin enough for him, given that he had numerous nieces and nephews? Why was it so difficult to talk frankly about such matters? Because the feelings could expand too readily into pain and frustration, perhaps, with a risk that they would overwhelm.

'We could go on a weekday instead,' she offered. 'Mum might want to come as well.'

'You mean when the murder's solved and we can all relax, I suppose.' This was clearly not what he had hoped. 'Meanwhile, I still don't understand what's happening.'

'I don't think you're up to date. I can never remember who knows what when these things are going on. I tried to tell Ben the latest, but he brushed me off. Moxon had some new information, and I was just getting the glimmerings of a theory, but it's very elusive. And there's a new person in the mix, which is likely to change things rather a lot.'

'Try your theory on me,' he invited. 'You don't seem to be in much hurry to get home.'

So she did, discovering in the process that it was much less of a cogent theory than a few disconnected suspicions.

'Jennifer Reade was either lying to Christopher on Wednesday, or else she had a major change of mind about the house and its contents. This Bennett man must have a lot to do with it, as well. He seemed to be saying he didn't know Jennifer existed, but I suppose he could be lying too. I think Moxon wanted me to draw him out – and I did get him talking for a bit. There's something much too neat about the timing.'

Russell listened for a few minutes, until Robin grew restless, and Angie came in from the garden, eager for a cup of tea which she expected her husband to make while she subsided onto the other end of the sofa from Simmy.

Russell dutifully went off into the kitchen but was gone a very long time. When Simmy went to investigate, she found him staring blankly at the fridge.

'I'm thinking about that body,' he said. 'Do we think it must have been a local? Someone without a roof over his head, dossing in the cellar of an empty house. Isn't that the most likely thing? Then some relative or friend noticed he was missing, had an idea where he might be, and found him, sometime after Christopher saw him – it. Decided to give him a decent burial somewhere nice, saying nothing to the authorities. Living off the grid, or whatever they call it.'

'Blimey, Dad – your imagination is working overtime. But it's not really a credible explanation. Nobody would do that. There are laws.'

Russell conceded the point reluctantly. 'I suppose they would have to register the death, at least. Which would lead to all kinds of other regulations and restrictions. Even so, it would solve part of the mystery.'

'It's better than anything Christopher or I have come up with,' said Simmy generously. 'And there's still a host of unanswered questions just about that body. It looks as if Jennifer Reade stayed on at the house, right through

Wednesday and Thursday. She'd have seen anyone taking the body away.'

'But she wouldn't have had any objection, would she? She'd have been *glad*.'

'Maybe. That woman's thought processes are a total mystery to me. She manipulated Christopher, didn't do anything she said she would, had some dopey objection to all things digital and then got herself murdered. If I'd ever met her, I'm pretty sure I would not have wanted to be her friend.'

'"Objection to all things digital", did you say?'

'Apparently. No phone or satnav or Facebookery or anything.'

Russell sighed. 'Would that more of us had such courage.'

'If she'd had a mobile, she probably wouldn't be dead now,' said Simmy severely. 'She wasn't killed outright. She could have called for help.'

'The killer would have taken her phone.'

'You can't possibly know that. One assumes he thought she was good and dead before he left her.'

'So – another crucial question is – did the same person kill her and the man in the basement?'

'It's a cellar,' she corrected him. 'There's a difference.'

'Minimal. Does it matter?'

'Not really. I don't think the man was murdered.'

'No,' said Russell thoughtfully. 'But he *might* have been. In some ways it would make the whole thing simpler. Jennifer Reade curled up quietly in one of the upstairs rooms, hears the killer creeping back to remove the body, interrupts and gets herself coshed for her pains. Completely straightforward.'

Simmy was about to voice her response to this when Angie called from the sitting room. 'Where's my tea? What's going on out there?'

'Did you even switch the kettle on?' Simmy asked.

'I think I did. It'll have to start again, though. Should we use a pot, do you think?'

'Absolutely. Then two teabags can do the three of us.'

'A girl after my own heart,' he said fondly.

They sat together, the five of them, Angie taking Robin onto her lap and Cornelia sliding onto the floor. 'She's too hot,' said Russell. Nobody moved to do anything about it.

'We've been brainstorming,' Simmy told her mother. 'Dad's come up with some brilliant ideas.' In the last few minutes, she had realised that there was no longer any sense of loneliness. Her father had filled the vacuum with an unerring instinct for what was needed. The quality of his attention, the wisdom of his theories, the sheer *reliability* of the man, were everything she had been wanting. 'We think we might go over to Borrowdale one day this week.'

'What about me?' said Angie petulantly. 'And your child? I imagine you'll be taking the dog.'

'We can all go,' said Simmy bravely.

'Let's see what happens, shall we?' said Russell, with a wink at his daughter.

'I haven't finished telling you all the other bits about Jennifer Reade,' Simmy said. 'I keep remembering there's more. There's the mysterious Julian and another man by the name of Warwick.'

'Is one of them the swine who scared poor young Lily?'

'Could be, but it's not likely. She wasn't scared, luckily. She said the man was really quite nice. She's a tough little

141

thing, anyway. I don't understand why Bonnie doesn't like her.'

'Don't you?' It was Angie speaking. 'I'd have thought it was obvious, if she's as tough and brave as you say.'

'You mean Bonnie's jealous, in case Ben takes a liking to her?' said Simmy slowly. 'But she's only sixteen.'

'Listen to yourself!' scoffed Angie. 'The way you talk about her she could be Tanya Harkness, or Bonnie herself. Girls like that are rare, and here you are, effortlessly hooking up with another one. If nothing else, it's bound to make Bonnie feel devalued. Plus, she hates being stuck down in Windermere when the rest of us have moved up here.'

'Oh dear,' said Simmy.

'Have you been keeping her informed of developments?' asked Russell.

'No – I told you. Ben says she wants to be left out of it this time. And I assume she's trying to keep him out of it as well.'

'She'll be out of luck there if I know our Ben.' Russell shook his head slowly. 'Poor girl.'

'If you ask me, she needs to get back on the metaphorical horse as quick as she can,' Angie asserted, giving her grandson a little bounce for emphasis.

'Give her time,' said Russell peaceably. Again, he sent a special glance at Simmy. 'Meanwhile we ought to be thinking about something for supper. Can you stay, Sim?'

'Better not. I should be tracking down my husband and hearing what his day's been like. I haven't had a squeak out of him since breakfast.'

'I don't imagine that's unusual,' said Angie. 'He was never much of a one for keeping people informed.'

This was true, but until now Simmy had not realised that her mother had noticed. Christopher had disappeared into the unfathomable realms of Central America for over a year, in his twenties, making very little effort to reassure his family that he was alive. He had acquired and discarded a wife at some point along the way, carelessly mentioning it on a rare postcard and expressing surprise when his mother later chastised him for it.

'He'd tell me if anything important happened,' she defended. 'Anyway, I'll pop over to the saleroom now and see if he's there. We can show Robin the statue from Sir John's garden.'

'And the rest,' said Russell. 'All that *stuff*, just sitting there.'

'I know,' said Simmy sadly.

Chapter Twelve

It was a very short drive from Threlkeld to the outskirts of Keswick, but Simmy had time to review some of the most pressing questions circling around the death of Jennifer Reade. Top of the list was – why had she so desperately wanted to stop the sale? Thanks to the stimulating brainstorm she had enjoyed with her father, she found herself coming up with a small collection of possible explanations, all to do with inheritance and the sudden discovery of a relative called Warwick Bennett. Had Jennifer been told about him – and if so, would that explain why she wanted to stop the sale? Even if she hadn't been killed, the sale might yet have been stopped by the belated appearance of Bennett, who should at least have been consulted about the fate of the Hickory estate.

Timing . . . that felt crucial. Had Sir John's solicitors not informed Warwick Bennett of the sale of the property the moment they discovered him? That was, after all, the whole point in searching for him in the first place. Or did they assume it was too late to make any changes, and the man should be content to inherit his share of the proceeds? That seemed entirely probable, on reflection. So why had somebody seen fit to kill Jennifer? And where did the dead man in the cellar fit?

All of which forced Simmy to consider the woman's final moments, and try to imagine what it must have been like to feel your life ebbing away whilst struggling to save yourself by crawling out onto the road. Perhaps every instinct would be focused intently on survival and the idea of actually dying would be kept very much at bay. When people miraculously appeared and doubtless made soothing noises and took charge with their phones and basic first aid, there would be a moment of hope. Enough to muster all your wits and repeat *Stop the sale!* Because at that moment this was the most urgent matter of them all.

She knew she should have phoned Christopher before landing herself, child and dog at his place of work. She had not done so because he might have told her not to come. That would have been frustrating because she badly wanted to see for herself how things were. Had the staff all turned up, even though there was nothing to do? Had Christopher himself stayed to stand guard over all the precious objects? There was a sturdy metal gate that could be locked, but one side of the car park was bordered by a very flimsy fence, which divided the auction house from its neighbour – a small printworks, which did not operate at weekends. It would not be difficult to scale the fence, nab one of Sir John's garden ornaments or set of tools or ornate metal candlesticks from the outside area, and be off with it. While most of the valuable items were indoors, anything that was deemed weatherproof had been placed amongst the outside display. There was no space for it all to be under the roof. Ben had prattled on about the huge variety of objects and the impossibility of accurately valuing everything. It was quite possible that a dull-looking piece of pewter or zinc had considerable appeal to arcane collectors of garden ephemera. Just look at the way the bids mounted up when it came to enamelled metal advertising signs, whether for chocolate bars or motor oil.

To her great surprise, the gate was closed and padlocked. There were no cars anywhere to be seen and no sign of life. 'Oh!' she said.

'Uh-oh!' echoed Robin behind her. Cornelia whined, recognising the saleroom as a place she sometimes went to be drooled over by admiring female people.

'Sorry,' said Simmy. 'We're not getting out.'

She sat there, with the engine still running, fumbling for the phone in her bag on the passenger seat. It was switched off, which meant that she could not have responded to a call or text from her husband, even if he had tried to keep her abreast of his movements. And why should he do such a thing anyway? They had agreed from the start that they would only make contact during the working day if there was something vitally important to say. Ben and Bonnie regarded this as sheer perversity; they exchanged texts at least ten times every day.

There were only two places she could think of where Christopher was likely to be: the police station or home in Hartsop. Any niggling idea that he might have gone back to Borrowdale was dismissed as oddly uncomfortable. Her father had wanted to go there, and she had resisted. If her husband had for some reason done what Russell had urged, that would put her, Simmy, in the wrong. Her own reluctance would be seen as a needless disruption of a perfectly reasonable line of action.

She acknowledged that she had a need to know. Activating the phone, she texted 'Where are you?' to Christopher, and turned the car engine off – not in that order. She was going to sit tight and wait for a reply, at least for five minutes or so. If none came, she had little choice but to go home and see what happened next. The child and dog in the back were evidently content to remain in limbo for a time. Robin was almost asleep anyway.

It came after four minutes, a single word 'Penrith'.

'Oh!' said Simmy again. This time, there was no answering echo from her son. 'Now what am I supposed to do?' she asked the void that she felt surrounding her. The curt message felt rude, excluding her and implying he was too busy with important matters to explain himself. It might also mean that he was being cross-examined again by the police, who only allowed him twenty seconds to attend to his phone.

Half a minute later, her phone rang. The screen told her it was Detective Inspector Moxon. 'This is unexpected,' she said, as she responded.

'I wanted to explain myself. That man, Bennett – he's not quite what he seems. I was wondering about your impressions of him. I'm afraid I was exploiting you a bit when I asked you to join us. I thought he'd talk to you, more than to me.'

'And he did. But I'm not much good at psychology, you know. I thought he was tired and rather stunned. His story was a bit garbled, but that's not surprising, is it, after everything that's happened.'

'Maybe not. He left quite a lot out of his account of himself. He might not realise how much we know about him.'

'Don't tell me he's a fraud. A dishonest claimant.'

'Not quite. He's the real article, according to the solicitors. They're in a real tizzy about him, knowing they should have tracked him down long before this. They're rushing to cover their backs, denying any sort of responsibility for Ms Reade's death, saying they did everything they reasonably could. Actually, they've done a bit more than that, in the past day. It turns out that Mr Bennett is a bit of a dark horse. He's got a prison record.'

'Should you be telling me this?'

'What harm can it do?' She heard a heavy sigh. 'We need every ounce of help we can get – and with you and Ben Harkness making clever connections, we might yet get the thing settled. At the moment, it's not coming together even a little bit.'

'So what was he in prison for?'

'Fraud. Apparently, he faked antiques.'

That, Simmy realised, was the real bombshell.

'Oh!' she said. 'Well thanks for telling me. I'm going now. It's time I got Robin home.'

'Keep in touch,' he ordered her.

She started the car and drove in a loop, past the printworks next door and back onto the road that led through Keswick. There was a handwritten sign on the entrance to the printworks, which she barely glimpsed, except for the word CLOSED. They'd gone on holiday, she supposed.

She had coincided with the afternoon tourist traffic, and took longer than usual to regain the A66. The meandering route back to Hartsop took forty minutes, causing Simmy to spare a moment of sympathy for Christopher doing the journey twice a day. He would never characterise himself as a 'commuter' but the fact remained that he spent well over an hour in the car five times a week, which Simmy knew must run counter to his self-image. Living in the Lake District permanently, watching the millions of transitory visitors scuttling about on the fells and milling around in the shops, he and Simmy regarded themselves as enjoying a lifestyle from an earlier time. They experienced all the seasons, knew secret corners and ancient legends that the tourists never glimpsed. Thanks to Russell and Ben, these undiscovered details felt like special knowledge to which only the true Lakelanders were privy. Christopher had gradually taken a deeper interest in all this, through his work with antiques and old artefacts from the mines and factories that covered the region in earlier times. Driving at speed along the A5091 through Matterdale and Dockray and the Other Troutbeck (as they always called it, given there were two places with the same name) he would have to accept that he had more in common with the ordinary twenty-first-century man than he had ever wanted.

The suspension of the auction came back to her, as a potential disaster that should not be downplayed. And it could only be Jennifer Reade's fault. Even if she had an excellent reason, that might even ultimately save Christopher's business from committing some dire mistake, his current feelings about it had to be deeply negative. All the same old questions that she had shared with her father flooded back. Who was the dead man? Where was his body now? Were they all ignoring some blindingly obvious explanation? Had they overlooked all kinds of clues in Christopher's meeting with Jennifer? And was Moxon going to enjoy a rare triumph this time, solving it all without Ben, Bonnie or Simmy assisting him? From his tone, that seemed vanishingly unlikely, but he was clearly doing his best, glad to be part of the investigation.

Robin and Cornelia were both suddenly acutely bored and hungry. The child wailed and the dog whined and Simmy pressed on faster than before. The final two miles, at the southern tip of Ullswater, were so familiar that she drove without conscious attention to the road. Turning into the home strait, she was back at the house before noticing a flashing light on her dashboard.

'How long has it been doing that?' she muttered. Issues with cars always threw her into a panic, all the more so since moving to Hartsop where one's own transport was essential to life. The light displayed tiny letters reading 'ABS'. Simmy had no idea what that meant. She doubted whether Christopher would know, either. Not just a reluctant commuter, but an even more resistant car mechanic, he relied on others to keep his vehicle roadworthy. Having two cars was the only safety net he and Simmy employed. Surely there would never be a time when both were out of action at once, they reasoned. But his work was always going to trump any need she might have to go somewhere – especially if her car was the defaulter.

Choosing to forget all about it until Monday, Simmy occupied the next two hours with food, washing and bedtime. She sang two nursery rhymes, read two books and deposited Robin into his cot by twenty to seven. His west-facing room was still filled with sunlight, and he was not particularly sleepy, but agreed to play quietly with his activity centre for a while before dropping off.

'Good boy!' Simmy applauded.

Meanwhile Christopher was having one of the more unusual days of his life. Having gone first to Penrith, he spent the rest of the morning and part of the afternoon at the auction house, trying to create some order out of the previous day's chaos. A few people phoned to ask if they could collect items they had bought on Friday, and others to double-check that the remaining lots would at some point be offered for sale as advertised. No fewer than three of these questioned the legalities of the situation – which Christopher had to admit were very uncertain. Just who actually owned it all was now a mystery, at least to him. He tried to explain this in simple terms, whilst giving as little as possible away about the Borrowdale murder, but could hear how unconvincing he was being.

On the third occasion he cracked and shouted, 'I'm as much in the dark as you are. Do you think I *like* being lumbered with all this stuff for the foreseeable future?' Only then did the ghastly implications fully sink in. He could indeed be 'lumbered' for weeks, if not months, while the lawyers wrangled over ownership and the police slogged doggedly away at the murder investigation. The stuff would have to go into storage somewhere if he was to stand any chance of proceeding with his normal auctions.

Which realisation finally took him back to Penrith to seek reassurances from the police there, as well as informing them of the man who had spoken to Lily right outside his house. He sent all the staff home, locked the gate securely and set off along the A66. He spent the twenty minutes of the drive trying to compose a logical set of questions and suggestions, for himself and for the investigators. Just waving his arms about and demanding satisfaction would serve no purpose whatever. It'd be counterproductive, in fact. But logic was not his strong point. He had come to rely on Ben Harkness for that sort of thing at times like this, restricting himself to a vague role as supporter and maker-of-random-suggestions. For the most part he had not found it difficult to remain on the sidelines and leave the real work to someone else.

But this time was different. He felt almost privileged in the central part he was playing. The whole thing revolved around him on more levels than one. The police had no choice but to take him seriously and treat him with at least a modicum of respect. Granted, he had withheld very important information on Wednesday and Thursday, but since then he had been of considerable help. He was atoning for his misdemeanour, a fact that was rather surprisingly acknowledged.

Question One – who was the dead man in the cellar? Question Two – where had he gone and who took him there? These were enough to be going on with. Forensic evidence, witnesses, hypotheses and brainstorming should all be called into play and Christopher was determined to help.

He was relieved to find himself admitted to the office of the Senior Investigating Officer, who offered him coffee and cake.

'So . . . ?' the detective said, when the preliminaries had been dealt with.

Christopher leant forward, eager to contribute. 'I've

been trying to remember more about events on Wednesday. More about the appearance of the dead man. It's a lot more difficult than you might think.'

'I doubt that. I put little reliance on human memory, especially after three days. Days in which a lot more has happened, in your case. Your imagination will have been fully exercised, along with a need for self-justification and a good deal of theorising.' The man was broad-shouldered, with a short haircut and very big hands. Almost the opposite of Christopher in all those respects. But he appeared to have some brains, and to be remarkably patient. 'But try me,' he invited.

'The trouble is, I only glanced at his face for a second. It was *chewed*. You couldn't have recognised anyone in that state. But I did look at his clothes and I think I can remember a few details.'

'Go on.'

'Well, given the situation, I assumed he was somebody down on his luck, homeless, probably an addict of some sort. But he had quite *normal* clothes. Nothing torn or dirty. A denim shirt, I think.'

The SIO shook his head. 'Not very detailed, is it?'

'Sorry. There was no blood anywhere. No signs of a fight or anything. Although it was quite dark. I think his hair was quite a light colour – light brown. His hands weren't very clean.' The effort of dredging up even this meagre description was gruelling. Forcing himself to conjure again the picture that had made him vomit was deeply unpleasant. And he had voluntarily put himself in this grim situation. For a moment he felt almost heroic.

'Perhaps we should go back there, to see if that jogs your

memory. We ought to have done that yesterday, by rights, I suppose. Not that it could have made much difference.'

'No,' said Christopher, trying to follow the man's train of thought.

At that moment the female officer with the Doc Martens tapped on the door and came in before being invited.

'Missing person reported, sir,' she said without preamble, eyeing Christopher with an alarming intensity. 'Might be relevant. He works at the next sector to Mr Henderson's auction house on the Keswick estate. His picture's here.'

Christopher went numb. The SIO reached out for the paper in the woman's hand and quickly read it. 'I see,' he said. 'Thank you, Emma.' The woman departed, leaving Christopher idiotically musing on the use of her first name. The man across the desk held out the paper. 'Do you know him?'

The picture showed a man with a clean-shaven oval face, light brown hair and grey eyes. He looked to be about fifty.

'Um . . .' he said, while his heart began to thunder inside his chest. 'I don't think so. What did she mean "next sector"?'

'I assume she meant one of your neighbouring businesses.' The patience was clearly wearing thin. 'What else?'

'Which side?'

'She didn't say.'

'One lot are printers and the others sell DIY stuff. We don't have very much to do with them. We meet at the sandwich van sometimes, that's all.'

'His hair looks rather like your description just now of the dead man – don't you think?'

Christopher nodded wretchedly. 'What does it all *mean*?'

he whispered. 'This is turning into a real nightmare.'

'Don't be like that. Look on the bright side – if this is your man, it's a bit of a breakthrough.'

'Not if you never find him. If you can't find the body, you can't be sure it's this man. He might be alive and well, and living in Costa Rica, but nobody will ever know. If only we – you – could track down that body.'

'We will,' came the confident reply. 'A human body is extremely difficult to hide for long. They very seldom disappear permanently.'

'Even if it's at the bottom of Derwentwater? Or down one of the graphite mines? It seems to me it might be rather easy to dispose of it for ever.'

The man drew a long breath. 'Mr Henderson, sir, you might not appreciate that this changes things rather substantially. It connects you even more closely than before to the events in Borrowdale. If this Mr Deeping is in fact your dead man, then he is almost certainly known to you. It casts a degree of doubt onto everything you've told us – do you see?'

'Not really.' Christopher struggled to follow even a flimsy thread of reason. 'If I'd killed him, I would never have told you about him, would I?'

'Perhaps not. But you weren't to know the body would disappear – unless you moved it yourself and threw it into Derwentwater.'

'I didn't.'

'I hope not.'

'I truly didn't,' Christopher repeated. He raised his head. 'Did you say Deeping? That's the printer, then. His name's over the door. And on the big sign listing all the businesses, where you turn off the road.'

'Right,' nodded the SIO.

There was a brief silence, before Christopher asked, 'Are we still going back to Borrowdale, then?'

'Let me think about that. Are you happy to wait for half an hour?'

It was all bizarrely polite. No hint of coercion and no real display of suspicion. Everything calm and cool and rational. And yet the man's actual words had been sinister and frightening. He had plainly stated that Christopher's testimony was to be treated as unreliable, even deliberately false.

'I don't expect I've got any real choice,' he said.

'Technically, you're free to leave any time you like. You came here of your own accord, after all. But I'm sure you understand that you have a significant contribution to make, at this point in the investigation. And I dare venture to say that it is in your own best interests to provide whatever further assistance you can.'

'Yes,' said Christopher weakly. 'Oh, and don't forget the other thing.' He reminded the man about what Lily had told him. 'It was yesterday,' he repeated.

'Right,' said the detective with a sigh. 'Wheels within wheels – is that what they say?'

'I don't know. But it's got to be important.'

'Indeed – which is why it might have been helpful if you'd said something yesterday. I'm starting to see a pattern here, Mr Henderson, if you see what I mean.'

'Sorry,' said Christopher meekly, biting back an urge to justify himself.

'So, sit tight, if you will, and I'll see what we think might be best to do with you. I'll find a room to put you in.'

It was approaching four o'clock when the man came to find him where he had been left in a small room, with signs and posters all over the walls. One gave a complete list, with photos, of everyone working at the Penrith station. The SIO was called Detective Superintendent Mark Price – which Christopher had been told at the outset but had not registered. The female officer that had struck him as somewhat Amazonian was Detective Inspector Emma Godolphin, which made Christopher smile. The name really did not match the person very well at all. But he admired the intention of the display – openness, even a hint of friendliness, to moderate the general perception of the police as authoritarian and prejudiced. He was not entirely convinced that he personally could trust them, except for dear old DI Moxon, of course.

'Are we going to Borrowdale?' he asked DS Price.

'Not today. Too much going on. Most of the team are collating all the bits and pieces coming at us from all sides. I haven't forgotten that you have a special relationship with Detective Inspector Moxon down in Windermere. He tells me he saw your wife there this morning and that she's eager to keep up to date with the investigation – as usual, apparently. To be honest, he's gone very much off piste where she's concerned. We've got a new witness and Moxon introduced her to him, gave them both lunch. That man's a law unto himself.'

'He's a good chap, though. And he does get the job done, most of the time. Look at how he sorted things out in Askham.'

Price nodded slowly. 'I have not forgotten the recent events in Askham, which I'm sure were very painful for you all at the time. The precedent was set long before that, but he really did excel himself with that one. Not that we can blame him – we all left him to his own devices. But it was plainly very disagreeable for your wife and her young friends.'

'That isn't relevant now,' said Christopher with a frown.

'It is and it isn't,' said Price heavily. 'When it comes to relevance, we have learnt not to make snap judgements.'

'Oh,' said Christopher. 'So what happens now?'

'We think it could be helpful if you'd hang on for a bit longer and help us go through everything you can remember about your encounter with Ms Reade on Wednesday – and whatever dealings you had with her prior to that.'

'Didn't we do that yesterday?'

'Up to a point. But we're going more deeply into the background now. Give us another hour or so of your time, if you can.'

'All right. I don't have anywhere else to be.' Weirdly, he found himself in no hurry at all to leave. There was a security to being amongst police officers, doing as they asked and being treated with such politeness. It was embarrassing, but true. He might be far more involved than he would like, but he felt very little sense of responsibility. Nothing, in the end, had been his fault.

He was in the middle of dredging up everything he could remember about Jennifer Reade when his phone buzzed. DS Price invited him to read and reply to the text from Simmy, then quickly went on to pursue the same line of questioning before it got lost. 'Your wife?' he asked, some time later, nodding at the phone that Christopher had left on the desk.

'Wondering where I am,' Christopher nodded.

'You hadn't told her?'

'It never occurred to me. We don't use our phones all the time, like some people.'

'Or not at all, like Ms Reade,' the detective flashed back. Christopher had made quite a point of conveying that piece of information, unable to discern whether or not it came as news to the police.

'You must have known she didn't use a phone,' he said now. 'Which has to make your job a lot more difficult.'

'Like old times. Some of our younger officers can scarcely credit it.'

'I can imagine,' said Christopher, thinking of Ben and Bonnie. 'So you did know?'

'It soon became apparent. If it hadn't been for her car, we'd have been hard-pressed to identify her.'

'Except she was in her own house, which has to have been a clue.'

'She was in fact out in the road, as I'm sure we told you. It wasn't immediately clear where she had been attacked.'

Christopher was tired and as hungry as his little son and dog had been, if he had but known it. 'Is this going to take much longer?' he whined.

The man waved a dismissive hand. 'No sense in pushing it. We've been well over an hour already.'

'Have we? I've lost all sense of time.'

'It's not even seven yet.'

'No wonder I'm so hungry. I hardly had any lunch.'

'We gave you some cake.'

'So you did.'

'We'll try not to want you again tomorrow, but no

159

promises,' said DS Price. 'Go back to that long-suffering wife of yours.'

There was a barb to the remark that rankled all the way home. Had he been a bad husband? Should he have updated Simmy every couple of hours through the day? He admitted to himself that he had given her very little thought since leaving the house that morning. If he had, it was to nurse a niggling irritation at the way she had persuaded him to deliver Robin to his waiting grandparents at the Rheged service station. By making it so easy for him, she had subtly conveyed the idea that he was falling short in his duties. The age-old assumptions about their different roles never quite went away, and Christopher had no more success in divesting himself of them than had most men. The resulting guilt was faint but persistent. Underlying it was a stubborn conviction that a young child needed its mother more than it needed its father. That was simple biology. If a woman was going to produce a baby, then did she not have a duty to give it the great bulk of her attention? With a sigh, he knew he could never voice such heresy. Besides, Simmy was a thoroughly excellent mother in every way. He just wasn't so sure that he was quite such an excellent father.

Chapter Thirteen

Ben and Bonnie drifted somewhat aimlessly around the centre of Carlisle for an hour or so, ending up lunching in a small pub. Ben had done his absolute best all morning to set aside any thought of the Borrowdale murder, giving all his attention to the present moment, browsing charity shops and encouraging his girlfriend to chatter about anything that came to mind.

Except hardly anything *did* come to mind, except Simmy, the shop and Christopher's troubles. 'I should be working,' she sighed.

'You were due a day off. Look – we can go and see the river. Or we could drive out to those woods we passed on the way. There's some great country round here.'

Bonnie sighed again. The attractions of 'great country' made less impression on her than they did on Ben. Where he saw evidence of former times and forgotten human activity, she only saw mundane stretches of trees and hedges, ponds and fences. She was content to let him explain how almost all of it had been affected, if not actually created, by mankind, but she had heard it all before, and no longer found it exciting.

'Yes, I know,' she had started to say, on recent excursions. 'You told me that before.'

Now, she said, 'I think we should just sit in a park and talk about murder. This isn't working, let's face it. Avoiding it, I mean.'

He held her gaze. 'Are you sure? I wanted to give you a break – a change from all that stuff. We've had far too much of it already.'

'It's what we do, though, isn't it? I can't just duck out of it because it might hurt my feelings. That would be cowardly. Besides, this time it's got nothing to do with me – there is no way I can get sucked in again, like the last one. It's very sweet of you to try and protect me, but I'm a big girl now. Look at me – I've just eaten a whole scotch egg!'

Two years earlier, such a level of food intake would have been unthinkable. She had somehow survived on the most minimal diet, afflicted by a teenage anorexia that almost killed her. Corinne and Ben between them had pulled her through the darkness to this point where she could consume nourishment at a level almost approaching normality.

He laughed. 'Still not exactly *big*, but I know what you mean.'

She smiled. 'So let's find somewhere sunny to sit. You can even phone Simmy, if you like.'

'Actually,' he was quite shamefaced, 'she did call me not long ago, when you were in the loo. I told her we were having a break from murder, and she'd have to wait till tomorrow. I thought—'

'Yes, I know what you thought. It doesn't happen very often, but you got me wrong. As I've just been saying.' She drained her glass of lemonade and lime. 'So what did she say? Simmy, I mean.'

'She's seen Moxon. He told her a whole lot of things, I think. I wouldn't let her say much. The body's disappeared and a man accosted Lily in Hartsop.'

'*Lily?* What's it got to do with her?'

Ben shrugged. 'Nothing, probably. I really don't know. I wouldn't let her explain any of it because I thought—'

'Okay, we've been through what you thought. You'll have to call her back and get her to say it again properly.'

He pulled a face, indicating resistance. 'She'll be driving. She'll want to get home after being in the shop all morning. And we can't do anything up here anyway, can we? Why don't we stick to Plan A and just have a nice day out?' His expression did not carry very much hope that she would agree to this.

'We *are* having a nice day. The town's quite interesting, with all these old buildings. That big hotel is amazing. The whole town square is brilliant. I like towns,' she finished with a rueful smile. 'Better than the country, really.'

'I know you do. That's why I suggested it. Next time we could go all the way to Glasgow if you like.'

She grinned. 'Blimey!' she said.

'There's a new cousin turned up,' Ben suddenly remembered, and in spite of himself could not refrain from voicing the fresh information. 'That must be why they had to stop the sale. If Jennifer Reade is dead, he's probably the next in line to inherit. Although . . .' he frowned. 'If he's the same generation as her, he might have an equal claim and they would have had to share out the proceeds anyway, fifty-fifty. So it's a bit greedy to kill her for the other half.'

Bonnie settled back in her seat and gave a little laugh. 'This is more like it,' she said.

'Okay – but not here. We've finished, haven't we? Let's go and find some sunshine.'

They left hand in hand, considerably more relaxed than when they had come into the pub. Both were anticipating one of their habitual sessions of sharing, guessing, leaping at conclusions and connecting random details.

'I wish I'd brought a notepad with me,' sighed Ben. 'It only really works on paper.'

'I've got one. You know I never go anywhere without it.'

'Oh joy!' sighed Ben happily.

The session in the park occupied well over an hour, threaded as it was with irrelevant observations on passing people and their dogs, the prospect of Simmy and Christopher managing another child, and whether Bonnie would ever get herself to the point of learning to drive. The actual brainstorming on the subject of events in Borrowdale remained somewhat thin and frustrating.

'We don't know enough,' Ben complained. 'It's all smoke and mirrors.'

'Shadows and suggestions.'

'Guesses and ghosts.'

It descended into a silly game for a few minutes, before Ben took up his pen again.

'Well, we know a man died, probably in the big house and then his body vanished. We know the owner of the house was attacked there. But by then she might not still have *been* its owner. We don't know who does own it now. There's a very distant cousin and a mystery man who found out where Christopher lives and went there to look for him.

Presumably. Why else would he be there? He must have thought Lily was part of the family or something. We know Jennifer Reade wanted the sale stopped, to judge by her final words.'

'We know quite a lot, really. I'm not sure where you got some of this from, though. Did you see Christopher yesterday? Or what? Have you found any of it online?'

Ben realised that he had been deliberately withholding almost everything from Bonnie, on the assumption that she would find it upsetting. Now she was only slowly catching up.

'Nothing online that I can find. Yes, Christopher came back to the saleroom after he'd been taken off to Penrith and gave us the bare bones of it. And Moxon found Simmy this morning and told her some more.'

'Yes. I knew that. It's a very weird story, though. I can't see any sense in it at all.'

'Well, I think it looks as if Jennifer killed the man in the cellar and manipulated Christopher into keeping quiet about it. Then some other person attacked her – maybe in revenge because they knew and loved the dead man. Then they'd have to dispose of the body somehow, because it would incriminate them once it was identified. But it wouldn't matter if they found Jennifer's body.' He frowned deeply, snatching at elusive ideas. 'They must have thought she was dead, and not just badly hurt.'

'Probably too busy to check,' commented Bonnie wryly. 'Lugging a dead man out of a cellar and finding somewhere to dump him – sounds exhausting.'

Ben chuckled. 'So we're looking for somebody big and strong.'

'Or two people,' said Bonnie.

He gave her an admiring look. 'I never thought of that,' he said.

'Maybe we can call Simmy now,' Bonnie tried again. 'She'll be home, won't she?'

'Probably. How about you do it, so she knows you're okay with it? She can tell you how it went in the shop, at the same time.'

So Bonnie tried, only to be sent to voicemail, both on the landline and Simmy's mobile. She did not leave any message.

'Can't think why anybody still keeps a landline, especially if they don't answer it,' she grumbled. 'And I think her mobile's turned off.'

'She probably just wants a bit of peace and quiet after a busy morning.' Ben found himself feeling a degree of relief at not having his mistake exposed, where Bonnie's frame of mind was concerned. 'She'll be out in the garden or upstairs or something.'

'It's only half past three. She might have gone to find Christopher instead of going home. Or could be she's in Threlkeld. We don't know for sure that she went home, do we?'

'We don't know where *anybody* is,' Ben complained. 'Her or Christopher, at least.'

'Or Moxon, come to that. It's such a pity you didn't let her tell you everything when she phoned you. Now it's all scattered about, and we're wasting all this time.'

'My bad,' said Ben, knowing this would make her smile. 'I'm thinking we could just go to a movie and forget the whole darned thing.'

They found their way to the Vue cinema in the wonderfully named Botchergate and chose the least awful film on offer, out of a deeply uninspiring programme.

'It must be us,' said Ben with a sigh. 'We're freaks because we don't find superheroes very entertaining.'

'We ought to try harder,' said Bonnie. 'And it's worth it for the popcorn. I've always loved popcorn. When I was fifteen it was about the only thing I would eat.'

'Come on, then,' said Ben. 'And after this I suggest we go over to Hartsop and do things properly. I did tell Simmy we'd call in tomorrow, but she won't mind if we bring it forward.'

'Thank goodness for that,' said Bonnie.

The film was of only moderate length, and the pair were on their way to the Hendersons' at around half past six, having failed to give advance warning of their intentions.

'They'll be glad to see us,' said Ben with confidence. As they drove the final mile, they realised they were following Christopher's car.

'Fancy that!' said Bonnie. 'He's been out all day, by the look of it. Poor Simmy's been on her own all afternoon.'

'You don't know that. He might have just popped out for something.'

'Bet you.'

'I hope there's some food. Popcorn isn't very filling.'

'It is to me. We might have to go to the pub for something if you're hungry. You can't expect Simmy to feed us. She's probably putting the baby to bed, and not in the mood for cooking.'

'I think Christopher can work an oven, if it comes to it.'

'Why didn't we come here earlier, instead of wasting money on that dozy film?'

'Because we were having a day out, and that's what people do. It's only seven, or a bit after. We can all sit outside and solve the murder between us. It's what we're good at, remember?'

'We'll have to park at the end of the road. There's no space there. He hasn't noticed us, look.'

Ben pipped the horn as he paused outside the converted barn. Christopher glanced up and took three seconds to register who they were. He smiled warily and performed a little pantomime to ask whether they were planning to come in. Ben opened the car window.

'Is it all right?' he asked. 'We'll park further up and walk back.'

'Does Simmy know you're coming?'

'No. But she phoned me earlier on, and said she's got things to tell us. She won't mind, will she?'

'Your guess is as good as mine,' said Christopher Henderson ominously.

'Not exactly hospitable,' muttered Ben as he drove to a spot where he could leave the car.

Chapter Fourteen

Simmy was in the kitchen when her husband came in. The dog ran eagerly to greet him, jumping up and grinning.

'Hi, pooch,' he said, rubbing her shoulders tightly in a gesture she loved. 'Had a good day?' he called through to Simmy, having spotted her by the sink. 'Ben and Bonnie are here. I gather they haven't given you any warning.'

She came out, wiping her hands on a tea towel. 'That's nice,' she said and meant it. She gave her husband a close inspection. 'Was it horrible? Where are the others, then?'

'Parking the car. It wasn't horrible at all, actually. The man's called Price and he's remarkably human. There have been developments.'

'So I gather. I saw Moxon.'

Ben and Bonnie arrived then, greeting Cornelia first, as Christopher had done. 'We went to *Carlisle*,' said Bonnie. 'And saw a rubbish movie.'

'In this weather? What a waste,' said Simmy. 'Do you want food? I could do a pasta thing with chicken. It wouldn't take long.'

'Sounds great,' said Ben.

All four of them herded into the kitchen and formed a

team. Christopher cut up meat and onions and started them cooking; Simmy made a cheese sauce, jostling amicably with her husband as they both stood over the hob; Bonnie chopped parsley and Ben laid the table. The pasta was boiled and the whole assemblage finally popped into the oven.

'Drink!' said Christopher. 'We've earned it.'

They sat in the central room, variously labelled 'living room' or 'big room', since it served a number of purposes. The Hendersons drank white wine and the youngsters had ginger beer.

'We should be outside,' said Simmy. 'But there aren't enough chairs. We don't get many of these gorgeous summer evenings.'

'Your roses look good,' said Bonnie, gazing out of the window at the flowers.

'Not bad for their first year,' agreed Simmy modestly.

'I got it wrong about Bonnie,' Ben blurted. 'She's quite happy to talk about everything that's been happening. I was being overprotective.'

'I did wonder,' said Simmy. 'When you were so abrupt on the phone.'

'Sorry.'

'Christopher's been in Penrith all afternoon, and I saw Moxon. I'm not sure whether we've both been told the same things. This is the first chance we've had all day to speak to each other.'

'You told me there was a cousin suddenly showed up. Should we start with him?'

'No,' said Christopher firmly. 'Because I know who the dead man in the cellar is – was. I think that trumps everything else.' Everyone gave him all due attention. 'He's called

170

Deeping and he's a printer. He ran the printworks next to our saleroom. I ought to have known him by sight, although I didn't recognise the picture they showed me. It's obviously not a coincidence, as the police soon figured out.'

'You're lucky they didn't ask you to identify him,' said Ben. Then he smacked himself lightly on the hand. 'Silly me – there's no body to identify, is there? Unless they've found it and we haven't heard.'

Christopher shook his head. 'To be honest, I'm overstating it a bit. I don't think they can ever be completely sure who it is, until they find the body. It's all circumstantial. But when they showed me a photo I thought it must be the same person. Although I didn't really look at the body properly.'

'Overstating it a *lot*, then,' said Ben. 'That's not evidence, is it?' He paused to think. 'And it's the wrong way round, somehow. The police hear that someone next to you in Keswick has gone missing and they instantly conclude it's the vanishing body in Borrowdale. That seems quite weird – and it puts you right in the centre of it all. I bet they were pretty heavy about it, weren't they?'

'Not at all, actually. I was just telling Simmy they were perfectly pleasant. I only really saw the top man, anyway. DS Price. He seemed to think I was being quite helpful.'

Ben was quiet again, and Bonnie spoke for him. 'He's trying to think himself into the minds of the police,' she explained.

'They haven't got much to go on, have they?' said Simmy. 'No dead body to identify. Jennifer Reade not having a phone to examine, and coming from somewhere miles and miles away. The only person they'd like to suspect has a cast-iron alibi.'

'What person?' demanded Ben.

'I told you when I phoned. A long-lost cousin has materialised. But he was on a plane when Jennifer was killed, and in India before that – so it can't have been him, even though he's the one who stands to benefit. He's not exactly a cousin. I met him and he explained it.'

'He could have paid someone to do it,' said Ben, with raised eyebrows as if to say, *Isn't that obvious?*

'We're forgetting the nameless man who came here yesterday and accosted Lily,' said Christopher. 'I nearly forgot to mention him to the police, which was pretty stupid of me. But my head was so full of the auction and everything, it's not so surprising.'

Simmy stared at him. 'But it's got to be important. I told Ben about it – almost the first thing I said, but he didn't want to listen to me.' She was still feeling sore at the way she'd been cut off.

'I've said sorry,' Ben repeated. 'I meant well.' Bonnie patted his arm, both consoling and warning. 'We all get things wrong,' Ben added, looking at Christopher.

'We talked about him this afternoon,' said Bonnie. 'Ben wrote down some ideas about it.' She pulled the notebook from her canvas bag and handed it to Ben, who had his computer on his lap. He put the notebook down beside his leg on the sofa.

In half a minute, they were all intently comparing findings and ideas. It turned out that Simmy had the most to say, reporting her relief in sharing the whole thing with her father and her admiration for his quick understanding. 'I can't remember all of it now, but he clarified things for me, at least. I was in a complete muddle until then.'

'I'm listing the main questions,' said Ben. 'First – why

did Jennifer want to stop the sale? That's the big one now, it seems to me. Lots of other bits point to that being crucial. The cousin who's a counterfeiter and will presumably now inherit the money from the house and all the stuff that was in it. I'm wondering if there's something amongst the lots that's worth way more than we realise and is the whole answer to everything.'

Christopher groaned. 'Don't say that. We've gone to all that trouble to find provenance and current value for just about everything in the sale. Even your precious *veilleuse*, which I admit to never having heard of before. First edition Hugh Walpoles won't fetch much. I don't remember any boxes of old papers or a manky old stamp album. And judging by how it was going yesterday, the hammer prices won't be anywhere near what we were hoping.'

'There is a stamp album, actually,' said Ben. 'It was Sir John's in the 1950s. But there isn't much in it.'

'No Penny Black?' said Bonnie.

Ben shook his head.

'Then there's the printer,' said Simmy. 'If it is him, of course.'

'Right,' said Ben uncertainly. 'I think I do know him slightly. He came to a sale a few months ago, and I think he put something in. Antiquarian books, or something.' He addressed Christopher. 'Don't you remember?'

'Not really. Did they make much?'

Ben tapped the keyboard of his laptop. 'Let's have a look. Yes – back in February. "Three small incunabula." They were just a few pages each – it's all coming back to me. We had to look up that word.'

Christopher closed his eyes, racking his memory. 'Okay.

I'm getting glimmers of memory. Wasn't that the day we sold the vintage tractor, and everyone went mad for it? Everything else got a bit overshadowed. Did they make much?' he asked Ben again.

'They did, quite. Some online bidders were fighting for them. Went to five hundred quid or thereabouts. Surely you remember now?'

'Sort of. It really isn't my field. I hadn't twigged that it was the printer man who was the vendor.'

Simmy had followed this with interest. 'Incunabula?' she repeated slowly. 'What a wonderful word! Like something from a Dan Brown story.'

'It just means a very old piece of printed matter. Quite dull, really. I think Dan Brown does mention them. If he doesn't, he should.'

'It's starting to connect up, though, isn't it?' said Bonnie.

'Who bought them? The incunabula?' asked Christopher.

Ben scrolled and tapped. 'Someone called Maurice Phillippson. Two ls and two ps. Lives in Salisbury.'

'Which isn't far from Swindon,' noted Simmy. 'Where Jennifer Reade lived. Isn't that significant?'

Ben was still tapping. 'Found him!' he announced after thirty seconds. 'He's got a shop there, and a bit of an empire, by the look of it. Places in Leeds and Aberystwyth as well. All very specialist and old-fashioned. Pictures of little shops in side streets. Sells stamps, postcards, antiquarian books, early broadsheets, letters, diaries. Probably does most of it online now, in spite of having the shops.'

'This is really getting somewhere!' said Bonnie happily. 'Look at all the connections we're finding.'

'Except we might be getting it all wrong,' cautioned Ben.

'Let's leave that a minute and try Question Two. Who was the man who came here and spoke to Lily? And what exactly did he say?'

Simmy and Christopher looked at each other, and then Simmy spoke, 'Something like, "Tell Mr Henderson, I know he's trying to find a body". Nothing else. We just assumed he had to be talking about the man in the cellar. But it's a funny way to word it. Like he was accusing Christopher of killing the man.'

'No,' said Ben slowly. 'More like he was on the same side – implying they both wanted to find it.'

Simmy thought about that. 'It's possible, I suppose. Lily said he wasn't unfriendly or scary. But it sounds like an accusation to me,' said Simmy.

'Maybe he was Maurice Phillippson,' said Bonnie hopefully.

'I smell food,' said Christopher suddenly.

Simmy jumped up in a panic. 'I *knew* this would happen,' she cried. 'We get so carried away we let the dinner burn. Come on – quick!'

It was not burnt, except for the very edges, and they soon demolished the whole lot, adding more wine and ginger beer, and finishing with some chocolates that Simmy had saved from Easter.

'I always did make them last,' she laughed. 'I have been known to keep some until Christmas.'

They returned to the big room, but the momentum was lost.

'This is a weird way to spend a Saturday night,' said Christopher. 'We should all be down at the pub.'

Nobody had anything to say about that. The fact of a baby asleep upstairs was enough on its own to make the remark unworthy of consideration. A feeling that it was Christopher who, more than all of them, should be pressing for a resolution of the matter in hand kept the three of them quiet. Ben's laptop had fallen asleep and Bonnie was looking tired.

'It's only eight o'clock,' Christopher went on. 'And the sun doesn't set for another hour or more.'

'So?' said Simmy.

'I don't know. I just think we're wasting time somehow. We haven't really got anywhere with all that talk, have we?'

'We've got everything down in one place,' said Ben. 'And we've identified a few more connections we hadn't got before. Plus names. What we *haven't* got is anything on Jennifer Reade. She really is completely off the grid.'

'You must have something from when she first commissioned you to sell all the house contents,' said Simmy.

Ben shook his head. 'No. it was all through her solicitor. We barely heard from her at all. It didn't seem odd, at first. We all thought she was an eccentric old woman who couldn't face the hassle. Then the solicitor told Fiona she was only thirty or so, which made us change our impression a bit.'

'I was stunned to see her at the house,' said Christopher. 'They told us for definite that she wasn't going to come up here in person. Something must have happened to change her mind.'

'Another question.' Ben made a note. 'Who did she know? Who did she speak to? And what on earth happened between Wednesday and Friday?'

'She seemed to know what she was doing. I mean – she wasn't shy or nervous or out of her depth – not much anyway. Perhaps at the start she was a bit off balance,' said Christopher. 'She was surprised to see me, and didn't seem to know what to do with me. But she soon got to grips with everything, so I felt like I was an intruder, with no business to be there. And then later on she talked me into staying quiet about the body. Well, you know all that already.' He subsided into a state of gloomy confusion. 'I think the police think I'm a bit of a fool. Too dim to have done a murder, even.'

They all laughed kindly at this, and made reassuring noises. 'You and Moxon both,' said Simmy fondly. 'I like my men to be a bit dim.'

'Corinne always says that about dogs,' said Bonnie. 'The clever ones are a real pain.'

Nobody picked up the reference to *my men*. It had long been accepted, even by Christopher, that Simmy and Moxon had a bit of a thing between them.

'All right,' said Ben assertively. 'Let's pack it in for today. Bonnie's dodging the car boot sale and staying over in Keswick, so what about tomorrow? What do you say we all go back to Borrowdale? If there are ever going to be any proper clues, that's got to be where we'd find them.'

Simmy quailed. 'With Robin? And the dog? *All* of us? It'll be heaving with hikers. We'll never find anywhere to park.' She had another thought. 'And my dad's going to want to come as well.'

'We'll use the bus,' said Ben. 'It leaves from Keswick. We can get an early one and beat the crowd.'

'Oh, God!' said Christopher with full melodrama. He put his head in his hands for good measure. 'We'll need a whole bus just to ourselves, at this rate.'

'My mother won't want to come,' said Simmy, as if this offered any reassurance.

Chapter Fifteen

Somewhat against Simmy's expectations, the entire group was boarding the Borrowdale bus soon after nine next morning. The sky was clear, and had been for the past four hours or more. Robin was co-operative, unlike Cornelia, who had never experienced a bus before.

After a short drive down the quiet country road, with dense woodland on both sides, they were set down close to the bridge leading into Grange.

'This is where Robin did his amazing walk,' said Simmy. 'He hasn't done that many steps since. I think he needs an audience.' She observed the cafe and the church and the old school as they walked in a gaggle up the road towards High Gates. 'I can't help feeling this is rather silly,' she said. 'What can we possibly hope to find? The house belongs to someone else now, presumably. It'll have police tape all over it, as well.'

'I imagine the sale never got properly completed,' said Christopher. 'It was still not quite done on Wednesday. Unless Jennifer and her solicitor got cracking on Thursday, it must still be in limbo.'

'You can sign documents remotely now,' said Ben.

'Not if you don't have the technology, like Ms Reade,' said Bonnie.

'Right. I forgot.' The boy waggled his head in bemusement. 'I can't think how that's possible. How did she ever *communicate* with anyone?'

'Landline. Postcards. Carrier pigeons,' said Russell, who was cheerfully enjoying the unexpected day out, grateful to be invited. 'I don't know how I can be of any use,' he had demurred. 'But I'd love to come, if you'll have me.'

'Another pair of eyes,' said Simmy vaguely.

'I like the idea of carrier pigeons,' said Ben now. 'If I was a terrorist, that's what I'd use.'

'I don't think anybody's imagining terrorism is a part of this,' said Christopher, humourlessly.

'I never said it was,' argued Ben.

'Stop being so literal, both of you,' said Simmy. 'How far are we going to walk?'

'We could get all the way to Honister, if we make a day of it,' said Russell. 'It's glorious up there.'

'That's *miles*,' moaned Bonnie. 'Uphill all the way.'

'And it's in the opposite direction,' Ben observed. 'We're going north, and it's down to the south, behind us.'

'Of course, I knew that,' blustered Russell, clearly disconcerted.

'I got confused about that as well,' Simmy consoled him. 'It feels wrong, somehow. But it all hinges on the river. You have to go back over the bridge to get to Seatoller and all those places.'

'There isn't much on this side,' added Christopher.

'Even so,' argued Russell, 'it can't be very far. And the bus must go all round everywhere picking up tired hikers.'

'You do realise that the reason we're all here is for Ben and Bonnie to see the house for themselves, don't you?' said Christopher impatiently. 'It's as simple as that.'

'Sorry,' said Russell meekly. 'I was only thinking it's a fine June Sunday and we can all benefit from a nice day out.'

'That's right,' said Simmy. 'Trust my dad to see the positive side.'

'We seem to be ahead of the crowd, anyway,' said Bonnie staring up at the fell to their left. 'I thought the place would be swarming with hikers. I can't see anybody.'

Everyone looked. The scrubby ground rose steeply behind the few scattered houses and gardens that lined the road. Pathways threaded between the rocky outcrops and sheep grazed the short grass almost to the top. Lambs gathered in small groups, constantly nagged by their watchful mothers.

'You must be able to see Derwentwater from up there,' said Ben.

'And beyond,' Russell confirmed. 'You can really watch the world go by. I remember I sat up there with Simmy's mother for a whole afternoon, about twelve years ago now. I haven't been back here since. Although . . . it was probably on the other road, now I think about it. I don't think I've ever been on this one before.'

They were progressing very slowly up the gentle hill out of Grange. Five adults, a child and a dog made a fair-sized group straggling across the little road; almost no traffic went past. The sun had not climbed very far above the high ridge to their east. Simmy kept pausing to look around.

'It still feels as if we're going south, for some reason,

although I know we can't be. The river runs into Derwentwater, and I know that's to the north.' She sighed. 'And I thought I was really getting the hang of how it all worked by now.'

Ben and Russell both opened their mouths to enlighten her, but Christopher forestalled them.

'We've done the geography already. Let's stick to the main business, okay?' He was pale and stiff, walking ahead of the others. 'The house is just round the next bend.'

Simmy tried to recall their first walk from the village to High Gates, thinking it had been further than *just around the next bend*. 'Are you sure?' she asked. 'We haven't gone very far yet.'

'Two bends at most.' His voice was thick and shaky.

'Hey!' Simmy hurried to catch him up, past Russell who was in charge of Robin's buggy. 'You look as if you're having a flashback or something. We don't have to do this, you know. Not if it's going to get you in a state.'

'Yes we do. It's too late to abandon it now. You're right, probably, that it's all very stupid, but it's gone too far, and now it feels horribly serious, all of a sudden. I guess it wasn't quite real before. I keep seeing that rat.'

'Rat?' echoed Bonnie. 'Nobody said anything about a rat. Where?'

'Don't make me explain it again now,' begged Christopher. He stopped walking and took some breaths. 'Actually – Bonnie, Russell – do you think you could hang back a bit, with the dog, when we get there? I know we can't go in or anything, but I'll get clearer in my head if I'm not surrounded with you lot. Okay?'

'No problem,' said Bonnie, oozing understanding and

compassion. 'I know how these things can get to you.'

Russell was not so generous. 'So, can we have a look after you've done your soul-searching? What's come over you, man?'

'Dad, have a bit of patience. You sound like Mum. Two people died right here, less than a week ago, and Chris was right in the middle of it. Give him some space – that's all he's asking.'

'Right, right. Sorry. I forgot.' The elderly man wheeled the buggy violently to one side. 'I'll keep out of the way, then.'

'No need for that,' said Bonnie, putting a hand on his arm. 'It's only that everything got a bit real for Christopher just then. We can all have a good long look, if that's what we want – *after* he's done what he came to do. He's the only witness to what happened on Wednesday, so it's important he tries to get the memories straight, don't you think? That *is* why we're here, you know. I'm keeping right out of it, as well. Although I'm not scared of rats. I quite like them, in a way.'

'Clever little beasts,' Russell grudgingly agreed. 'Angie says that's why people fear them. They feel like a kind of competition for domination. Like ants.'

'Right,' said Bonnie vaguely, flashing a smug smile at Ben. 'So, we're all right again, aren't we?'

Russell was rueful. 'Forgot myself for a moment,' he mumbled. 'I thought all that sort of thing was over and done with, but it catches up with me now and then.'

Simmy heard some of this, despite her attention being almost entirely on her husband. Her father had gone through a spell of neurosis two years or so before, exhibiting severe

182

anxiety and compulsive behaviour. Therapy and medication had calmed him down, identifying the probable cause as the loss of Simmy's first baby and the exhausting rigours of running a Bed and Breakfast guesthouse with little or no respite. But it had aged him more than his family fully realised, and there were still moments of confusion and anger.

They walked on for two or three minutes and there, somehow darker and larger than before, was High Gates House. In front of it were not only two lengths of police tape, but gates that must have been closed with a determined effort, and a police car parked inside them, containing two officers. Standing in the road outside were four people.

'Uh-oh,' said Ben.

'Now we're a crowd,' muttered Bonnie. 'Gawpers. This is embarrassing.'

Christopher had stopped dead. 'They'll recognise me,' he said softly. 'It's worse than embarrassing.' He looked at Bonnie with a ghastly smile. 'Help!'

'We've every right to be here,' said Ben stoutly. 'Out for a day with kid and dog. That sort of thing.'

'Nonsense,' said Russell. Simmy was forced to agree with him.

'Do you know them?' she asked Christopher, nodding at the officers in the car.

'I can't see them properly. But they'll know me, won't they? I've been in that blasted police station for hours since Friday. They've all had a good look at me. We should have known there'd be someone here.'

'Not necessarily,' said Ben. 'What do they hope to achieve?' He stared at the car, and went on slowly, 'They're standing guard. Presumably the place is stuck between owners, and there's legal considerations. But that's not the job of the police.'

'They're doing what Moxon did in Askham,' Simmy realised. 'Showing a presence, in case somebody wants to come and tell them something. It's easier to do it out here than in the Penrith station. It's a bit like an incident room, only in a car.'

'Except they've shut the gates, which can't have been easy. One of them's missing a hinge, look. How would anyone get in?'

Christopher was hanging back, completely flummoxed. 'They'd let anyone in if they thought they had something to tell them,' he said. 'Obviously.'

The four people who had been there before them were shamelessly watching and listening to all this, shuffling excitedly at the dawning realisation that the newcomers might actually have some involvement in recent events. Quite how this had become apparent was unclear to Simmy, but there was little doubt – and the explanation was soon forthcoming.

'You're the auctioneer!' accused one man. 'This affects you, doesn't it. I heard they cancelled the auction on Friday.'

'Are you local?' Ben asked, scanning the foursome. 'You don't look like hikers.'

'Jill works at the hotel down there, and I've got a shop in town,' said the man, nudging the woman at his side. 'These two are from the slate mine museum. They need to get back to work in a minute.'

'You haven't walked all the way from there, have you?' asked Russell.

A woman shook her head. 'Car's in a gateway just back there.' She nodded up the hill. 'Just wanted to come and see what the fuss was about.'

'So you're not here to help the police, then?' Russell went on, with increasing belligerence. 'Just gawping, so to speak?'

'Dad,' sighed Simmy, at the same time unable to repress a flash of admiration. He was, after all, speaking for them all.

'I knew Sir John,' said the original man. 'Nice old chap. Lonely. He'll be spinning in his grave with all this carry-on.'

'Serves him right,' said the Jill person. 'He should have made a proper will and saved everyone a whole lot of bother. If you ask me, there'd never have been a murder if he'd done it right.'

'The auction isn't cancelled. Just postponed,' said Christopher.

'Must be a right old hassle for you, then. All that stuff sitting there like that. My mate Joe wanted to bid on some rugs. Came all the way from Leeds for them, he did, and now he's gone back empty-handed, saying he won't bother again.'

'He can bid online,' said Ben.

The man gave him a withering look. 'You don't know Joe,' he said. 'Thinks computers give out poison waves that rot your brain. Won't go near the things.'

'Not another one,' sighed Ben. Bonnie poked him gently, warning him not to say any more.

Robin chose that moment to make it very plain that he had had enough. The buggy was too confining, the people

185

too boring and his immediate prospects too unappealing for him to tolerate.

'Hey . . . hey . . . hey!' he shouted and drummed his heels on the footbar.

More people were approaching, walking up the hill out of Grange as Simmy's party had done. There would soon be a veritable crowd loitering mindlessly outside the gates.

'We can't stay here,' Simmy said quietly to her husband. 'It's horrible – and it'll get worse. There'll be people like this hanging around all day. Oh!'

She had recognised the couple coming up the road, as they got closer. 'Isn't that . . . ? The people at the cafe in Grange, remember?'

'Bloody hell, that's all we need.'

Steve – the man was called Steve, and he knew about mining and geology and who knew what else. The woman had been patronising. They had got the bus out of Keswick on the day they'd met, and presumably had done the same thing again today. *We're here for a week*, he had said. The way it all came back to her was a surprise. Was Christopher experiencing a similar total recall of his encounter with Jennifer Reade? Being in the same geographical location did seem to be an effective prompt, at least in Simmy's case.

There was no hope of going unrecognised by the couple, given the presence of Robin and Cornelia. There was a gleam of triumph in the woman's eye.

'You again!' she cried. 'Fancy that!'

'Hello,' said Simmy.

The original people paused their intended departure at the prospect of something interesting. 'You know each other?' asked the man with the shop. 'How come?'

Nobody answered.

'Hurry up, Phil,' said the Jill woman. 'We're really late now.' In submission to her will, the four of them walked off with no more than a few feeble waves of hands.

Ben and Bonnie were eyeing the newcomers curiously, trying to guess where they fitted, having heard what Simmy had said, but still not clear. Christopher's words, however, had been enough of a clue as to how to behave. Bonnie bent over Robin, talking at him in an effort to appease him. Russell took the dog to the other side of the road, where she found something interesting to sniff. A sense of aimless dithering prevailed, which could only frustrate Steve and his missus.

Except it didn't. It would take more than that to deter the man, who started to talk urgently.

'The thing is, we know the people who found the dying woman on Friday. They're staying at the same guesthouse as us, as luck would have it. They're a gay couple from Essex. Bert and Lawrence. Lovely people. Awful thing, though. Hit them badly, it did. They cancelled the rest of the holiday because of it. It wasn't until last night that we got the story from the landlady. It was all on the news, of course. I expect you saw it. Well, it's human nature to come back for a look, isn't it? Here you are, with the same idea. I mean – look at that house. Could be something from *The Munsters*. Edgar Allen Poe. That sort of thing. All dark and gloomy and full of ghosts.'

'Stop it Steve,' said his wife, aware of undercurrents and something worse than inappropriate.

'What's *The Munsters*?' murmured Bonnie to Ben, who shrugged.

'What? Why? What did I say?' demanded Steve.

'The *police* are here.'

'So? We're not breaking any laws, are we? They're not taking any notice of us, anyway. They'll just be here to keep people out of the house.'

'We should go,' said Simmy, hating to be taken for the same ghoulish sightseer as these people. She joined Bonnie beside the baby buggy. 'My turn to push,' she said.

'Looks as if he wants to get out,' said Mrs Steve. 'Poor little man.'

'Your hubby seems to be in a bit of a fix,' said Steve, gazing raptly at Christopher. 'He's gone a funny colour.'

It was true. From pale, his face had turned to a mottled mixture of pink and green. To Simmy's alarmed eyes he looked on the verge of collapse. Russell and the dog came back from their short stroll along the verge and both peered at him, Cornelia wagging uncertainly.

'Tummy trouble,' said Russell heartily. 'He's been bad for a day or two now. We thought some fresh air might sort him out, but it's obviously been too much. Come on, son. Back to the bus stop for you.'

'Are you his father, then?' asked the woman.

'That's right, dear. We're all one big happy family. Niece, nephew, son, grandson – the works.' He waved a patriarchal arm at the group. 'Lovely day, too. Look at that sky!'

Nobody looked, and Bonnie stifled a giggle. Simmy lifted Robin out of the buggy and set him down on his bandy toddler legs.

'Walk, then,' she told him. 'Christopher – come and hold his hand. I'll take the buggy.'

Somehow they all got into motion, heading back the way they'd come.

'Hey, but wait—' Steve tried vainly to stop them.

'Have a good day,' Russell called back, after a few yards had separated them. He had a supporting hand under Christopher's elbow, and Robin staggered crookedly on the other side. Christopher was holding him so tightly that when he missed a step he dangled from his father's hand, legs waving in mid-air. It made for slow progress, which suited the sickened man very well. Ben and Bonnie went ahead, talking intently to each other.

'That was ghastly,' said Simmy. 'Those people!'

'Coincidence,' said Russell. 'Them being in the same guesthouse as Bert and Lawrence. But it happens a lot. We saw it all the time in Windermere. I remember once there were two sets of guests from the south somewhere, who turned out to have been at school together. The wives, that is.'

'Yes,' said Simmy absently. 'How are you now?' she asked her husband. 'Did you remember anything new?'

'It *was* ghastly,' he told her. 'Worse than I could ever have imagined. I kept seeing the man's horrible face, and remembering Jennifer, and *those people*.'

'They're just ordinary folk,' said Russell. 'Most are just like that. You learn that when you run a B&B. Drove your mother mad at times. They can't help it.'

'It's brought back a whole other lot of stuff. The thing in Grasmere, for one. I thought that was dealt with long ago, but there it is, sitting like a toad somewhere in my head. I was pretty unaffected at the time, that's what's so weird. Why did this one knock me sideways? It doesn't make any sense.'

Russell offered an answer: 'Could be that things are

different now – for you, I mean. You've got this little lad to think about, for one. And you're not flavour of the month with the police this time, either.'

'You were brilliant, Dad,' Simmy congratulated him. 'One of your finest performances. I just hope it doesn't come back to bite us. We might not have seen the last of that couple. What if they find out who we are?'

'Let them. What does it matter?'

'It doesn't, I suppose. Not really.' But she chafed at the prospect of being exposed as the daughter of a fantasist.

Christopher was still looking tormented, which all the others saw quite clearly. Bonnie had rejoined them, hovering on the other side of Robin, making a straggling foursome taking up much of the road. A car hooted behind them and they all shuffled awkwardly to one side.

'Let me take Robin,' said Simmy. 'He's done enough walking for now.'

'He likes it,' said Bonnie. 'Look at his face.' The child was beaming and pink with achievement, crowing every time he had to be saved by his father, holding his breath as he stepped out, his chest puffed up.

'He's too slow,' Simmy insisted. 'We need to find somewhere we can all sit down.'

'You'll be lucky,' said Russell.

'We can go into the church,' said Simmy. 'But at this rate we won't be there till lunchtime.'

'What's the hurry?' snapped Christopher. 'What are we planning to do now? We've bashed our faces up against a brick wall and made fools of ourselves.'

Nobody disagreed with him, and after a moment, Ben tried to sum up the situation. 'Brick wall is exactly right.

You do realise that none of us has ever met a single one of these people, except Christopher, and he only saw Jennifer Reade – once. They're just names. How can we hope to make any sort of sense of the thing like that?'

'Time to stop asking questions and start *doing* something,' said Russell. 'If you ask me.'

'That's why we came here, isn't it?' said Ben. 'To make ourselves feel we were doing something. But it's hopeless. Silly, as Simmy said.'

Christopher had almost forgotten his little boy, taking two long agitated strides before the whimpers reminded him.

'Sorry, kid. Better go to your mother now.' The handover was made, and Christopher took two more strides, as if gripped by a sudden purpose. 'We need to find that body. We need to know how he died and when, who he was for certain. The whole thing is stuck without that.'

'The only one of us who stands the remotest chance of doing that is Cornelia,' said Ben. 'And she's not much of a bloodhound.'

'They should be dragging Derwentwater,' Christopher persisted.

'Not to mention Buttermere and Loweswater,' sighed Russell.

'And every crevice of these fells. Mine shafts, too. Car boots. Acid baths.' Ben was brainstorming rather too enthusiastically.

'Stop it,' said Simmy.

'We're at the mercy of fate,' said Bonnie, which drew everyone's attention. 'I mean, we just have to hope the police find him, or the person who took him has good intentions.

He might just have wanted to save him from those rats.'

Christopher shuddered. 'That's what I should have done.' He looked round, with sunken eyes. 'This whole thing really is my fault. . I've been kidding myself till now. That's what hit me at the gates. I could have saved Jennifer Reade's life if I'd been anything like decent. It's all my fault.'

Chapter Sixteen

Ben had convinced himself that somewhere in all the wild ideas that had been voiced lay the truth of the whole matter. He was also of the opinion that it was important to be here in Borrowdale, on the spot. When Simmy and Christopher wimped out, he and Bonnie opted to stay longer.

'We're not ready to go yet. I'd like to explore a bit more. We can get a bus back to Keswick any time,' he said. 'And Bonnie likes fell walking once she gets going.'

'Do I?' The girl frowned. 'When did that happen?'

'In Hawkshead, you got quite into it, remember?'

'That wasn't fells. It was mostly level ground. I'm not big on stamina, you know.'

'Just humour me, okay?' he persisted.

So the Hendersons and Russell Straw went back on the next bus, promising themselves lunch somewhere in town and an hour in the park for the child and dog.

'What's all this?' Bonnie asked, when they were left on their own. 'I smell a plan.'

'The house. If I've got the geography right, we can walk along by the river, more or less parallel with the road, and sneak up from there. Those policemen looked half asleep to me. They won't have anybody watching the back.'

'Hang on. Why do we have to avoid the road? The house isn't on the same side as the river – it's tucked under the fell on the *other* side. We could go back the way we've just come, walk on past and then go through those woods. Although the back of the house looked as if it's pretty much squashed against the fell.'

'That's all true, except there's bound to be some space behind the house for ventilation and light. But they'll see us if we do that, and there'll be people who might remember us. We need to stay out of sight. Plus,' he gave her an uneasy glance, 'I thought we should have a good look at the riverbank. Just in case.'

She caught on instantly. 'In case we find the body.'

'Right.'

'That would be a miracle.'

'Not really. Isn't that what anyone would do if they wanted to dispose of a body? Unless they bundled it into a car, they'd have to carry it and bodies are heavy. And what then? You can't leave it in a boot for long. So best to drag it over the road, across a field or two and dump it in the river at a quiet spot. All at dead of night, obviously.'

'I think the car theory is a lot more likely.'

'Just humour me, okay, and be thankful I'm not really taking you to the top of the fell in those flimsy shoes.' Bonnie had taken to wearing 'barefoot shoes', which she vowed were supremely comfortable for every sort of activity. Fell walking had not yet been tried, however.

'I am truly thankful,' she said.

'Come on then.'

They felt conspicuous as they scrambled down from

the road just before it crossed the bridge at Grange, and pushed their way along the riverbank through reeds and rushes that soon gave way to shrubs and trees. There was no proper path and the ground was boggy. They could not easily look into the river itself, due to all the vegetation.

'How will we know when to start crossing fields?' asked Bonnie.

'We'll see the house, I think. It's visible from most places. We need to get past that big hotel and on a bit further.'

'Somebody's going to see us. We're not meant to walk along here.'

'They won't take any notice. I wish we could get closer to the water. This isn't how I imagined it.'

'Nobody could get a body through all this, anyway.'

'It looks a bit clearer further along.' He led the way, holding tree branches aside for her once or twice. 'There's an old water mill around here somewhere. People have to trek across a field to get to it, if I remember rightly. If anyone sees us, they'll think we're looking for that.' He stopped to look round. 'Although it might be much further up. Or even the other way, towards Rosthwaite. I can't remember now.'

'Look at your phone, why don't you?'

'Good idea.' He produced the mobile and sidestepped into the shade of a tree in order to see the screen. 'Ah – right. Silly me. It's a long way from here. Up by Seatoller. That's where the serious walkers go.'

'They'll think we're trying to find a quiet spot to have sex,' she said with a giggle.

'They can think what they like. Just so long as those policemen don't see us.'

'Oh – what's that?' There was a smudge of off-white behind a hawthorn tree. 'A tent, look. Hiding away by the wall.'

'Clever.' Ben peered through the tree. 'No one could see it from anywhere but here.'

'Do you think . . . ?'

'We shouldn't jump to any conclusions. Probably a birdwatcher. Or a homeless person. All perfectly innocent.'

They were speaking in a whisper, only twenty yards from the tent.

'I'm going to see,' said Bonnie. Ben made no attempt to stop her, but followed close behind. There was no easy way to approach, so they went in a loop around the prickly tree and then had to cross a stretch of mossy stones that revealed the sporadic presence of a small rill trickling down to the Derwent. The tent was pitched on a rare piece of level ground, with a stone wall at its back. It was very small. A man sat on a low stool, a knife in his hand. Strewn around his feet were two plastic boxes, a tripod and a book. On his lap was a plate holding a piece of bread and other food.

'Hello,' said Bonnie. 'You look very organised.'

'Not as organised as I thought. Nobody was supposed to be able to find me.'

'Sorry,' said Bonnie. 'But it's only us. We're quite good at this sort of thing.'

'What's in the boxes?' asked Ben with rude curiosity.

'Mind your own business. What are you doing here, anyway? This isn't a public right of way, you know.'

'Nobody seems to care much about that sort of thing out here, though, do they?'

The man shrugged and smiled. '*Touché*,' he said.

The pair examined him with frank interest. He was quite young, with straggly black hair and beard, wearing a grey, short-sleeved shirt and light green cotton trousers. He was tanned and thin and looked strong. 'How long have you been here?' asked Ben.

'Nearly a week, I think. I gave up trying to keep track. It was raining the day I came, but it's been nice and dry since then.'

'How do you manage for food – and drink? You can't have carried a week's worth all down here.'

'Well, I did. This is the last of the bread, though. There's water in the river, in case you haven't noticed. Remarkably unpolluted.'

Which reminded Ben and Bonnie of their quest. 'So you must have seen all the goings-on just up there at High Gates House,' said Ben.

'What?'

'A woman was murdered there, probably early on Friday. Two days ago. It's Sunday now. The police are still there, and all the hikers are going to gawp.'

'And a body's gone missing,' said Bonnie. 'We thought it might have been dumped in the river.'

The man looked from face to face, as if they were two small children recounting the story of Little Red Riding Hood or Hansel and Gretel.

'You're joking,' he said.

'Not at all.' Ben was offended. 'It can't be more than a quarter of a mile from here. How could you miss it?'

'Well, I did,' the man said for a second time. 'Things are clearly not as you think. My name's Peter, by the way – just about the only one of my generation.'

'Sorry? The only what?' frowned Ben.

'Peter. Have you ever met one under the age of fifty? Or even sixty?'

'I don't know. I never thought about it.'

'Oh well. People often comment, that's all. Anyway, I take photos. You'll have noticed the tripod. And you'll have scared the otters, not to mention the water rats. I should be ranting at you about it, but what's the point?'

Ben leant excitedly towards him. 'Is the camera motion-sensitive? Do you have it set up overnight? Where is it?'

'In the tent. You're not serious about this murder malarky, are you? Things like that don't happen in places like this.'

'Actually, they do,' said Bonnie. 'Quite a lot.'

'So tell me, then. You'll have to sit on the grass, but it's quite dry. I can offer you a drink of best river water.'

'No thanks – we've got our own.' Ben produced a bottle from his rucksack and he and Bonnie settled onto the spongy grass. 'Have you looked at your night recordings?'

Peter shook his head. 'Have to conserve the batteries. Some of it works with solar, but it's not very good. I'm taking it all back to civilisation in another day or two. I'm hoping I've got enough material to keep me going through the rest of the summer.'

'You sell the pictures?'

'Right.'

'Can we see the video from the nights of last Wednesday and Thursday, then?' asked Ben.

'What? Just like that? No, you can't. What would be the point? If somebody did a murder right beside my camera, I'd have heard them.'

198

'That's not what we said. The murder isn't what we want to see. It's the disposal of a body – a man who was dead *before* the murder.'

Peter reverted to his earlier sceptical expression. 'Oh yes? Disposal of a body, not the murder victim, down here in my quiet little spot? How?'

Ben maintained his dignity. 'By throwing it in the river, of course. It's the obvious thing to do.'

'Okay. So you're looking for film of a person slinking through these trees, past my tent, with a dead body over his shoulder, in the dead of night. As I said before, I'm pretty sure I would have heard something like that going on.'

'How wide-angled is it? How far from here do you set it up? You could have caught *something*. Is it facing the river? If you're looking for otters and water rats, it must be.'

Bonnie spoke up, then. 'If you won't let us have a look, will you at least show us a way down to the water? We wanted to see if there's a place . . .' she tailed off, daunted by Peter's expression. 'It sounds daft, I know. But honestly – it's all absolutely real.'

'It sounds totally bonkers. But who am I to judge? I'm not going anywhere, but I can tell you that if you follow this wall a little way, then go through the gap, past a big willow tree, there's a place where the riverbank's fairly open. I guess it flooded there not long ago and any trees that were there got washed away, leaving a hole. That's where I go for my water – and where I set the camera up at night. I take it down every morning, for obvious reasons. It's only for backup, anyway. The real work's in taking stills during hours of daylight. I've got about fifty highly marketable shots of red squirrels, for a start.' He sighed happily. 'And about the same of birds. Kingfishers, herons, baby ducks. Plus,' his eyes shone, 'there's a family of fox cubs in the next field.'

'It's a hard life,' said Ben enviously.

'If there's a dead body in the water, I should probably stop drinking it.'

'Not if you stay upstream of it,' laughed Ben. 'Sounds as if you believe us, after all.'

'I'm suspending disbelief, as they say.' He finished his bread and sat quietly waiting for someone to say something.

Ben broke the short silence. 'We really should have a look at your recordings, though. You can't be sure you'd have heard anything. There must be all sorts of night noises – owls and things – so you might not have taken any notice even if you heard a splash or grass rustling. There are sheep everywhere, for a start.'

'I'm not setting it up now. But I promise not to delete anything for a few more days, okay? Look – here's my number. If you think I can be helpful, give me a call. But it's not very likely, is it? Your baddie would have seen the camera and made sure he didn't get caught by it. All the same, I don't want to be obstructive. I don't approve of murder. That's one law I guess we can all agree on.' He opened a plastic box, took out a wallet and extracted a business card from it. 'The website's on there, too. Give it a week or so and you'll see some of my pictures.'

Ben took the card and read aloud: 'Peter Hinckley. Photographer. Website. Email. Mobile. At least you're not off the grid.'

'Pardon?'

'Oh – just that we keep coming across dinosaurs who

don't do anything online. It's unnerving.'

'Well, that's not me.'

'When you get back to civilisation, you can check everything we've said. The murder was in the news. The victim had just inherited about a million pounds worth of property.'

'You amaze me.'

'The house is just up there somewhere,' Bonnie told him again. 'You can go and have a look any time you like.'

'And why would I do that?' asked Peter Hinckley.

Ben and Bonnie followed Peter's directions and found the stretch of riverbank just as he had described it. They also found footprints, both human and ovine, and holes where the tripod must have been set up. The river was wide and shallow.

'You'd see a body easily if it was in there,' said Ben. 'We've got this all wrong.'

'How about down there?' Bonnie pointed. The river narrowed slightly and was dotted with rocks. The water swirled around them. Scrubby trees once again clustered right to the water's edge. 'It's worth a look.'

Ben was suddenly pessimistic. 'We won't find anything. That would be too much to hope for.'

'So where's the house from here? I've lost my bearings.'

'Me too. Let's have a look.' Once again Google was consulted. 'The map isn't very detailed, but I think we must be almost directly below it. And not very far at all.'

'So it *could* work. It does make sense.'

'Let me think before we do anything. We might be missing something. What if that chap isn't at all what he

201

seems? He could be an undercover detective, or an escaped prisoner, or . . .'

'The actual murderer,' said Bonnie, eyes wide.

'This business card – it's all a bit too good to be true. Why would he have them with him out here? Like a good cover story, ready for all eventualities. And stringing us along like that, not believing us one minute and then seeming to the next.'

'I think he's what he says he is, though.' Bonnie's excitement subsided. 'It's the most likely explanation, after all.'

Ben was scouring the ground in Sherlock Holmes mode. 'I can only see one set of footprints, which must be Peter's. If a person carried the body down here, we'd see signs.'

'What if he wasn't really dead at all? Or it was a dummy? Christopher said it was dark in the cellar and he was scared of the rats. You have to think of everything,' she added before Ben could pour scorn on the suggestion.

'You do – and that had not occurred to me. But it sounded pretty real to me. Chris was *sick*, remember. And look how he was just now – he went *green* just thinking about it.'

'I thought that was more about Jennifer Reade than the man in the cellar. Because he feels guilty about her.'

'Both, presumably. He's a mess, either way.'

'There's a lot of men we need to think about. I make it six, at least. And not a single woman.'

'Except Jennifer,' Ben said. 'So who are all the men? I can only get four.'

'The man who spoke to Lily. The long-lost cousin, Warwick something. The dead one. Julian something-or-

202

other. Mr Deeping the printer – and Peter the photographer. And the one who bought the incunabula in Salisbury. That makes seven. Too many,' she sighed.

Ben gave her a reproving look. 'Deeping and the dead one are almost certainly the same person. And the one in Salisbury doesn't count. And the Julian person isn't likely to matter. Which brings it down to three.'

'No it doesn't. You can't make all those assumptions.' She lifted her chin. 'That's lazy thinking, which isn't like you. We could even count Jennifer's solicitor – is that a man?'

'I think so. I never had any dealings with them, so I'm not sure.'

'The trouble is, we've never seen any of them. They're just names.'

'Except Peter. And Simmy met the cousin-who-isn't-a-cousin.'

'True. Can we go now? There's nothing much to see here, is there?'

Ben shook his head. 'We should try and follow the river a bit more. It might get deeper further along.'

'Can we get through those bushes?' More hawthorns and alders were growing close to the water.

'We can try.'

They shouldered their way past a few trees, but it was hard going. Bonnie got scratched on her face and they both had wet feet from when they had to step sideways into soft mud.

'I'm not going any further,' said Bonnie after a few minutes.

'Okay. Let's go back, then.' He looked up at the almost

vertical wooded escarpment on the other side of the river. 'It's still remarkably wild around here, isn't it. Borrowdale's always been famous for hard rough living. They've tamed it massively now, of course, but it's still pretty inhospitable.'

'You could do wild swimming down this river,' she mused. 'Except it's not deep enough for proper swimming. You'd get all bashed by the stones.'

Ben shuddered. 'What made you think of that? It'd be brutal.'

'I don't know. Some people think it's fun. You have to keep an open mind.'

'Careful. You sound a bit priggish.' It was a word they had adopted a year or two earlier, as one of their specials. It always made Bonnie giggle.

They went back to Peter's piece of riverbank, and headed in the original direction, skirting the trees and soon encountering another stone wall. There were sheep on the further side of it. Ewes and half-grown lambs were scattered over the field, contentedly browsing.

'You'd think the foxes would get the lambs,' said Ben.

'The mothers wouldn't let them. They can eat squirrels instead. Or rabbits.'

A faint squealing drew their attention to some sort of activity near the wall, a little way to their right.

'Look!' whispered Ben, leaning over to see. Bonnie joined him and they discerned three young foxes tussling over something, exactly as puppies would do, and making quite a noise about it.

'Oh! Sweet!' breathed Bonnie. 'What is it they're playing with?'

'Can't see. Let's get closer.'

They got over the wall slowly, trying to stay low and inconspicuous and crept towards the cubs. They need not have bothered too much about scaring them, so intent were the animals on their game. All three had their teeth fixed on the plaything pulling in three different directions. There was no sign of a parent fox. Then Bonnie kicked a stone, which hit another stone with a crack that must have triggered the cubs' survival instinct. All three dropped their toy, looked up, saw the humans and vanished into the vegetation.

'Oops!' said Bonnie.

'Might as well see what they'd got,' said Ben, trying not to sound excited. He trotted the last few yards and gingerly lifted an object from the ground. 'It's a shoe,' he said. 'A man's shoe.'

Chapter Seventeen

It took almost two hours to get from Grange to Penrith police station. They just missed a bus to Keswick. Ben's car had been boxed in by a large four-wheel-drive thing, which delayed them by a quarter of an hour. There was a sign on the windscreen saying BACK IN TEN MINUTES. They used the time to go to his digs, find a plastic bag for the shoe, snatch drinks and crisps, and go to the loo. The vehicle was still there when they went back, but a harassed woman turned up five minutes later.

'Sorry, sorry,' she panted. 'There wasn't a space to be had anywhere, and I thought it was worth the risk. I had to go and see my daughter. She said it was an emergency.'

'And was it?' asked Bonnie coolly.

'Not at all. She's just crying wolf again. Next time, I'll leave her to stew.'

'Took more than ten minutes, all the same,' said Ben.

'More like an hour. Have you been waiting long?'

'Long enough,' said Ben.

They wasted no more time, speeding along the A66 much faster than Ben normally drove. 'I guess there isn't really a huge hurry,' said Bonnie in a small voice. Fast driving frightened her. 'They know we're coming, after all.'

Ben had phoned the police moments after finding the shoe, to be taken only moderately seriously. 'Bring it in, then,' the woman on the phone said.

'They'll have to search the river, set up all sorts of liaison points, close it all to the public – it'll take them the rest of the day.'

'They won't do that unless they're sure it's the dead man's shoe, will they? They'll have to show it to his wife and see if she recognises it. Do you think it could have been there for ages? We could be all wrong about it.'

'I don't think so,' said Ben. 'But I suppose they'll have to justify the trouble and expense.'

'Especially on a Sunday.'

'Right,' he sighed.

It took several minutes to explain the events of the morning to the detective constable who was detailed to interview them. 'So you were actually looking for something like this – am I right?'

'Pretty much, yes. We worked out that the most likely scenario was that somebody dragged the body down to the river, probably sometime between Wednesday and Thursday night, because that had to be the quickest and safest. If it got washed down into Derwentwater it wouldn't be found for ages, if ever.'

'But you didn't see a body, did you? Just this?' The shoe lay in its bag on the desk between them. It was surprisingly clean and only minimally damaged by the teeth of playful fox cubs.

'That's right,' said Ben with exaggerated patience. 'But

we think it's quite significant, don't you?'

'Could be,' said the man. 'Not a lot to go on, all the same.'

'It will be if Mrs Deeping can identify it.'

This was a mistake. It revealed a degree of knowledge that encroached on police territory and raised suspicion. The DC was new and young and did not have a full grasp of the history behind Ben Harkness and Bonnie Lawson and numerous previous murder investigations. It was Sunday and not everyone was working, despite the fact of Jennifer Reade's killing. Leads were in very short supply and DS Mark Price saw no reason to keep everyone away from their families just to make them go over old ground. Price himself was making numerous phone calls to people in Wiltshire, constructing as detailed a picture as he could of Jennifer Reade's life. He had not been informed of the arrival of two young people and a shoe.

'You know Mrs Deeping, do you?' said the constable.

'Not at all,' snapped Ben. 'But we know her husband is missing. Listen – could you perhaps inform one of your superiors that we're here? I think you'll find they'll be very interested.'

It all happened eventually, the constable fighting with his own inclination to dismiss these cheeky amateurs as nothing but time-wasters. His training had insisted that all such contributions from the public should be treated with respect and due consideration. He felt threatened by Ben's obvious intelligence, daunted by his accurate knowledge of the investigation and worried that he might get into trouble if he did anything wrong.

The change of gear was startling. The detective

superintendent himself came into the room and greeted Ben and Bonnie with impressive enthusiasm, having despatched the constable and the shoe.

'I heard all about you from DI Moxon recently,' he said, taking the chair recently vacated. 'He and I have been getting to know each other better, ever since . . . well, for a little while now. So – you found a shoe. We need to ask Mrs Deeping if she recognises it. I've got someone ready to go there now. We can't proceed any further until we've got a response from her.'

'Will you tell us what she says?' asked Ben, trying to assemble his thoughts.

'More than that – you'll be needed to show us exactly where you found it. Is there access for vehicles anywhere close?'

'Not really,' said Ben. 'So you think it actually might be his shoe, then?'

The detective gave a rueful smile. 'I'm reserving judgement. It's been my experience that shoes turn up in the strangest places for the strangest reasons. Let's just say it's the first cause for hope we've had all day.' He cleared his throat. 'Have you told Mr Henderson about it?'

Ben looked at Bonnie, wondering what the expected answer to that might be.

'No, I haven't.' He refrained with difficulty from giving any further account of Christopher's movements that day. The impulse to splurge a mass of irrelevant detail had gripped him on previous occasions, and he knew he should keep it under control.

Bonnie merely smiled vaguely and said nothing. She had, for a moment, felt overawed by the presence of the senior detective, and nervously avoided saying anything ill-advised. The theories concerning all the various men they kept hearing about were far too flimsy to put into words. And besides, it was never a good idea to raise suggestions to the police until you had some facts to go on. You could never be sure how they'd react.

The shoe had at least gone from the desk and was perhaps on its way to the home of Mrs Deeping, who was a completely unknown quantity.

'Where do they live?' asked Ben. 'The Deepings, I mean.'

'Outskirts of Keswick. We set up an incident room there on Friday, as you probably know. Standard procedure, of course. Still a distance from Borrowdale, but it seemed more practical.'

'We saw the car at High Gates, but we didn't know you'd set up in Keswick,' said Ben. 'We thought people might go and have a word to the officers in the car if they've got anything to tell you. It's caused quite a stir up there, anyway.'

'Really? All I hear is that hikers often stop for a minute to have a good old nose, before schlepping off to the tops of the fells.'

'Something like that,' Ben agreed without argument. He didn't think the description quite covered what Steve and his missus were doing. 'We chatted to a few of them this morning.'

'So – are you happy to wait until we've got some news about the shoe? It'll be an hour or more, probably.'

'Well . . .' said Ben with another look at Bonnie. 'We might go for a stroll and come back, if that's all right. Or you could phone us with any news. Then we'll all have to go back to Borrowdale, I suppose.'

'As I said.' Price got out of the chair. 'Lucky we've got the long light evenings. Even so, it's probably going to be tomorrow before we really get it organised properly.'

Ben and Bonnie left the car where it was and walked into the middle of Penrith. On a Sunday afternoon, it was not at all busy. Even on a weekday it was never exactly thronging.

'Funny little town,' said Ben, looking round. 'I've never taken much notice of it before.' They found a seat at the bottom end of a street where they could chat quietly.

'We have to phone Simmy,' said Bonnie. 'And see how Christopher is, and what they want to do next, and whether they've heard anything from anyone. And tell them about the shoe, of course.'

'I suppose. I'm wondering how much they really want to know, though. Not while it's all still up in the air like this. If we can prove the body was the Deeping man, that's going to be big news – even more if they actually *find* him. I'm sure he's stuck under those trees somewhere. The foxes probably dragged the shoe off him. It would be a careless murderer to let it just fall off in a field.'

'Rats *and* foxes. The poor man. Do foxes chew dead things as well?'

'Probably. I hadn't thought of that. They won't let the wife see him if he's really mangled. It'll be DNA, which takes ages.'

'It won't be that bad. Clothes. Scars. Teeth. Anyway, they haven't even found him yet. We're jumping ahead again.'

'You're right.' Ben wriggled his shoulders. 'It's all so *slow*. Whoever killed Jennifer could be in Australia by now.

I can't see that they'll ever work out who did it.'

'Why did we come all the way here if there's an incident room at Keswick?'

'Ah – because nobody told us otherwise. Because there is in theory a police station in Keswick, but it's not been functioning lately, so I just assumed everything came here.'

'You didn't think, did you?' she accused. 'You took it for granted that because of the thing in Askham, they'd know us here and it would all be easy and straightforward.'

'I think that's about right, but this Price person seems to be pretty much on the ball, so maybe we did the right thing, even if it was careless. Don't forget we've been here before, when Simmy and Christopher got married in Threlkeld. That all got dealt with here, even though it's practically in Keswick. Moxon knows them here . . .' He tailed off. 'Does it matter?'

His question was intended purely as concerned the arrangements of police provision, but Bonnie seemed to take it as more widely meant. 'It does a bit, when I want to work out how things connect up. Penrith's an awfully long way from Borrowdale, after all. And it's *all* a terribly long way from Windermere.'

He had forgotten for the moment how infrequently Bonnie had been to the northern reaches of the region, leaving her unsure of how everything worked – so many people she hadn't met, conversations she had missed out on. Given their detailed explorations of areas around Hawkshead and Grasmere, this was difficult for him to fully appreciate. He cocked his head at her, wondering what she was thinking. 'I know,' he said. 'But what can we do about it?'

She stared at the floor for a few seconds, groping for an honest answer. 'Nothing, I suppose. It's okay most of the time – until I stop to really think about it. All the interesting things are happening up here these days and I'm always going to be left out.'

He put a hand on her arm. 'No, you're not. You're here now, aren't you? Besides, I can never keep up with things in Hartsop or Troutbeck, either, especially in the summer when the roads are so slow. And, basically, everywhere around here is a long way from everywhere else.'

'Yes, well, I'm here now,' she agreed with a brave smile. 'And we've got until about nine o'clock this evening to get everything sorted.'

'Why nine o'clock?'

'That's when you've got to take me back to Windermere. I'm not staying another night in your horrible digs.'

'Oh,' said Ben.

Detective Superintendent Price was true to his word and texted Ben at half past three. 'Identity confirmed. Please come back.'

'Like an old-fashioned telegram,' said Ben happily. 'Come on, then.'

The next three hours were busy, confused, frustrating and finally exhilarating. A man's body was almost miraculously discovered wedged between two large rocks some distance from where the River Derwent merged into the lake of the same name.

Chapter Eighteen

In Threlkeld, Mr and Mrs Straw were harmoniously discussing recent events. Angie had done her best to stay clear of it all, but her will had wilted in the face of her husband's eager report of the morning.

'Poor Christopher!' they kept sighing, turn and turn about.

'We can't just ignore it all and leave it to sort itself out,' said Russell.

'Which you have not in any way been doing,' she reminded him. 'First you go in a huddle with Persimmon in the kitchen for ages and then you actually go with them to the very scene of the crime. How much more involved do you want to be?'

'I know. But nothing became the slightest bit clearer as a result. It was a complete waste of time, in fact. The only good thing is that I think I do have all the facts now. Although there are so *many* of them, I might be missing something. There's a new person shown up a day or so ago that I'm not sure about. But it strikes me that we ought to be much more focused on the woman who was unambiguously murdered, and not the mysterious dead man who died before her.'

'Because she must have killed him?'

Russell blinked. 'I hadn't thought of that. It would make her extraordinarily devious, given how she was with Christopher on Wednesday.'

'Women *are* devious. You know that.'

'Yes, but—'

'So talk it through, a step at a time. I'll sit here and listen. Should I make notes?'

'Wouldn't hurt.'

They started in good earnest, with Jennifer Reade's last words and what they might imply. This diverted into the new information gleaned at High Gates about the two men who witnessed these words.

'They came all the way down from the Slate Museum just to gawp at the house,' he sighed. 'Some people!'

'Returning to the scene of the crime, do you think?'

'Probably not. I'm never convinced that people really do that. And they weren't the witnesses themselves, just people who knew them. I think.' He shook his head. 'Now I've got it in a muddle. It was difficult to follow everything with the baby and the dog, and the five of us. People talking over each other and Christopher having the vapours.'

'Lucky I didn't go, then.'

'You didn't miss anything, really. The house is handsome but depressing. Nothing like as appealing as Borrowdale Gates – if you remember that?'

'I don't. But I did read *The Herries Chronicles* in my teens, and have quite a vivid impression of it all. Nobody seems to remember poor old Hugh Walpole now.'

'And yet he lived right there. He almost certainly visited that very house. Sir John's old dad was probably his chum.

215

It's tempting to try and fit him into the story somehow.'

'How about there was a priceless original manuscript of one of his books and Jennifer Reade found it?'

Russell pushed out his lips, considering the question. 'For one thing, I doubt poor old Hugh's manuscripts would be worth much now. But it's a thought. Especially with that missing printer in the mix. That could imply something about manuscripts, I suppose. And Ben burbled a whole lot about incunabula on the bus from Keswick. He thought he'd found a kind of link or clue, but he wasn't very clear.'

'Incunabula? Aren't they zombies or something?'

'My dear woman – where have you been? How can you be so ignorant?'

'I do apologise. Please enlighten me.'

He proceeded to do so at some length and with great enjoyment. 'They sold some in one of the auctions earlier this year. They're very collectable, but not massively valuable. I wouldn't imagine they were grounds for murder. And how in the world could we make it fit the facts?'

'I'm writing it down, all the same,' said Angie. 'I like the sound of it.'

'It *is* rather romantic,' he agreed with a smile.

'Is all this just a repeat of what you and Simmy were saying yesterday?'

'No. Not at all. That was mostly about the body and how it was probably a vagrant, and how the person who killed Jennifer Reade had perhaps come back for some reason and she interrupted them. Plus, we talked about how the woman refused to have a phone or anything else electronic.'

'Really?' Angie's eyes shone. 'How old did you say she was?'

'Thirties, I think. Yes, really. Simmy thinks she could still be alive if she'd been able to phone for help when she was attacked.'

'Pooh!' said Angie, not very convincingly. 'It would take forever for an ambulance to get there. She did the best thing she could, crawling out into the road as she did. Do we know the nature of her injuries?'

'Not exactly. Cudgelled rather than shot or stabbed, I believe.'

'It has to be important, though, don't you think? It shows what sort of a person she was. Strong-minded. Independent.'

'Eccentric.'

'Resourceful.'

'Or just plain crazy,' Russell finished with a sigh. 'How did she manage her money? Or train tickets? Or . . .'

'People do, you know. They use cheques and landlines and maps and do their tax returns on paper. A dwindling minority, admittedly, but none the worse for that. It could yet happen that they'll turn out to be the clever ones, if somebody manages to nobble the Internet. I have to say I rather look forward to that.'

'It's never going to happen, but it's nice to dream. We'd probably be sorry if it ever did come true. We'd be back to the Dark Ages, only worse.'

'The people of Borrowdale would survive, I'm sure. It's all there in Walpole's books. The living up there's never been easy.'

Russell mused for a few moments. 'Do you think we

217

should find out more about Sir John Hickory? This is very likely to be all about him, after all. Secrets. Discoveries. Connections. All that sort of stuff. Maybe the Reade woman knew more about him than she admitted, right from the start.'

'Maybe she even killed him,' said Angie again.

'You've really got it in for that poor girl, haven't you?'

'Not at all. I just wish she hadn't managed to stop poor Christopher's sale. We mustn't forget what a blow that's been. He doesn't know where he is, and it obviously matters enormously. All those priceless things hanging in limbo. They could get stolen or destroyed in a fire – or anything.'

'They'll be insured,' said Russell vaguely.

'I doubt it – nobody knows who they rightfully belong to, do they?'

'Good point. Even the house sale might not have been finalised, without Ms Reade to sign all the papers.'

'How funny if it ends up in the hands of the National Trust.' Angie was no great fan of that organisation, ever since she got chastised for proceeding around a stately home in the other direction from that indicated by the large authoritative arrows.

'That's not going to happen. There's this man from India poised to take it all over. Simmy met him yesterday. The solicitors will be getting the paperwork in order as we speak. We all think he's the prime suspect, except he didn't land in this country until after Jennifer Reade was killed.'

'So he paid somebody to do it for him.'

Russell nodded. 'Maybe he did. But who? Paid assassins are notoriously difficult to catch.'

Angie looked at him from over her glasses. 'Is that really true? Did anyone tell you that?'

He bowed his head. 'No – but it's in all the books. Seems reasonable, though, don't you think?'

'Should I write it down? "Man from India paid the killer, so he could have the whole estate"?'

'With a question mark beside it,' he nodded.

'We've got a whole lot of ideas and connections now. It's really coming along,' she boasted. 'Do you think we've come up with anything new? What should we do with it when we've finished?'

'I expect we should go over to Hartsop with it. After supper, maybe. They'll be doing the same sort of thing, I shouldn't wonder, and we can all pool our findings again like we did yesterday, and Ben can make one of his dossiers and then show it to the Moxon man, and between us we might make some headway. Except,' he paused and drooped a little, 'we won't have a smidgeon of evidence for any of it, will we?'

'I seem to remember it's acceptable to first form a hypothesis and then seek out supporting evidence. In a case like this, what other option is there?'

He gave her an admiring look. 'I thought you wanted to stay out of it this time, and now see how engaged you are. It's a joy to see.'

'Never mind that.' Angie was brisk again. 'We're not done yet. Now – let's get into details. Did Jennifer Reade know about this person from India? If she didn't use a phone, she could hardly have been told anything while she was in Borrowdale. The house won't have a landline and I bet there isn't a working phone box for miles.'

'Unless a person came to tell her face to face.'

'Right! A person who then killed her.'

'Because?'

'Well, because there was going to be a tremendous fight for Sir John's estate, of course. Do we know what the law of inheritance would have said about it?'

'I assume that if they were both in the same generation, going back to old Grandpa Hickory or even further back than him, they'd have to share it fifty-fifty. That'd leave them both millionaires, pretty well, so not much cause for complaint.'

'Do they both go back to Grandpa, though? How?'

'No idea,' Russell admitted. 'But Ben has it all at his fingertips. So does Christopher, I presume.'

'Anyway, that's all easily discovered, and probably counts as evidence. It would explain why the sale had to be stopped, as well.'

'Hmm. I've been thinking that there must have been one specific item amongst the lots that hadn't been properly valued, because nobody in the saleroom recognised it for what it was. Which brings us back to incunabula – or would, but Ben doesn't think there's anything that could possibly come under that heading.'

'I thought they'd shipped in experts, to avoid anything like that?'

'They did. And it's pretty hard to imagine any single object worth so much that a person would kill over it.'

'It wouldn't be the first time, would it? It involves reputations and obsessions and rivalries.' She nibbled her pencil. 'Collectors get absolutely insane over this sort of thing. If there was an object that filled a gap, made their collection complete, they might be tempted to kill to get it.'

'We're drifting away from details again,' he pointed out. 'Not to mention our quest for evidence.'

'There's no harm in coming up with theories,' she insisted. 'Haven't we already decided that?'

'Simmy calls it brainstorming. And you're right, of course. I'm just finding it all a bit exhausting. If you'd shown an interest from the start, I wouldn't have to fill you in with all these details now.'

'Stick at it,' she urged. 'What else did Ben say about these incunabulas?'

'That's not a word. It's already plural. The singular is incunabulum.'

'Russell . . .' she said warningly.

'Sorry. He said they sold some to a person in Wiltshire, some months back, and Jennifer Reade lived in Swindon, which is Wiltshire, and he thought there could well be a connection.'

She wrote it down. 'And is he following that up? Has he told the police?'

'I have no idea, but I imagine he's going to, if he hasn't already.'

'You're right that we all have to get together and make sure we're not duplicating efforts, and all hitting the same brick wall. With any luck, we'll have come up with a lot of different ideas, which make a logical picture when they're all combined. Are Ben and Bonnie in Hartsop now?'

'Who knows? They stayed in Grange when we all came back to Keswick. They could still be there – although that seems unlikely. Whatever they're doing, it won't occur to them to tell us about it.'

'Don't be bitter. We've never been part of their amateur detection gang, have we?'

'Well . . . I was pretty much involved in Askham,' he demurred. 'I was right there with Simmy, when we talked to that man.' He drifted into a momentary reverie, recalling the brief time when he and Simmy were a team. 'But I suppose you're right, when it comes down to it.'

'What time is it?' she asked suddenly. Their living room did not contain a clock, since they decided that retirement should be sufficiently relaxed that there was never a need to know the precise time. In reality, this led to frequent frustration.

'Must be time for some tea,' he said. 'My guess is that it's well past five by now.' He got up and went into the kitchen where there were two clocks. 'Five twenty-five,' he called back, pleased with his accurate guess.

'I'm putting the news on, then. Local radio might have something about Borrowdale at half past. You never know.'

Russell brewed tea and was back in time to listen to the headlines.

'There is breaking news of renewed police activity in Grange-in-Borrowdale, believed to be in association with the recent murder of an heiress to the Hickory Estate,' lumbered the newsreader. 'No formal statement has been made, but a witness has informed us that it seems as if in the last few minutes preparations are being made for the dragging of the River Derwent. Many questions remain to be answered.'

'You can say that again,' Russell remarked. 'I detect the hand of young Ben Harkness, if I'm not very much mistaken.'

222

Angie laughed. 'You mean he and Bonnie found the dead man from the cellar? In the river? Amazing!'

'Well, it sounds as if they found *something*. Enough to get the police sufficiently interested to send the divers in. I doubt if there's need for actual *dragging*. That's a major operation. I'll phone them and see.'

'Who exactly?'

Russell paused. 'Simmy, I suppose. She'll know what's been going on.'

But Simmy had no idea. She was completely bemused. 'We haven't had the telly or radio on,' she said. 'We've been far too busy. It's all happening over here. Too much to explain.'

'Well. It's all happening even more up at Borrowdale. It's in the *news*.'

He tried to summarise what he had heard, but Simmy cut him off.

'I can't cope with any more now,' she pleaded. 'I know it's bad of me, and I will want to know everything when I've got a bit of space. It does sound important, but so is what went on here this afternoon.'

'We need to pool our findings,' said Russell ponderously.

'Yes, Dad, I know. And we need Ben and Bonnie as well.'

'Can we come over, then? We need to hear it all from each other. And where are Ben and Bonnie now?'

His daughter made a moaning noise, as if about to drown. She ignored the last question and focused on the first. 'I suppose you can come. There's never any escape, is there? Wait until we've got Robin to bed, okay? I'll take him a bit early. Should be free by about seven o'clock – and don't expect any food.'

'It's a date,' said Russell. 'What about Ben and Bonnie?'

'I don't know, Dad. I have absolutely no idea.'

Angie surprised him by saying, 'Don't include me in all this,' when he'd ended the call. 'I've done my part. I do want to know how it turns out, obviously, and it was fun getting it all down on paper, but I don't fancy sitting around half the night with all you amateur detectives talking at once. It'd give me a headache. Besides I want to watch my antiques programme this evening. There might be something relevant to Christopher's sale.'

'I don't see how,' frowned Russell.

'I've got the catalogue here. There are all sorts of things I don't know anything about. I feel ignorant.'

'Surely not. After all those years glued to the *Antiques Roadshow* and the rest?'

'Just go without me,' she said.

Chapter Nineteen

Sunday afternoon for the Hendersons had indeed been quite eventful. The drive home was bad enough in itself, with Robin wailing and Christopher still shaky. Simmy was driving, and before they even got to Keswick, she pulled into a layby and ordered her husband to sit in the back and pacify their son. 'Cornelia can come in the front. She's the only one who isn't causing trouble.'

Christopher struggled to behave normally. 'Isn't there a law against dogs in front?'

'Who cares?' snapped his wife. Normality was a distant memory for her at that moment.

Within five minutes of arriving home, Lily was at the door.

'That man's here again,' she hissed. 'He says he's got to see you, and he's going to wait for you. He's in his car up at the top. He gave me his phone number.'

'Damn it,' said Simmy. 'We've got to have some lunch first. We're all starving.'

'He wanted to watch out for you, but I said he couldn't park here. He'll be lucky if he's found a spot that's allowed, but I guess he must have done. He's been gone about half an hour.'

'Thanks, Lily. It's a pity you've got dragged into whatever this is.'

'No problem,' said the girl cheerfully. 'He really is quite nice. You'll see.'

Christopher was standing behind Simmy, listening to everything that was said. 'I could go up and talk to him,' he offered.

'Oh no!' said Simmy firmly. 'I'm not going to be left out now. Not after this morning. We'll have some food and then phone him. Well done, Lily – see you tomorrow, I expect.'

'Just give me a shout.'

'What a girl!' sighed Simmy when she had shut the door. 'I was never that capable at her age.'

'You were fine,' said Christopher daftly.

'I feel absolutely worn out,' she admitted. 'Which is ridiculous as I've hardly done anything.'

'Emotional exhaustion,' he diagnosed. 'And all my fault. I just want to slump in front of a silly film all afternoon.'

'Well, you can't, because there's a man who wants to see you about a body.'

'Can't we just give his phone number to the police and forget all about him?'

Simmy did not dignify that with an answer. They were both in the kitchen, as was Robin, and random bits of food were being consumed as they spoke. Bread, cheese, tomatoes and carrot sticks predominated.

Christopher changed tack. 'I wonder if Ben and Bonnie are finding anything useful. I didn't really understand what they were proposing to do.'

'Not much they *can* do, I imagine. Just mooch about in the sunshine and enjoy themselves. I think they were rather sick of us and all our fuss. And who can blame them?'

'There were too many of us. We should never have taken your father, for a start.'

'He was glad to see the house. Presumably it'll be changed out of all recognition once the new people get their hands on it.'

'It's listed, so they can't do anything too drastic.'

'So we'll phone that man, then. He'll come banging on the door if we don't.'

'All right,' sighed Christopher. 'What shall I say to him?'

'Tell him to walk down to us and we'll talk to him in the garden. Robin might have a nap with any luck. Actually, wait till I've got him down, or I'll miss everything.'

Less than fifteen minutes later, three people were enjoying the weather in the Hendersons' garden, despite the uncertainty as to what might be disclosed.

'I'm sorry to seem so mysterious,' said the newcomer. 'My name is Julian Baxter. I live in Swindon and I was Jennifer Reade's friend. Boyfriend, if you like. I've been up here for a few days.'

'So you've been interviewed by the police?' asked Christopher. 'They didn't mention you.'

Mr Baxter shook his head. 'I've been keeping out of their way, to be honest. It's easier than I expected.'

He was about thirty, with symmetrical features and nice cheekbones. His unremarkable brown hair was of unremarkable length and he was of medium height. Simmy could see that he might readily disappear from view. Few people would remember ever having seen him. But he did have a voice that might linger in someone's mind. Deeper and richer than seemed to fit his slight frame, it had an attractive accent that might be Dorset or Somerset.

'Why?' Simmy asked.

'They'll think I killed her, won't they? Or at the very least that I know who did. And I really don't like being treated with suspicion.'

'You were acting suspiciously here on Friday when you tackled our dog-walker girl,' Simmy accused.

'Not really. I was so sure I'd find you, I didn't know what to say to her. I messed up, but I wanted to let you know I'm involved, and that someone else knew about the dead man in the cellar. He looked at Christopher. 'Did you say anything about him to the police?'

'Of course I did.'

'But you told Jennifer you wouldn't.'

'Yes. So it wasn't until Friday that I broke my promise to her, if you want to see it that way. Once they told me she was dead, everything got a lot more important.'

'Did they believe you?'

'Absolutely – why wouldn't they? They even think they might know who he is – was.'

'Careful!' muttered Simmy, hoping the man couldn't hear. She and Christopher were together on a garden seat and Baxter had been given a folding chair that wobbled slightly.

'I didn't kill either of them, I assure you,' said the visitor.

'Glad to hear it,' said Simmy.

'We don't really think you did,' added Christopher. 'It would be a very bold murderer to come here like this in broad daylight, after letting Lily see you – twice. She can probably give a pretty good description.'

'No need. I've told you who I am.'

'So why did you want to see me?' asked Christopher.

'Why do you think? You're selling Jenny's stuff. You met her on Wednesday and saw the body. The police will be treating you as a very interesting person. And when I got chatting to some folk in the pub up at Patterdale, they told me you've both had plenty of experience as amateur detectives along with some young couple from Windermere. I was hoping you might lend a hand in finding out who killed my girl – because I'm damned if I'm going to let them get away with it.' His face crumpled, and he dashed a hand across his eyes. 'I didn't know until last thing on Friday. Funny how people say it hasn't sunk in and they don't believe it. It took about three minutes for my entire view of the world and life and the future to change completely.'

'Wow!' said Simmy. 'Really?'

'Yes, really,' said Baxter irritably. 'And I can't begin to explain to you exactly what I've lost.'

'And yet you haven't spoken to the police? Not at all? That seems incredible,' said Simmy, who was making an effort not to be intimidated. 'They must be looking for you, as Jennifer's partner.'

'How would they know? Who's going to tell them? They're not clairvoyant. If I don't come forward, they won't even know I exist.'

'She mentioned you on Wednesday,' said Christopher. 'I could have told them that.'

'Yes. That's why I had to come and find you. Partly, anyway. They'll have spotted the printing press in the cellar by now, I expect. And they'll be starting to make a few inspired guesses about how things connect up.'

Christopher exchanged a bemused glance with Simmy, and then he held up a finger.

'Let's take this slowly. We'll come to the printing press in a minute, because we've no idea what you're talking about where that's concerned, and there are other things that should come first. You saw Jennifer after I met her on Wednesday – right? You know there was a dead man in the cellar of the house. You probably know where she was and what she was doing on Thursday, before getting killed early on Friday. You have a lot of crucial information that would surely help the police in their investigations. At every point, you've broken rules, in fact. And now it seems you've had something going on with the printer man.'

Julian Baxter cocked his head teasingly, most of his apparent grief already out of sight. 'And you?' he said. 'You went along with Jenny's advice to keep quiet about the dead man. You're just as bad as me, let's face it.'

'It was a bit more than "advice". More like blackmail. I've got a business to consider.'

'And see where it's got to now. Everything hanging in the air, nobody knowing a thing about what happens next.'

'So everything Chris just said is right, then?' Simmy put in. 'About Thursday?'

'More or less.'

'When did you last see her? Assuming for the moment that it wasn't you who killed her.'

Baxter expelled air in a huff of exasperation. 'Now you see why I'm steering clear of the police. It looks impossibly bad for me. Anyway, the fact is, I last saw her at eleven o'clock on Thursday. After we'd dealt with the body. She stayed behind at the house, and I took myself off to somewhere more comfortable for the night.' He flushed, making himself look boyish and irresponsible. 'Which I realise is a crime in itself, and makes everything even worse for me where the law is concerned.'

Christopher and Simmy merely stared at him, lost for words. Finally, Christopher managed a single word: 'Why?'

'Why what? Why dispose of the body? Perhaps I'd better not say any more about that. I was a fool to mention the printing thing, I suppose. I can't tell yet how far you two can be trusted. I came, basically, to appeal to your good natures, to make you see that justice and fairness conflict very starkly with law and retribution, in this particular case. I've told you my name and that Windermere boy you consort with could probably track me down – but it wouldn't be easy. Jennifer and I have always been careful about that.'

'And yet the solicitors found her when they'd figured out that she was heir to High Gates,' said Christopher.

'They did. And there they stopped, thinking their work was done. Little did they suspect that another distant third cousin or whatever he is might crawl out of the woodwork with no warning.'

'Warwick Bennett,' said Simmy. 'Did Jennifer know about him, then?'

'She did. He sent a letter that arrived on Tuesday, saying he was on his way to the UK and he had always known he was related to Sir John. But he didn't know he had a claim to the estate, and had only just found out the old boy was dead. He's always lived in India.'

'What about Maurice Phillippson?' said Simmy suddenly, for no better reason than that the name had suddenly occurred to her, much to her own surprise. 'He lives near you.'

'Ah!' said Baxter. 'That's annoying. Nobody was supposed to know about him.'

'Like the fact of a printing press in the cellar,' Simmy realised. Baxter kept his lips tightly together, but did raise a teasing eyebrow.

'Have you spoken to the Bennett man since he arrived in the country?' asked Christopher, after a frustrated few seconds.

'Hmm. No comment. The water's are getting a bit deep all of a sudden. I think I'm going to go now. It might have been a mistake to come, but I didn't have anybody else to consult. I hadn't factored that in – how lonely everything is without Jenny.' Again his face crumpled. 'I suppose I just wanted someone to talk to, and you two sounded feasible. And that nice little girl with the dog . . . I hope I didn't scare her.'

'She can cope,' said Simmy. 'You're not very scary.'

Simmy was herself starting to feel something beyond apprehension. The careless dropping of the Phillippson name carried a few implications that she hoped had not yet occurred to Baxter. She remembered her little boy upstairs, and felt vulnerable. The man wasn't big and didn't look especially strong, but he had reason to fear what they could do to him – such as reporting his existence to the police. 'You should go,' she said.

'I should,' he agreed. But he made no move. 'Where do we stand, then?'

'You'll have to go to the police,' said Christopher flatly. 'Anything else is unthinkable. Don't you want to know who killed your girlfriend? Don't you want the whole thing settled? They might suspect you at first, but if you didn't do

232

it, you needn't worry. As for disposing of the dead man, I suppose that is a crime, but they're not going to throw you into prison for that, are they?'

'Such a trusting nature!' murmured Baxter. 'Can you really be so naive after everything you've seen? I heard all about the woman at your work being bumped off a year or so ago, and the thing in Askham – is that the right place? I know nothing of the geography around here. It's a whole different world.'

Simmy was still assembling implications. 'Do you *know* who killed Jennifer?' she asked with a frown. 'And *why*? Is there a whole side to this, connected with the printer and the fake manuscripts or whatever they are, that we've been ignoring?' Again she heard the name *Maurice Phillippson* echoing around her head.

His smile was bitter. 'I see you've still got a lot to untangle, and I can't help you, because I don't know. On the face of it, it strikes me as being pretty obvious. There's a person who had motive – but he must have done it by magic or remote control, because I know for a fact he wasn't in the country until yesterday. Which is very inconvenient.'

'The cousin,' Simmy supplied. 'Because then he'd inherit the whole estate.'

'How do you know he wasn't in the country?' Christopher interrupted.

'Because I was at the airport yesterday when he arrived. I was just about to go up and greet him when another bloke got there before me. Looked like a plain-clothes policeman to me.'

Simmy laughed in sheer amazement. 'How did you know what he looked like?'

'He sent a photo of himself in the letter I told you about.'

'Why did you do that – go and meet him, I mean?'

'Because you wanted to hide him away,' said Christopher slowly. 'Maybe even kill him. Isn't that right? Because of whatever was going on in the High Gates cellar.'

The man got up and moved towards the door. 'That would be very neat, wouldn't it? All I can say is "No comment" and I'm glad to have met you. I have a feeling we'll meet again.'

Simmy also stood up. 'You haven't answered half our questions, have you? And I can think of about twenty more. Why did Jennifer want the sale stopped? What on earth were you both doing at High Gates in the first place? Why are there all these weird coincidences about old documents and printers? What really did you hope to get out of coming here like this?'

Christopher put a hand on her arm. 'I think he's told us most of it, if we stop and think it through. We should let him go now.'

Something in his tone made her step back quietly, while Baxter almost ran the remaining distance to the door and pulled it open.

'Don't keep on,' he begged her, turning back for a moment. 'The truth will out, sooner or later. I just don't want it to involve me. I'm not one to boast, but I'm confident you won't be able to find me, at least until the whole thing's settled.'

Simmy gave herself a little shake, and called after him as he walked swiftly back to his car, 'It's not a game, you know!'

There was no response, and she went back to Christopher,

who was slumped on the sofa. He looked up at her. 'For him, I think it is. A game, I mean. What on earth are we going to tell Ben? He'll say we've made a complete mess of things.'

'And he'll be right,' said Simmy.

Chapter Twenty

When Russell phoned, an hour or two later, Simmy lacked the energy to try to describe Baxter's visit. Robin had woken up after a very short nap, Christopher had taken the dog out, Ben had remained silent and her head was hurting with it all. Her father's news about events in Borrowdale felt like another brick on a teetering pile that was sure to topple over and damage them all. *We should call Moxon,* she thought desperately. Or the Penrith man. But what were they to say? It felt equally impossible to withhold the latest developments as to try to describe what they had learnt. Or vice versa. Christopher was reduced to his earlier state of panic and guilt, with an added dose of bewilderment mixed in.

'What did he really *tell* us?' he repeated.

'That he and Jennifer disposed of the body you saw. That's the only definite thing. I got the impression that Jennifer might have killed him, but he never actually said so.'

Time began to do strange things. She played with Robin, put a quickly made lamb stew in to cook, and wondered where Ben and Bonnie could be and to what extent they

236

really had found some answers. Christopher cravenly went upstairs for a lie-down, which she found irritating and self-indulgent, even while she knew he was genuinely distressed.

Russell's phone call had thrown a massive new element into her already turbulent thoughts, even with the few words she had allowed him to utter. It went without saying that Ben and Bonnie had been instrumental in mobilising the police into launching some kind of operation at Borrowdale. *They might even have found the body*, she realised. In fact, that was surely the only possible conclusion to draw.

Christopher ought to be told, but she hesitated to disturb him. He'd be sure to get all excited and want to go off to see for himself, or else phone police, Ben, local radio – who knew what? Robin would be unsettled and the schedule for the next few hours thrown into chaos. Better to let Christopher doze his cares away for a bit, and wait passively to see what happened next. The only thing she made herself do was to send a text to Ben.

'Come here this evening after seven, if you can.'

It was five-fifteen when another man came to the door. This time it was the familiar and very welcome DI Moxon, with his customary diffident smile. 'I always come at a bad time, don't I?' he said.

'Not always. And today nothing is remotely going to plan – we didn't even *have* a plan. It's just one thing after another. But we seem to be making headway, somehow. We've all been busy, one way and another. We should have reported some of it to you, but . . .'

'I'm here now,' he said comfortably. 'When in doubt, this is the place to come. I learnt that a long time ago.'

'That's nice. Do you want a cup of something?'

'Tea would be most welcome. Shall I hold the young master while you make it?'

Moxon had no offspring of his own, but his wife had two grown up sons who had never felt like his, having been reared largely by their father. The ambivalence of the situation had never been resolved and he tended to keep things simple by describing himself as childless. The subject had been intensely painful, especially as he was foolishly fond of babies and small children.

Simmy handed Robin over without hesitation. 'Christopher's having a little nap,' she explained. 'He's taken all this very hard. Worse than ever before. He feels guilty. He thinks if he'd done it differently, Jennifer would still be alive.'

'That'll be Price's doing. He has that effect on people. Best let him alone for a bit, then. I do need to have a word with him at some point, though.'

The next half hour was nothing like a police interview, and yet the conversation was all about death and suspicion and evidence and investigation. Moxon had a notebook on his knee and a pen in his hand. Each enlightened the other, fitting the new information together to create something like half a picture.

'The body was that of Mr Deeping the printer,' Moxon said at the outset. 'He was in the river below High Gates. Your Ben and Bonnie found his shoe.'

'Was he murdered?'

'Too soon to say. Seems likely, though.'

'A man who says his name is Julian Baxter came here this afternoon. He and Jennifer almost certainly put the body in the river. They know the man who bought incunabula

238

from Christopher's auction back in the spring. He lives in Swindon.'

'Inkoo . . . what?'

Simmy explained inadequately, finishing by saying, 'I don't know, exactly. But it must be relevant, seeing that Mr Deeping was a printer. And he said there was a printing press in the cellar for some reason.'

Moxon smiled. 'We're ahead of you there, at least. There is indeed a strange old handmade printing press in a part of the cellar at High Gates House that was blocked off by some sheets of hardboard. We found it late yesterday. It didn't seem particularly significant until we worked out the dead man's profession.'

Simmy's eyes widened. 'Gosh! That must explain a lot. What else was there?'

'Nothing. No papers, if that's what you mean. Just the dirty old machine spattered with black ink stains.'

'Have you seen it yourself?'

He shook his head. 'But now you've told me about the in-cun-ab-ul-a' – he pronounced the word very carefully – 'things are making a lot more sense. Deeping must have been faking the things for quite a while. Since before Sir John died, possibly. A nice little sideline, I shouldn't wonder.'

'So when Jennifer Reade showed up, she caught him at it, and took umbrage,' Simmy theorised. Then she stopped to think. 'Although there's something rather pleasingly old-fashioned about a primitive printing press that she might have liked.'

'I can't see how it fits with her being killed, though.'

'No,' said Simmy slowly. 'But didn't you say that the Bennett man was in prison for counterfeiting? That can't possibly be a coincidence. What if he knew the Deeping man – was even selling his fakes – and Jennifer Reade was a highly inconvenient nuisance, marching in and claiming ownership of the whole caboodle?'

'Plausible,' nodded Moxon with a smile. 'I don't know how you do it.'

'Nor do I. It's usually Ben, not me, that fits things together. It feels as if I did it by accident.'

'You always were an accidental detective,' he said fondly.

She grinned at him, and then forced her brain to stay on track. 'We're still not there, though, are we? Why was Jennifer Reade so desperate to stop the sale? Doesn't that mean there was something being sold that shouldn't be? That's what Ben thinks.'

'Could be, but I'm not convinced. The police thinking is that she didn't want the proceeds to go to whoever the next in line might be. Which means she knew who that was, and that he probably killed her because of it. And with this new idea, that feels even more probable.'

Simmy nodded. 'Yes, but Warwick Bennett was in an aeroplane when she died, so it can't have been him, even though it keeps looking more and more obvious that he's the one it really ought to be.'

Moxon voiced the same reply that others had done already. 'He could have paid someone else to do it.'

'That's it, I suppose. I just hope it wasn't Julian Baxter. I rather liked him. But he's put us in a very difficult position.'

'Go on.'

'He doesn't want to be interviewed by the police. He's doing everything he can to stay out of your sight. He might know who killed Mr Deeping, but I'm sure he didn't kill Jennifer. He loved her.'

'We know the name, of course,' said Moxon carelessly. 'And we'll find him if we need to.'

'How?'

'He has a driving licence, a National Insurance number, and a bank account. He'd have to go to considerable lengths to evade us, given all that. The question is – what's he afraid of?'

'I don't know, exactly. Hassle, from the sound of what he said. Because he's sure you'll try to pin both murders on him.'

Moxon smiled irritably. 'How childish.'

'Me or him?'

'Both, to some extent. You for taking his side and him for thinking we're out to get him without any evidence. Although evidence might materialise, of course.'

'Sorry,' she said, and sighed. 'I still rather like him, and I don't want to think he's a murderer.'

'He could have a motive, if Ms Reade left any sort of will with him as beneficiary. There's a great deal of property at stake,' he reminded her.

'She wouldn't have left a will, though. She was too young for that.'

They fell silent, each trying to assemble the disparate elements of their conversation. Then Simmy went back a few steps, 'Contract killers are very difficult to catch, I suppose.'

Moxon would not be drawn in that direction. 'Indeed,' was all he would say.

She sat back, watching her little boy playing with a

bunch of keys that Moxon had produced. The notebook had been set down on the sofa beside them. Was Robin understanding any of their talk? Could it harm him to be hearing words about murder and dead bodies? She supposed not, but it made her uneasy. Angie had said, more than once, that the child ought to be shielded from the darker aspects of life until old enough to manage them. Simmy had been surprised – her mother was ordinarily the first one to reject euphemism and evasion.

'All in its rightful time,' Angie had insisted when challenged.

But Robin could have no concept at all of death and criminality. If he was unsettled at all, it would be due to the tones of voice and levels of stress. Which took her back to Christopher and the state he had been in earlier that day. Moxon, by contrast, was phenomenally relaxed.

'We're getting close, though, don't you think?' she pressed on. 'I think everyone's going to be here again this evening, pooling all our findings from today and hoping to get the full picture.' She stopped, a hand to her mouth. 'Gosh! I sound as if we're doing all the things the police are meant to do, don't I? How impertinent of me.'

The detective gave her a long patient look. 'Since when did that worry any of you? When I think back to those first cases – Bowness, Staveley and the rest – it's always been the same. Ben Harkness and his dossiers are famous now across the whole of Cumbria, and beyond. Carry on, with my blessing. Even DS Price knows when to step back and let the famous florist and her sleuthing carry on undisturbed.'

'Oh dear,' said Simmy, torn between relief, apprehension and amusement.

'All we ask is that you keep us informed.' His voice had dropped to a more serious tone. 'DS Price feels there is reason to emphasise that point in particular. Not that he has any argument with the youngsters. They have been more than forthcoming, going out of their way to share everything they found today. I gather the constable on the desk was inclined to dismiss them at first.'

'Typical,' said Simmy automatically. 'Keeping everyone informed has got weirdly difficult, apparently. You should have a big poster on the wall with Ben's name and picture, saying *Listen to him!* I expect he was cross about it.'

'Probably. I'll pass on your suggestion.'

'No you won't.'

The banter was wasting time, she supposed, and yet there had been little urgency to this investigation all along, once Christopher's auction had been suspended. People at the police station would be trawling the Internet, looking for connections and incriminating evidence. Names would be cropping up, theories tested, testimonies sifted.

'So the body is identified,' she said, hoping to prompt him into further revelations. 'Did the wife recognise the shoe? Or what? Oh – I know. My dad phoned and said they were dragging the lake. Hasn't it all been remarkably *quick*?'

'They didn't drag the lake. Mr Deeping was in very shallow water under a dense piece of vegetation, about fifty yards from the place they began to search. It took less than ten minutes to locate him. The person who called the media got everything wrong. The DS isn't best pleased about that – Mrs Deeping might have heard it too soon.'

Simmy tried to put herself in the widow's place. 'She

wouldn't have been surprised, though, would she? Does she know now that it was him?'

'Oh yes. As you say, it all moved rather quickly in the end. Thanks to your young friends, that side of the picture is explained – more or less.'

'I'll have to tell Christopher. That's the thing that's been bothering him more than anything.'

'Nobody doubted him, you know. When he said there'd been a body. It was just that it didn't make very much sense . . .'

'I can hear you, you know,' came a voice from the top of the stairs. 'Why didn't you call me?'

Chapter Twenty-One

Moxon got up, placing Robin on the floor, where he started taking wavering steps towards his mother. 'I've been here a few minutes,' he said. He took up his notebook again. 'We'd more or less finished, really.'

'It was Mr Deeping,' said Simmy. 'The printer chap from Keswick.'

'Right,' said Christopher, as he reached the bottom of the stairs. 'So what happens now?'

Moxon consulted his notepad, with a little frown. 'Well, there are a few points we need to clear up. If you've already been over them with DS Price, just say. But while I'm here, I ought to make sure. It might save you having to come back to Penrith again. There are one or two inconsistencies.'

'To say the least,' laughed Simmy, whose mood had lightened dramatically.

Christopher sat in an armchair. Simmy got up and plonked Robin on a playmat with some books and bricks. 'Play with these, there's a good boy,' she said. The child half-heartedly began to arrange bricks into a wobbly wall.

Moxon waited for her to sit down again, before continuing. 'We spent a while working out the significance of Ms Reade's car, seeing that we need to know all her movements since Wednesday. One tyre was completely flat, and from a quick bit of forensic magic on Friday afternoon, it would seem it hadn't been moved for at least two days – which takes us back to Wednesday. So if she went anywhere, it must have been in a taxi or on a bus. None of the taxi or Uber people saw her, so that just leaves the buses.'

Simmy was following closely. 'Don't the buses have cameras?'

'Not the one that goes to Borrowdale. We've spoken to the drivers of the whole fleet, and nobody remembers a woman of her description. But they're busy at this time of year and scarcely notice any individual passengers.'

'She would have paid with cash – would that help them to remember, I wonder?' said Simmy.

Moxon shook his head. 'Three buses an hour, packed with tourists and dogs, it's all just a blur. It only costs a couple of pounds. Half of them would use cash.' He did a double take. 'How do you know that, anyway?'

'She was allergic to everything electronic or digital. You surely picked that up?'

'Oh yes. But the implications keep hitting us afresh, and we hadn't thought about how she paid for a bus ticket. In fact, she did have a bank card, but only used it once in the past month. There's no record of any payments for petrol or accommodation or food. We have tried, believe me, but she's been virtually invisible all her adult life.'

'Nice to know it's possible,' said Simmy, thinking of her parents.

'It's turned into a game with some people – to see how far they can stay off the grid. You can't really blame them with all this talk of identity theft and bank fraud.'

'I suppose nearly everyone likes the idea of living like that,' said Christopher vaguely.

'Of course, if we set up a nationwide search, pulling in every second of CCTV, we'd find her car driving up here, and see her in shops and walking down the street. But it would be a massive exercise, way beyond the budget, and probably wouldn't tell us anything useful anyway.'

'Um . . .' said Christopher. 'What else did you want to ask?'

'The big puzzle, of course, is – did she or did she not know that body was in the cellar before appearing to find it for your benefit? You were there first, she showed every sign of never having been to the house before, and yet it was she who discovered it. You had already been down there and yet you never noticed him. She went down for half a minute and spotted it right away. It's all rather neat, don't you think? As if she was acting out a script she'd already rehearsed. How convincing was she? Did she seem to know her way around? There's nothing to say she hadn't been there previously.'

'And killed him herself, you mean?' said Simmy.

Moxon waved at her, keeping his eyes on Christopher's face. 'So? What do you think?'

Christopher slumped in his chair. 'You're putting ideas in my head. Any of that's possible. I explained it to myself at the time as being about the rats. I've got a thing about them. When I saw one in the cellar, the first time I went down there, I came rushing back without looking at anything else.' Simmy, watching his face as intently as Moxon was doing, saw the greyness return, with the feelings of responsibility

247

and inadequacy. 'It all started with the rats, really, and my stupid phobia.'

There was no good answer to that, and Moxon let it lie, waiting for more of Christopher's impressions. Robin abandoned his playmat and crawled from one adult to another, seeking attention. 'He needs his supper,' said Simmy. 'And I was hoping we'd have finished ours before people start arriving.'

'People?' said Christopher.

'My dad, and I've asked Ben and Bonnie as well. I don't know if they'll come. He might have texted me by now.'

Moxon made a little sound of concern. 'Give me a few more minutes. I need to ask about the auction. One idea that keeps cropping up is that there could be something being sold that has a special importance. Something you haven't fully identified. Is that feasible?'

'We did wonder about that,' Christopher nodded. 'But I can't think of anything. It's nice stuff, a good variety, but nothing that stands out as particularly valuable. Even Ben's *veilleuse* isn't likely to be worth more than a few hundred. It'll probably go to America. They collect them there more than here.'

'Don't ask,' said Simmy, seeing Moxon's face. 'I've already had to explain incunabula,' she told Christopher.

'Which we have not got in the sale,' he said quickly.

Moxon picked this up. 'So – it could be something of sentimental value to the relatives, such as they are. Something precious to Sir John or his forbears that ought not to be sold. Something that had been forgotten until now. It's likely that the chap from India – Bennett – contacted Ms Reade and asked her about it. Some old family legend, maybe . . . ?' He stopped with a rueful smile. 'I think I might be getting a bit carried away. And now I think about it, it's not nearly so likely now we've connected up the business with the printer.'

'But it's such an appealing idea,' sighed Simmy. 'A medieval chalice hidden behind the brickwork in the cellar is just the sort of thing that could be real. The house must be full of hiding places like that. I mean – you've already found one, haven't you? There might be others.'

'It's Victorian, not medieval,' Christopher reminded her. 'What hiding place?' he asked belatedly.

'I'll tell you later,' said Simmy.

Again a small silence fell, before Simmy admitted to her husband, 'I've told him about Julian Baxter. Not that I know how to find him or anything. And they seemed to know most of it already.'

'Not the main fact,' Moxon reminded her. 'That he helped to dump poor Mr Deeping in the river. By his own confession, evidently. That's a crime in itself.'

'Which is why he's lying low,' said Christopher. 'Who can blame him?'

Moxon sighed. 'I suppose you liked him as well.'

'I did rather. And at least he has a mobile phone. I can give you the number.'

'Thanks. It's nice to know you're not hiding anything.'

'We're not,' Simmy flashed at him. As if we would. We're on the same side as you – obviously.'

Christopher was having a worrying thought. 'Does Mrs Deeping know the whole story? About him being in the cellar, and me seeing him there and not saying anything? What will she think of me?'

'I can't say how much she's been told. I gather she's a strong character – that's all I know. But there'll be some concerns about letting her see the body.'

Christopher shuddered. 'The rats!' he muttered.

'And being in water doesn't help,' said Moxon.

'She's bound to want to see him, though,' Simmy realised, thinking suddenly of her stillborn daughter. 'Everybody does.'

'Not everybody,' Moxon corrected her. 'But I agree it's the best thing – usually.'

'I ought to go and talk to her,' said Christopher. 'Don't you think?'

The others looked at him with similarly uncertain reactions. 'In a few days, perhaps,' said Moxon.

'You can go to the funeral,' Simmy suggested.

'But – I just *left* him there. I threw up over him. I was a stupid cowardly traitor, and I should go and apologise.'

'Why should she care?' Simmy said, suddenly angry. 'What difference would it make if you grovelled and tried to justify yourself? It wouldn't be for *her* benefit, would it?'

Moxon took a quiet step backwards, eyeing little Robin who was now on his father's lap. Christopher had gripped the child like a shield, which was having an unsettling effect.

'Enough,' said the detective suddenly. 'We're starting to get heated. It's time I got out of your way.' He looked at his notebook, to which he had added very few words more than when he had arrived. 'And I need to think.'

'Will you go back to Penrith tonight? It's Sunday,' said Simmy. 'You seem to be spending more and more time up here. Poor Windermere's going to feel neglected.'

'Where Mr and Mrs Henderson go, the policeman has to follow,' he said, rather clumsily.

'Sorry about that,' said Simmy, with a pang. 'But it's not really our fault, is it?'

'Of course not,' the detective reassured her. 'And don't worry about me.'

A quirky association formed in Simmy's mind and she blurted, 'Do you know what an ABS is, in the car? The light came on in mine, today. Is it important?'

'Brakes,' said Moxon readily. 'Best get someone to have a look.'

'Honestly, Sim,' reproached Christopher. 'What does that have to do with anything?'

'Quite a lot, if it means I won't be able to use it,' she snapped at him.

'It's not going to be dangerous, if you go carefully,' said the detective. 'Just get it seen to soon.'

All three of them looked at Robin, each entertaining alarming images of a defective car careering down a Lakeland lane unable to stop.

'I will,' said Simmy. 'Thanks.'

Simmy was rather relieved that her mother had not added herself to the assembly in her living room. 'She's swotting up on antiques,' Russell reported. 'With the help of Fiona Bruce.'

It was half past seven and everyone had gathered as instructed. Ben and Bonnie sat on beanbags that had been brought down from the spare bedroom, Russell on the best armchair and the Hendersons side by side on the sofa. Robin had gone fractiously to bed, aware that he was

251

missing something, but also aware that his parents were in no mood to indulge any protestations. His head was full of impressions from the day, along with a handful of new words. The sound of voices coming up from below was soothing and he resolved to make the best of things.

Cornelia too was content to lie on her blanket in a corner and let everything wash over her. She'd eaten a big dinner and had her own experiences from the day to process.

Ben produced a large notepad and turned to a clean page. 'So, we pool our findings from the day,' he announced. 'I get the impression that we've all got plenty to contribute.'

'Too much, if anything,' muttered Christopher. 'Where on earth do we start?'

'Known facts, probable guesses, connections, theories and provisional conclusions,' Ben listed confidently. 'If we stick to that and don't get diverted into irrelevance, we should get somewhere.'

'Go on, then,' Russell invited with a happy sigh.

'Right. Major fact number one – the dead man has been found and identified. He was Mr Deeping, the printer who has the unit next to Christopher's auction house in Keswick. His wife has been informed. They'll do a post-mortem tomorrow. Foul play exists, at the very least in concealing his body, if not in actually killing him.'

'Poor man,' said Bonnie softly.

'Yes,' said Simmy.

'Post-mortem,' echoed Christopher with a shudder. 'I hope they didn't let his wife see him.'

'They might not be able to stop her. She has rights,' said Ben. 'They don't protect people like they used to, because it's seen as patronising. Or something.'

'Tricky,' said Russell.

Ben wrote 'Deeping' at the top of his page. 'And we met a photographer called Peter, who pretty much pointed us in the right direction. He had a camera set up on the riverbank, which could possibly have caught whoever it was dumping the body.'

'Jennifer and Julian,' said Simmy. 'He effectively admitted it to me.'

Ben patiently extracted details from her and wrote them down. 'Moxon says they'll catch him in the end, although Julian was sure they wouldn't.'

'He'll have to face charges,' said Russell knowingly. Everyone nodded in agreement.

'What next?' Bonnie prompted Ben.

He looked at Simmy. 'Your turn.'

'Have we finished with Julian Baxter? He came here, you know. I liked him. He's as keen as we are to know who killed Jennifer. He was her boyfriend and he's very sad she's dead. Yes, he helped her dump Mr Deeping in the river – at least, I think that's what he was trying to say – but I really don't think he helped to kill him. Moxon and I wondered if she did that on her own, in some sort of rage when she found him doing his criminal counterfeiting in her cellar.'

'He's definitely part of the whole picture,' said Ben. 'But I don't think we need to say any more about him now.'

'Just one or two more things,' Simmy insisted. 'Julian's the same as Jennifer in rejecting technology and so forth. And he knows the Phillippson person in Wiltshire, who collects incunabula.'

'Wow!' Ben sat back and gazed at her. 'You kept the best bit till last. Well done!'

253

'I didn't do anything. He came to us.'

Bonnie bounced on her beanbag. 'Talk about connections!' She was glowing with excitement. 'That's fantastic!'

'Has anybody seen the man from India since yesterday? What's his name?' said Ben.

'Warwick Bennett,' Simmy supplied. 'He seems to be the one most preoccupying Moxon. I have no idea where he is now. We all want him to be the one who killed Jennifer, but he can't possibly be. Christopher thinks he paid a contract killer.'

'Don't we all think that?' said Christopher.

'Wait!' Ben ordered. 'We're getting muddled. I've got to write it all down. This Thingummy Phillippson. What's his first name?'

'Maurice,' said Bonnie. 'You found him in the auction database, remember?'

'Of course.' Ben looked irritated at his own lapse of memory.

'Excellent piece of detective work,' beamed Russell, who had begun to lose the thread and was wondering what his own role might be in this intense piece of investigation. He wasn't at all sure he knew anything about a person called Phillippson. 'I'm afraid my contribution amounts to nothing more than wild theories.'

'We'll come to them later,' said Ben, and Bonnie rewarded Russell with a warm smile. Ben went on, 'So – Jennifer Reade and Julian Baxter were living in Swindon, off the grid. Did they live *together*?'

Nobody knew. 'Probably,' said Christopher. 'Much easier to survive without Internet or anything if you're both in the same house.'

Everybody took some moments to contemplate what that lifestyle might be like. 'We know they had a landline,' said Ben. 'The number's the only thing we've got stored at work. We don't even know their address because Jennifer's solicitor handled everything.'

'We don't know who owns High Gates House now, do we?' said Bonnie.

Ben waved his pen at her. 'That comes under motives. We're not there yet.'

'We know who witnessed Jennifer's final words,' Simmy reminded them. 'Two men on holiday who are staying in Keswick. Are they important?'

Ben waved the pen again. 'Outside our remit.'

Simmy nodded submissively.

'I think it's wonderful that they've found the body,' Russell enthused. 'That must surely answer lots of questions.'

'Let's hope so,' said Christopher. 'Everyone seems to have forgotten that my business hangs in limbo through all this. I'm starting to feel like the real victim here. I mean – that's the whole reason I didn't report the body last Wednesday. I was worried it would affect the sale. Jennifer told me it would. She persuaded me it was in my interest to stay quiet until we'd finished the auction.' He groaned. 'And now look where it's got me.'

The others gave him a variety of looks: Ben was impatient; Bonnie was sympathetic; Russell confused and Simmy tending to Ben's side. 'Yes, yes,' she said. 'But haven't we moved on from that by now? Something happened to change Jennifer's mind about the auction going ahead.'

Her husband shrank back slightly, looking hunted. 'I

have to think about the implications for the business. I could lose a whole lot of money if it isn't sorted out soon.'

'We might know tomorrow what happens next,' said Ben briskly. 'Once we know where the proceeds are to go, there'll be no reason to delay any more.'

'Half the buyers will have lost interest,' moaned Christopher.

'Not at all. And the publicity's going to bring in a whole lot of new ones,' predicted Ben.

'Ghouls,' muttered Russell. He looked round. 'I was rather hoping we would find some sort of link with the past. Like Hugh Walpole and the Margaret woman in Grange. That's what I hoped we'd turn up this morning. Nothing went as I expected.' He sighed.

'Hard to imagine how Hugh Walpole might fit,' said Simmy, who was the only person in the room who knew what Russell was talking about. 'Hasn't he been dead for about a hundred years?'

Russell smacked the arm of his chair crossly. 'Not at all. He died in 1941, after his reputation was trashed by Somerset Maugham. He's a very interesting character, let me tell you.'

'Not much short of a century ago,' said Ben pedantically. 'I think we did mention him, didn't we? Sir John Hickory's father quite probably knew him, but it's definitely not relevant now.'

'It might be,' Russell insisted. 'What if that printer chap was in possession of a lost manuscript and was going to publish it, and it had something defamatory about the Hickorys, so the Reade lady decided it couldn't be allowed and had to be stopped?' He looked round proudly. 'There's a theory for you.'

'Very impressive,' said Bonnie kindly. 'Make a note, Ben.'

Ben ostentatiously flipped over to a fresh page and wrote a few words. 'We might come back to it,' he agreed. 'Now – there are more people we haven't covered. The man at the house with his wife.'

'Steve,' said Bonnie helpfully.

'Yes. He seemed suspiciously abreast of everything. He's been lurking at the back of my mind all day. But even more intriguing is the man in the tent—'

'Peter Hinckley,' Bonnie contributed, like a super-efficient secretary.

'Okay, Bon,' said Ben tightly. 'I do remember his name.'

'No problem,' said Bonnie imperviously.

Ben proceeded to report in detail the encounter with the photographer in the tent, who had – whether inadvertently or not – pointed them in the direction of the dead Mr Deeping. 'I doubt if we'd ever have found him otherwise,' he concluded.

'"Inadvertently or otherwise"? I like that,' said Russell. 'Very subtle.'

'He was just a bit too good to be true,' said Ben.

'Could he have killed Jennifer, then?' asked Christopher, with a flicker of hope in his eyes.

Ben pulled a thoughtful face. '*Could*, I suppose. But when, why, how – and surely he wouldn't just hang about a couple of fields away? He claimed to know nothing whatever about the goings-on at the big house.'

They then went back over all the names that had occurred, with special reference to Julian Baxter.

'I keep wondering if *all* these people knew each other,'

said Bonnie. 'We've been guessing at links in various ways, but what if there's just one big gang, all wanting the house or the mystery object in the auction? I see Jennifer Reade as the big boss, pulling all the strings. And,' her eyes sparkled, 'what if it all goes back much further than we think? She might have known all along she was the heir to High Gates and bumped the old man off to get it? That would make sense of her staying off grid, so nobody could track her contacts and movements.'

'It's certainly a theory,' said Ben, non-committally.

'Surely it's much more to do with what Deeping was up to,' said Christopher, and Simmy gave this a vigorous endorsement. 'That gives us a pretty solid theory to work with, as I see it.'

The next twenty minutes began with an effort to construct just such a theory, before it descended into realms of fantasy that had Ben begging for order. Bonnie shamelessly abandoned him, giggling at some of Russell's more outrageous ideas. Even Christopher lightened up a bit and threw in a suggestion that everything that had happened had been orchestrated by Jennifer Reade, right down to her own death.

'Suicide by vengeful cousin,' he summarised. 'With me there as some sort of fall guy.'

'She couldn't have known you'd be at the house on Wednesday,' said Ben humourlessly.

'Drat!' said Christopher.

'It's nine o'clock,' Bonnie realised, when things had calmed down. 'We should go.' Ben was driving her home to Windermere and then returning to his Keswick digs. 'It'll be midnight before you get to bed, at this rate,' she added.

'We resume tomorrow, then,' said Ben brightly, looking from face to face. 'We're nowhere near done yet.'

'No provisional conclusions,' said Russell. 'Pity about that.'

'It's all so impossibly *complicated*,' moaned Simmy. 'We've got no idea what happened on Thursday. A whole day that's blank.'

'That Steve could probably supply a few of the missing facts, don't you think?' said Christopher.

Ben stared at him. 'That never occurred to me. Do we know he was back in Borrowdale again that day?'

Simmy interposed with, 'He didn't say, exactly, but it sounded as if they did keep going back to walk more sections of the crags right through the valley. They got the bus to and from Keswick.'

'But they were going *south*,' Christopher pointed out. 'And our business is all north of Grange. I think I'm just clutching at straws.'

'Ha!' said Russell, whose surname was Straw.

Ben flipped his notepad back to where it had started and tucked it away in his rucksack. 'More tomorrow. I'll see you at work,' he told Christopher. 'And I can phone Bonnie with any developments.'

'And me?' said Russell. 'Don't leave me out now I've got the bit between my teeth. I'm going to go and research Hugh Walpole and . . . those manuscript things.'

'Incunabula,' said Simmy, always happy to utter the word again. It felt like a magic incantation every time. 'You knew really,' she accused her father. 'You just wanted to hear me say it.'

'You do it so beautifully, darling.'

Even Christopher giggled at that.

The gathering dispersed quickly, the light outside having turned to the unearthly late-summer-evening glow that always came as a surprise. Looking up at Hartsop Dodd, Simmy could discern every small detail of bush and stone on the side of the fell. Trees had become silhouettes in some places and vivid images displaying every leaf in others, according to which direction one looked.

'Midsummer,' she murmured. 'Doesn't it seem magical!'

'Makes you realise how many useful hours of daylight there are, if you want to get up to mischief in the remoter regions,' said Ben pragmatically.

'And it's light again at four in the morning,' Bonnie added. 'I don't think nature intends us to sleep at this time of year.'

'Speak for yourself,' said Simmy, who liked her sleep.

There were few words exchanged between the Hendersons before they both sank into oblivion. 'Dad was funny, wasn't he?' said Simmy.

'Hilarious,' Christopher agreed. 'At least somebody's enjoying himself.'

Chapter Twenty-Two

Even Ben could detect a peculiar atmosphere when he arrived at the auction house on Monday morning. He had adopted the habit of cycling to work on dry days, weaving through the smaller streets of Keswick to the industrial estate on the outskirts of town. On this morning, he had been delayed by a new set of roadworks, perfectly timed to catch tourists, workers and school-run traffic in considerable numbers. Cyclists were accorded no special dispensations, although he did manage to creep past most of the cars and trucks to the front of the queue. This evidently irritated the driver of a big delivery van, who accelerated past him, leaving barely two inches between them, and then pulled in so that Ben had nowhere to go. He stopped, heart beating at double the normal pace, half expecting the van to reverse right over him. Impatient drivers surged past, making up the time lost at the temporary lights. Not until the next batch were stopped did he venture into the roadway again, having lost four or five minutes. He rode slowly the rest of the way, vowing to use his car for the rest of the week.

When he got there, he found the saleroom staff

clustered in the entrance, in earnest discussion. Fiona, Jack, Hughie and Kitty were all there, but no sign of Christopher.

'A woman came to see him,' Fiona explained. 'They're in the office.'

'Who is she?'

'Well, Jack thinks she must be the wife of the printer bloke they found in the river last night. He thinks he recognises her. She's certainly in a state – though not quite how you'd expect.'

Ben went very still, his brain whirling. Mrs Deeping, of all people! She had not featured at all in their evening discussion. Surely she'd be much too busy coming to terms with her loss to show up here first thing on a Monday morning?

'Blimey!' he said.

'I know. Everything just gets more and more bizarre in this place,' said Kitty with a sniff. 'What I want to know is – when can we resume the sale? If it's not going to happen, we may as well all go home.'

'You can say that again,' snapped Hughie. 'I was supposed to finish up here today and get onto the next place.' Nobody asked him where that might be.

And then Christopher appeared and focused on Ben. 'Can you come and talk to this lady?' he said, with a feeble attempt to look authoritative and discreet. 'She wants to hear about yesterday.'

'It's all right,' said Ben. 'They know who she is.'

Christopher frowned and turned back to his little office. Ben followed. But before they got inside the room, a red van pulled up outside and a postman jumped out with a bundle of mail held together with a rubber band. Fiona took it from him and followed Christopher and Ben. 'Hey, Chris – the post's here,' she called. Ben took it from her and handed it to his boss. On top he noticed a white envelope with a stamp, the address handwritten. Such an object was a rarity and he smiled to see it.

In the office a middle-aged woman in a thin blue jacket was sitting on an ornately carved chair in front of the oak desk. All the furniture in the side rooms was old and handsome, having been in the auction at some point, only to find itself unclaimed for one reason or another. Bidders would change their minds, or the item go missing thanks to a wrong number somewhere along the line. The previous proprietor of the business had nabbed this nice old chair before it even went up for sale, paying the vendor peanuts for it and installing it in his office. Such practices were standard and unremarked.

'This is Mrs Deeping,' said Christopher, putting the newly arrived letters on the desk and forgetting about them.

'Rosemary,' said the woman. 'Hello.' There was no wobble in her voice and her eyes were clear.

'Pleased to meet you,' said Ben. 'I'm sorry about your husband.'

'Yeah, well, serves him right. I *told* him he'd come to a sticky end.'

There was no answer to that, and Ben, with his shaky grasp of emotional nuance, was left with his mouth half open.

Christopher came to the rescue. 'You need to hear what Mrs Dee – I mean Rosemary, has to say. She came to us before going to the police.'

'They'll be back this morning with a long list of questions. So I came here first thing. It's awkward, you see,' the woman elaborated.

There was nowhere for Ben to sit, so he leant against a bookcase and tried to look receptive. Rosemary Deeping went on, 'Klaus was a printer, as you probably know. Mostly leaflets and calendars and funeral service sheets, but people sometimes got him to do booklets and even proper books now and then. He did pretty good business because he gave proper old-fashioned service and didn't make mistakes.' She smiled slightly. 'You can't imagine how rare this is, these days. The newer businesses rely entirely on computers, which is very stupid.'

'Klaus?' said Ben. 'Was he German?'

'His mother was half-German and half-Danish. Scottish father. A good mixture as it turned out. He was a perfectionist, very skilled, very focused. Organised. Ambitious. With a good dash of imagination.' She was using her hands to illustrate this list of attributes, ticking each off on a finger. It seemed to Ben that she had done it before, probably several times, and that it was not just something she'd worked out since learning of her husband's death.

'How long was he missing?' he asked.

'What? Oh – since last Monday. I contacted the police after three or four days.'

'Where did you think he was?'

'I had no idea. We'd not been speaking much for months. He'd go off to sales around the country, collecting old broadsheets, mostly. Always had to see the thing for himself and handle it. But he'd always told me how long he'd be away. We've got a boy to consider. Somebody needs to be there for him. Christian. That's his name.'

Ben detected a subtext concerning the 'boy', but opted to set it aside. 'So – you wanted to tell us something,' he prompted.

'Klaus was a counterfeiter.' The words came out flat and rather loud. 'He faked medieval stuff. What they call incunabula. He even sold some here, a few months back.'

'Ah!' said Ben, looking at Christopher and acting the innocent. 'Did you know about that?'

'I hadn't realised who the vendor was,' said the auctioneer. 'It's a shock.'

'Implications,' nodded Ben, aware of the reputational risks attached to selling bogus artefacts.

'Yes, well,' said Rosemary. 'He was extremely good at it. Careful, too. Never did too much. Spread it out across the country, hardly ever using the same saleroom twice. Avoided the specialists. I didn't realise for years, what he was up to, but then, earlier this year, it started to catch up with him.'

Connections, Ben was thinking. The Phillippson man in Swindon, known to Jennifer Reade and Julian Baxter, who bought the faked incunabula. A much better picture was coming into focus, and he beamed at Mrs Deeping. 'It's very good of you to come to us like this,' he said.

'Yes, it is,' echoed Christopher.

'Well, I didn't think it would be fair not to. To you, or to Klaus, in a way. He couldn't see that he was doing anybody any harm, and I think he had a point. He was a real artist, using all the old processes, taking weeks over a single page.

It wasn't even especially lucrative. And he always insisted he was making people happy.'

'But it made at least one person angry,' said Ben. 'Because they killed him.'

'Precisely,' said Rosemary Deeping. 'Which is why I'm going to have to report all this to the police, much as I hate to. As I said, Klaus should have known better, but he never thought there was any actual *danger* in it. He was a difficult man to live with, but we jogged along and I'm going to have a much harder time without him. Because of the boy, you see.' Ben cocked his head invitingly. 'He's got muscular dystrophy. He needs full-time care. Klaus was very good with him, always took Mondays off work to take his turn, give me a break.'

'How old is he?'

'Thirteen. He was going to a care centre attached to a school, a marvellous place, but the funding dried up somehow and now it's only two days a week instead of full time. Just as we were getting into a much better routine, they went and wrecked it all.'

'Stressful,' muttered Christopher, who did not appear to be keeping up very well, leaving everything to Ben.

'You have no idea. Anyway, it all started to go wrong for Klaus when he sold those things here. The buyer was thrilled and demanded more. Offered big money. Klaus got a bit scared, but kept his nerve – told the man he couldn't just magic such things up – they're fantastically rare, and only turn up very occasionally when someone opens an old box in an attic after four centuries or whatever. But it turned out that this bloke knew perfectly well what was going on, and wanted in on it. Said he had contacts in Asia and South America, with collectors who'd go mad for the stuff. It was all too tempting, and Klaus gave in. He would spend whole nights up at that house with his old printing press. Poor old Sir John just thought he needed more space, and let him use the cellar without asking any questions. Klaus didn't think I knew about it, but he wasn't very good at covering his tracks.'

'The police have found the press,' said Ben. 'They'll have worked most of this out for themselves by now.'

Mrs Deeping looked confused. 'You think? But they only found him last night.'

'They gave the place a proper search once Mr Henderson told them about a dead man in the cellar.'

'Oh.' She played a silent tune with her fingers on her leg. 'I can't work out what must have happened. When he went missing, I thought he'd probably gone to meet this bloke that bought his fakes, and had got right out of his depth. The trouble is, I have no idea who it is – or where he hangs out.'

'Maurice Phillippson,' said Ben. 'In Salisbury.'

'Oh!' said Rosemary again. 'Really?'

'We looked him up. Basically, you've just confirmed a theory that we were already considering. But we can't work out for sure why he was killed at High Gates House.'

'Or why somebody murdered Jennifer Reade,' said Christopher. Both men looked hopefully at Mrs Deeping, as if expecting her to supply the answer.

'Don't ask me,' she said. 'And I have to go. I left Mrs Next Door with Christian, and she doesn't like me to be out for long. Plus I've got the bloody police due any time.'

She and Christopher both stood up. 'Thank you very much for coming,' said the auctioneer. 'I really appreciate it.'

'Well, I thought you should know. With your auction suspended and all this High Gates business causing you grief, I thought you should be in the picture a bit more. It all links up, doesn't it?' she finished vaguely. 'Somehow or other.'

'So it seems,' said Christopher miserably. 'Well, I am sincerely sorry for your loss. It obviously isn't going to be easy.'

'Thank you. He wasn't the greatest husband in the world, but life will be a lot harder without him. I have friends and a sister and some scraps of state assistance, so I'll muddle through. It's just not what I'd got planned for myself, twenty years ago. Funny how things turn out.'

'You'll be all right,' said Ben, as if stating a definite fact.

She looked at him for a long moment. 'Let's hope so,' she said.

Ben stayed in the office with Christopher for a few more minutes after the visitor had left.

'That letter looks interesting,' he pointed out. 'Can I stay while you open it?' Already he was having inklings as to its origin.

Christopher did as bidden, unfolding a single sheet of good-quality notepaper and reading the last line first. 'Jennifer Reade!' he gasped. 'It's from Jennifer Reade.'

'I thought it might be,' said Ben, holding back his excitement. 'What does she say?'

'I'll read it.

"High Gates, Thursday morning.

Dear Mr Henderson,

I am really very sorry to have presented you with such an impossible dilemma yesterday. A lot has happened since then, and I am now in some real trouble, which I hope is only temporary. I want to be present at the sale tomorrow, but it might not be possible. I daren't leave here for the moment. I'm hoping to find someone to post this letter for me. I think a friend will be joining me today. I know I have no right to be here now. I'm sleeping in my car and trying to be inconspicuous. You will think me insane not to have a phone with me, but the truth is, none of this would be easy to say to you. A letter feels better. I write a lot of letters.

Please don't worry about me. By the time you get this, I expect everything will be over and done with, and we'll all be the richer. Let's hope so.

Meanwhile, I simply wish to apologise and hope to meet you again in calmer times.

With very best wishes,

Jennifer Reade."

That's it. What are we meant to make of that?'
Ben took a deep breath. 'Well – the visitor must have been Julian Baxter. The trouble must have been the presence of the dead Mr Deeping. Or perhaps whatever she means by a lot happening since she saw you. If she didn't have a

phone, how could she know Baxter was coming? Did they use carrier pigeons, or what? I wonder who posted it for her – and when?' He was articulating random thoughts with little sense of understanding any implications. 'What about you?' he finished.

'I'm still reeling from what Mrs Deeping told us. It's all too much at once. I can't work out what it all means or what I'm supposed to do about it. For a start, the police should see this, I suppose. Although I can't see that it'll be of much help.'

'No,' said Ben slowly. 'There are still a lot of gaps. For one thing – who owns the Hickory estate now? You could call Jennifer's solicitors maybe, and see if they can answer that. You've got every right to be informed, given that the auction's still in limbo.'

'Yes.' Christopher shook himself. 'Sleeping in the car! Isn't that totally bizarre? Why would she do that?'

'Did she think she had to guard the house for some reason? Or was she hiding out? Or just waiting for Baxter to show up. Maybe she wrote letters to other people as well.'

'Did she know about the cousin – Warwick Bennett? Was she hiding from him?'

'Quite possibly. And don't forget Maurice Phillippson.'

'Good God, Ben. It's quarter to ten – everyone's still hanging around out there wanting to know what I want them to do. And I have no idea what to say to them. It's like Friday all over again.'

'Don't ask me,' said Ben. 'Perhaps if you phone the solicitor, he'll have some suggestions.'

'What about the police? They have to see this.'

'It doesn't tell us much, does it? They can wait. And you're right – the top priority now is what happens here. You should probably send everybody home. Hughie's making a fuss and Kitty looks as if she agrees with him. In fact, Hughie's a bit of a problem. He was only meant to be here until today, helping people collect their stuff. I doubt if he's going to want to stay much longer.'

'He'll want paying. I said he could have it in cash.'

'Not another one!' sighed Ben.

'Happens all the time in this business,' said Christopher absently. 'I'm phoning that solicitor now.' Which he did, waving Ben out of the room first. 'Go and say I'll talk to them when I've done this.'

Ben did as instructed, feeling important. He could feel Fiona's eyes on him, not altogether friendly as she wondered why he was suddenly the messenger instead of her. Fiona had worked at the saleroom for even longer than Christopher, aware of the chequered history and taboo areas. She had been forced to transfer loyalties, which she had done with a good grace, but now and then it was plain that she was wondering whether former times had been preferable to the regular pickles that the new boss got himself into. She liked Simmy, adored Robin and deplored the dog. Her own home life was shadowy and seemingly very unexciting, given that she lived with an elderly mother. Fiona was forty-five and her mother was eighty-six. There were no siblings.

The other person who manifested exasperation was not Hughie, but Jack – the general factotum, as Ben had labelled him. He went ten years further back than Fiona and knew even more of the history of the place. He was small and strong and silent, speaking only when strictly necessary. He had adapted to the new management with difficulty; any changes brought his disfavour down on Christopher's head. To have an auction suspended in mid-flight, so to speak, was unprecedented and deeply resented. It smacked of poor judgement in his eyes. For Jack, nothing mattered more than that the sale should run smoothly, with all vendors and purchasers going away happy at the end. The fact that this time there was only one vendor already made him uneasy. The alteration in layout, the unusual mixture of items for sale and the overall feeling of depression had soured his mood for the past two weeks. And some of the ructions, if he was not very much mistaken, stemmed from this upstart boy Ben and his clever ideas. 'What's happening, then?' he demanded.

Ben had little idea as to how he was regarded by the various staff members. He did his best to be civil to them and not get in anybody's way.

Now he gave a brave smile and said, 'Christopher's trying to find out. It depends, probably, on who now owns the estate – I mean, who gets the proceeds when we sell it all. Once that's settled, we can carry on.'

Kitty made a sceptical sound. 'That could take months. If there's a dispute over the inheritance – which is highly likely – everything could be in limbo indefinitely.'

'I think there's some progress on that,' said Ben awkwardly.

'Otherwise it'll all have to go into storage somewhere,' said Hughie. 'Which'll be expensive if it goes on for long.'

Ben winced. The idea of packing everything up again, unsold and abandoned, was painful to contemplate.

'Let's hope it doesn't come to that, then. Meanwhile, let's just wait until Christopher's got some news. Chances are, you can all have a few days off – though someone's got to be here to man the phones, I suppose.'

'That'll be you, mate,' said Hughie with a nasty laugh.

Ben smiled again. 'I expect it will. Lucky I haven't got anything else to do.'

'It's all so *awful*,' moaned Fiona. 'That poor woman, bashed to death. Why don't the police arrest somebody?'

'And why was Mrs Deeping here just now?' It was Jack, speaking softly, almost to himself.

Ben realised that the news of Deeping's demise had already emerged. Jack clearly knew the couple, which came as no surprise; Jack knew everybody. Ben did a rapid risk assessment, and then said, 'Her husband's body was found yesterday. She came to talk to Christopher about something he'd been doing, involving us. It all seems to connect, somehow.'

'They found him, then? That thing on the news – it was him, was it?' Hughie pushed forward, his expression intense. 'This gets more and more sinister. Was he murdered as well?'

Ben leant away from the importunate young man. 'I don't know. I can't tell you any more. Everything's still being investigated.'

Kitty gave a long sigh. 'Well, hurry up, Christopher, that's all I say. I can't abide hanging about doing nothing like this, murder or no murder. It's nothing to do with me, whichever way you look at it.'

'Nor me,' said Fiona.

Hughie and Jack both nodded in agreement.

Nobody said much more until Christopher joined them five minutes later.

'Not much progress, I'm afraid,' he said. 'Nobody knows anything for certain, but we're probably suspended for at least the whole of this week. I suggest you all take some days off. Don't disappear altogether, though. No last-minute flights to Benidorm. I'll keep you updated every morning. Be ready for this to change. Fiona – I might need you at some point to take over from Ben. He can do the phones and stuff for the time being, but it's not fair to leave it all to him. Is that all right with everyone?'

Jack raised his hand like a schoolboy. 'If it's all right with you, boss, I'll stick around. There'll be folks turning up at the gate and it's only fair to keep them informed, don't you think? There's always some bits and bobs I can be getting on with.'

This was true. The further end of the yard, where weatherproof items were displayed for viewing, had long been a repository for broken and abandoned lots. A day devoted to tidying it up was long overdue.

'That's fine, Jack. I should have thought of it myself.'

'Can I take my pay and go, then?' said Hughie. 'I've got another job waiting for me.'

Christopher glanced at Ben, before saying, 'Of course. Although there won't be enough cash. I'll have to go and get some.'

The young man sighed. 'So you do that, and I'll pop off and get a few things done, and see you back here after lunch. Is that all right?'

'Fine,' Christopher nodded. 'Sorry you'll have to come back.'

274

'No problem – the bike needs a bit of a run. It's been good working here. I hope it all works out for you – auction-wise.'

'Thanks. I'll be sorry to see you go, I must say.'

Hughie did not reply in kind, but his look suggested that the feeling was not entirely mutual, despite his earlier words.

'He talks about that bike like it was a horse,' remarked Ben.

Chapter Twenty-Three

It dawned on Ben quite slowly that the auction house was not the best place to be. While Christopher seemed to feel it was a welcome bolthole, away from any upsetting action, Ben wanted something quite different. He understood that he was feeling very much the same as Bonnie often felt, stranded as she was in Windermere. Not to mention Simmy, stuck with a baby in the cul-de-sac that was Hartsop. Russell and Angie Straw, by comparison, were poised on the busy A66, able to hurtle off in any direction at a moment's notice. Russell had been particularly engaged with the Borrowdale events and should not be underestimated if it came to a final crescendo. Wouldn't it be only decent to update him on the morning's developments? As Monday slowly trundled on, Ben decided he might profitably pop over to Threlkeld in the lunch hour, such as it was.

'Did you call the police about Mr Deeping?' he asked Christopher, at eleven o'clock.

'Not yet. I've had that man about the statue on again, demanding that we ship it to him today. He's transferred the money for it already, the idiot – and not deducted the cost of transport.'

The statue – of a pixie sitting on a mushroom – had been an early lot on Friday, and had sold for ninety pounds, hammer price. Ben had wondered what such a piece of kitsch had been doing in Sir John's small garden in the first place. It hadn't looked very old. When unloading it with other outdoor lots, Jack had paused, and said, 'What's this doing here?'

Hughie, who had been helping him, said carelessly, 'Probably somebody gave it to him or his dad and he couldn't refuse. It's quite nicely made – and a good size. Heavy, too. Looked nice sitting under the side window, it did.'

Jack had cocked his head at that, in puzzlement. Later he said to Ben, 'It wasn't under a window when we loaded up. Everything was in the parking area.'

Ben had taken very little notice, well aware of the organised chaos up at High Gates for the past week or more.

Now some of this came back to him as he listened to his boss.

'There's something about that pixie,' he said slowly. 'Something to do with Hughie and Jack.' He forced himself to think back. 'It sounded as if Hughie must have seen it before they started loading everything up. If I remember rightly, it was the first time he'd been out with the truck, but Jack said it wasn't where Hughie said it was.'

'What?' Christopher was paying scant attention.

'Probably nothing. Just a bit odd that it's cropped up again. I wonder if the police have caught the woman who took that vase last week. Fiona says she reported it.'

Christopher tutted. 'That's the least of our worries.

Don't get all distracted now, for heaven's sake. I'm still trying to make sense of Jennifer Reade's letter. I think that Price man's going to be here soon. He said it'd be better if we did it face to face.'

'Did what?'

'Catch up, I suppose. Show him the letter. Fill him in about the Deepings. *You* know.'

'Right. Can I sit in as well?'

'You'll have to ask him. I don't see why not.'

It was not DS Price, but DI Moxon who arrived a short time later. He had a plain-clothes officer with him, who he introduced as Detective Sergeant Smith.

'He's just come to us from Norfolk,' said Moxon. 'First day with us. I thought he should get to meet the best amateur detectives in England before going any further.' They were in the saleroom, which provided more space than the office. Smith and Ben both sat on dining chairs that were part of Lot Number 468.

Ben simpered and Christopher gave no reaction at all.

'First things first, then,' said the inspector briskly. 'You've had a letter, right?'

Christopher proffered it. 'Have you seen Mrs Deeping?' he asked.

Moxon nodded. 'She's been very helpful.'

'Beyond the call of duty,' said Ben. 'She doesn't seem too upset about him dying.'

'You can never judge,' Moxon told him severely, with a glance at his sidekick. 'My impression is that she just wants to keep everything straight. Gave us plenty to think about, anyhow.'

'Any progress?' asked Ben. 'Have you found Julian Baxter? Or Maurice Phillippson?'

Moxon sighed. 'See what we're up against?' he said to DS Smith. 'No sense of boundaries or areas of responsibility or good old-fashioned discretion. Just wades in and asks the most pertinent questions.'

'Very unorthodox,' agreed the newcomer. He was late twenties, not very tall and showed no signs of any sense of humour. He was frowning slightly as he looked at Ben.

'As it happens, we can exclude Mr Phillippson from our enquiries. At least, he can probably provide some helpful details, but he's not under suspicion. He spent all last week in hospital having a rather nasty procedure performed on his nether regions. Someone's interviewing him today as he recovers at home.'

'And Baxter?'

'Nothing so far.'

'What about the cousin? Bennett? Where's he now?'

Moxon looked down his nose, eyes narrowed. 'Don't worry, he's keeping us informed of his movements. Everything that happens in the coming days will affect him more than anybody – even you.' He turned to Christopher. 'He's particularly concerned with what happens next regarding your sale.'

'Yes, I know,' said Christopher. 'I spoke to the solicitors for the estate this morning. They wouldn't say much, but I understood that they were examining Bennett's claim to the property, or verifying it, or something – it looks authentic so far.'

'Which makes him prime suspect,' said Ben. 'Without a doubt. Who *else* is there?'

279

'Not so fast,' said the detective. 'There's the matter of Mr Deeping's death to consider, remember. The post-mortem results should be through any time now. First indications were extremely ambivalent.'

'Did she see him? His wife, I mean?' asked Christopher, sounding suddenly choked. 'She didn't say, this morning. I didn't like to ask her. I didn't know if she'd been told about the rats.'

Moxon nodded at the question. 'She insisted – but in the event, when the mortuary man had a word with her, she just checked his clothes, and dodged the actual body.'

'Thank goodness for that. He must have looked ghastly.'

'It's odd that she didn't want you to tell her all about that. She knew you'd seen him last week. She must have wanted the whole story. Most people do.'

'Actually not. She wanted to do most of the talking. She didn't seem too concerned with how he died. That's odd, now I come to think of it.' Christopher shook his head. 'There's such a *lot* to think about.'

'There's sure to be all kinds of clues around, but we can't spot them because of all the other stuff,' complained Ben, slightly defensively. 'It's like trying to focus on something through thick fog.'

'We all got together again last night,' Christopher told Moxon, 'and thrashed out everything any of us had gleaned since Wednesday. It went on for ages. There seems to be no end to it.'

'And?'

'Plenty of theories, which got wilder as time went on. We think it highly likely that Jennifer – or perhaps Julian – killed Mr Deeping. They must have done, because then they

280

disposed of his body in the river. But . . .' – here Christopher lost much of his momentum – 'if that's right, then why on earth did she show me his body the way she did? It would have been so easy just to steer me away, so I would never have had any idea it was there.'

'Ms Reade's motives and mental processes are mystifying everybody,' said Moxon. 'Of course, she never expected to get murdered.'

A snort from Ben alerted the detective to the unconscious humour of his words, but he pressed on, 'That's to say, she must have had a plan which was fatally interrupted. Knowing what that plan was would probably be the key to the whole business.'

'Right,' Ben nodded. 'And we think it must be to do with the incunabula that Mr Deeping was counterfeiting.' Ben turned to Christopher, on a sudden thought. 'We should tell Mr Straw about that. He'll be fascinated.'

Moxon waved at him to stick to the point.

'Well, it would make sense if Jennifer Reade found out about the faking and took exception to it. In a rage, she bashed the Deeping man to death. We know she knew the Phillippson man, who had bought faked incunabula from our saleroom. So what if he realised it would come out that they were bogus, and that would reflected badly on Jennifer somehow?'

'And Julian,' Christopher interrupted.

'Okay. So they both came up here to confront Deeping, and used the empty house as a meeting place, and it all kicked off from there. With me so far?' He looked at the three men, one by one. They all signalled for him to carry on. 'Right. Meanwhile, there's a last-minute appearance of a cousin from India, who also seems to have some sort of links to falsifying old documents – which can't just be a coincidence. It suggests that Jennifer knew about him all along. But perhaps *he* didn't know about *her*. So, when he finally figures out that he could stand to inherit half the Hickory fortune, he dashes over here to stake his claim before it's too late.' He sighed. 'And then it falls apart because she died before he reached this country. That's more than enough to eliminate him as a suspect.'

'There must be someone else we haven't even thought of,' said Christopher, whose head was up again like a horse waiting for the starting pistol. 'But – gosh, Ben – that was a brilliant summary. I don't know how you do it.'

'We need this Baxter person,' said DS Smith. 'Surely he can't be all that hard to find?'

'He's doing his best. He's playing the Scarlet Pimpernel,' said Ben.

'Now you're channelling Russell,' Christopher reproved him. 'Nobody else has read those books.'

'But we all know who we mean,' said Ben.

'I don't,' admitted DS Smith.

'The theory holds good much better if he and Ms Reade attacked Deeping together,' said Moxon. 'But we still can't explain why Mr Henderson was shown the body.'

'Was it some kind of test, do you think?' suggested the sergeant. 'After all, she was relying on Mr Henderson's services as an auctioneer.' He looked around the big saleroom, packed with items that had belonged to the murdered woman. 'She needed him to work in her best interests. Is it possible that she thought she would have a hold over him if she showed him the body?'

'It did feel like that,' Christopher confirmed.

'But it gave *him* more of a hold over *her*,' Ben argued. 'Why would she give him that?'

Nobody had an answer to that.

'And then, of course, there's that photographer chap, Peter,' said Ben, as if speaking to himself. 'There's something suspiciously *neat* about him.'

Both detectives raised their eyebrows. 'Who?' said Moxon.

'Oh! Sorry – didn't we mention him? Yes, we must have done, when we took the shoe to Penrith. When we talked to Superintendent Price. It'll be in the file somewhere.'

'Remind me.'

Ben gave a quick resumé of Sunday's encounter. 'He insisted he hadn't heard or seen anything going on at High Gates. But he did point us in the right direction,' he concluded. 'I gave DS Price his details, from his card. And you should be sure to have a look at what's on his camera. It might be the only proper evidence you get.'

'I dare say the super has all that in hand,' Moxon said.

'And Steve, don't forget,' said Christopher. 'Him and his missus. They popped up at crucial moments, too.'

Again, there had to be an explanation. Christopher reminded Moxon that Simmy had mentioned the hikers, prompting him to complain, 'You can't drag in everyone you've met since Wednesday. 'How could this couple possibly be relevant?'

'They were right there, that's how,' said Ben forcefully. 'They could have seen the killer's car, heard shouts, spotted goings-on from the top of the crag through binoculars. That sort of thing.'

'They knew the men who rescued Jennifer,' added Christopher.

'Hardly *rescued*,' muttered Smith. 'The woman died on them.'

'Do you have Steve's business card as well?' asked Moxon.

Ben shook his head. 'Sorry.'

'What now?' asked Christopher. 'I can't see what else there is for you to investigate, apart from giving me the go-ahead for the sale. We're living in limbo here.'

There was a *ping* from Moxon's pocket and he fumbled for his phone. 'Post-mortem report,' he said. 'Preliminary findings. Cause of death a number of blows to the head. Also several contusions on the body and legs.'

'Pushed him down the cellar steps, most likely,' said Ben. 'Then finished him off with a blunt object.'

'That's probably it,' said Moxon heavily.

'No hope of establishing which day he died, I suppose?' said Christopher.

'Not a hope in hell,' said DS Smith. 'Not after everything it's been through. I'm surprised they can identify contusions, under the circumstances.'

There was a hint of relish in his tone that made both Ben and Christopher decide they didn't much like this man. Moxon appeared to feel the same. 'Poor man,' he said.

'They'll have told his wife, I assume?' said Ben. 'Though I don't suppose she'll be very surprised.'

'We didn't really finish talking about her, did we?' said Smith. 'And there's more. The way the Reade lady said "Stop the sale" like she did. I mean – if she had enough breath for that, why didn't she say who'd attacked her?'

'Because stopping the sale was the most important thing on her mind. And perhaps she thought that would somehow make it obvious who her killer was,' said Ben thoughtfully. 'You're right that it's important. And we haven't given it enough attention.'

'They told me she was attacked in her sleep,' said Christopher. 'So she'd have no idea what had happened or who'd done it.'

Moxon stared at him. 'Who said that? How could they *know*?'

Christopher had to think. 'It must have been one of those uniformed officers who came and stopped the auction. They told me quite a lot in the car, when they took me to Penrith. More than they should have, most likely.'

'Well, it was only ever a vague theory. It's not proven,' Moxon told him.

Smith looked smug. 'Typical,' he said. 'And while we're at it, we need to remember there were *three* deaths at that house. The old man, who died all alone in his bed. Who found him? Was there a post-mortem? Does all this go back further than we've been thinking?'

'That was *months* ago,' said Christopher. 'For heaven's sake.'

Smith opened his mouth to speak, but Moxon stopped him. 'I think we've said enough for now,' the detective decided. 'Looks to me as if all the effort now is going into finding the Baxter person. His phone's untraceable. You didn't see his car registration plate, I suppose? We thought we'd got details of his car, but it turns out that one's still sitting outside his house. He must have used a different one.'

Christopher shook his head. 'Sorry.' Then he looked up. 'But I bet Lily did.'

'We'll send one of the girls to talk to your friend Lily,' said Moxon, sounding authoritative.

After they'd gone, Ben remarked, 'Moxon seems to have found a foothold with the Penrith lot, doesn't he? A few months ago, he was being treated as a bit of a joke.'

'And yet he did the business in the end, didn't he? That'll have earned him some respect. And that Price person seems to have an unusually open mind, which probably helps.'

'Witnesses, forensics and confession,' said Ben.

'Pardon?'

'That's what's needed to solve a crime.'

'I thought it was means, motive and opportunity.'

'That too – sort of. That's when you're formulating a theory and have a suspect in mind.'

'Makes you wonder how they ever manage it,' said Christopher. 'Especially in a place like Borrowdale. If I wanted to murder someone, that's probably the first spot I'd choose to do it in.'

'Which might work for Deeping, but I'm not so sure about Jennifer.'

'Stop!' begged Christopher, as people quite often did when Ben was in full flight. 'My head can't take any more. Aren't we supposed to be doing something?'

'Having lunch? It's half past twelve.'

'And not a single phone call.'

'There'll be masses of emails instead,' said Ben. 'I'll just go and have a quick look.'

'I'll see you at the sandwich van, then. And don't tell me if there's anything nasty in the emails.'

Chapter Twenty-Four

Simmy spent a lot of Monday morning on the phone. Bonnie, Russell, Lily and Moxon all called her between nine and eleven. Bonnie had more to say about the shop than the events in Borrowdale. Verity had broken a tooth, and needed to go to the dentist that afternoon, leaving Bonnie to cope on her own.

'I'm not worried,' she said bravely. 'But I thought you should know.'

Broken teeth always seemed to choose the worst possible moment to happen. Simmy was reminded of her mother who had the same problem on Simmy's wedding day.

'I expect I could come and help you, if necessary,' she told Bonnie, with some reluctance. 'There doesn't seem to be very much happening here so far. But I'm not keen on driving over Kirkstone with my brakes not working properly.'

'Better not, then. Ben thinks it's coming to a climax today. He thinks we've got all the facts – they just have to be assembled logically.'

'He's such an optimist,' said Simmy. 'I wouldn't be surprised if it drags on for weeks and weeks yet. I can't see how they'll ever work out who killed Jennifer.'

'They will. Have faith,' her young assistant adjured her.

'I'll try,' said Simmy.

Russell was also optimistic. 'I have every confidence that'll it'll be sorted soon,' he said. 'I had a dream last night involving that Steve individual. I bet he knows more than he was letting on. Someone should try to find him.'

'He'll have gone home by now. They were only here for a week. We don't even have a surname. Besides, I think he'd have said if he had any useful information. He was very keen to talk.'

'Ah! But he won't have known what was useful, will he? Some detail that he never thought to divulge.'

'Too late, Dad. There'd be more sense in tracking down the Baxter man. He's more or less admitted to killing Mr Deeping, or at least helping to dispose of his body. He is rather awful, the way he treats the whole thing like a game. Actually, now you mention it, I think I had a dream about him. He had face paint on and a funny hat.'

'The Joker!'

'No, not really. Although I suppose that might have been lurking in my unconscious. I never did see those films.'

'Nor me, but they're in the culture now. It's such a strong image.'

'Yes, well . . . I suppose we'll just have to wait and see whether Christopher and Ben get anywhere. They're more in the middle of things than we are. You, me and Bonnie have been pushed to the sidelines.'

'Speak for yourself. I can get to Keswick in five minutes, remember. And I will, if I think I can be of any use.'

Simmy made agreeable noises, having no intention of

either encouraging or discouraging her energised parent. It was good to have him so involved and functioning so well, after a spell when everyone feared his mind and body were both irreversibly slowing down.

'Well, keep me posted,' she ended by saying.

Lily phoned from a distance of a hundred yards, saying she was too busy to come in person. 'We're going on holiday tomorrow,' she said, not sounding too happy about it. 'Dad got some last-minute deal to Sardinia, of all places, and we're leaving here at six in the morning. So I can't walk Cornelia for you. I can't do her today, either, because I've got to make three new bags before five o'clock.'

'Lucky you,' said Simmy sincerely. 'Don't worry about the dog. I should be here most of the time. How long are you away for?'

'A week. So what happened about that man?'

Simmy made no pretence of not understanding. 'He came here, and we talked. He's nothing to worry about, and he won't be coming back.'

'I wasn't worried. I thought he might turn out to be quite nice – it's just that people don't usually talk about bodies, do they? That threw me a bit. My mum thinks it's suspicious – especially with all that in Borrowdale. There's got to be a connection, she says.'

'Well, she's right. But he's gone now, and it's for the police to worry about.'

'Did you tell them about me?'

Simmy hesitated. 'You know – I honestly can't remember. Christopher might have done. But the man came here, so all you did was direct him.'

'Like a signpost,' the girl giggled.

'Exactly. And have a lovely time in Sardinia. All that wonderful sea and sun. I'm jealous.'

'Thanks,' said Lily with a sigh.

Moxon's call, shortly before eleven, was brief and friendly. 'I'm going to have a chat with your husband in Keswick,' he told her. 'And Ben, if he's there.'

'He will be.'

'There's a new detective sergeant, just started. He's spent the weekend with the Borrowdale files, so I'm hoping he might have some insight to contribute. A fresh eye is always a good thing.'

'Mm,' said Simmy.

'How did it go last night? Did they all show up?'

'Oh yes. It was quite good, really. Lots of mad ideas and people's names flying about. They'll fill you in when you see them. I don't think we arrived at a single convincing theory – just a lot of possibles. My dad had a dream about Mr and Mrs Steve – they're hikers you won't have heard about. And I dreamt that Julian Baxter was the Joker.'

'I seldom find that dreams are very helpful,' said Moxon.

Simmy laughed.

The rest of the morning was uneventful but busy with mundane tasks that were refreshingly mindless. Too much thinking about murder could not be healthy, after all. Let the men sort it out. The only woman in the case was a murder victim, she realised – unless you counted Mrs Steve. Simmy's own mother had remained detached from the start, which had probably been very wise. Even Lily was off to a sunny island.

With the nagging worry that some annoying person was planning to bring the whole thing to her door again, she decided to take the child and dog for a good long walk after lunch, leaving her phone firmly at home. Bonnie would have called again if she needed her, and everyone else could wait. At least her mother would approve, even if some others might consider her irresponsible. After all, hadn't Jennifer Reade eschewed all such devices? But then, she had got herself murdered, so she might not be a very good role model.

They were out for over an hour, Robin getting some walking practice in a field close to the river where there were sheep and rocks and brambles, but also a few flat patches. Cornelia found herself tied to a blackthorn bush, which she judged to be most unfair and annoying.

'I can't trust you with the sheep,' Simmy explained. 'And I can't run after you if you get into trouble, because of Robin.'

'Huh!' sniffed the disgruntled dog.

When they got back, quite a lot had changed.

For a start, the house was full of men. Christopher, Ben, Moxon and a strange detective were gathered in the living room. Ben and Moxon were both on their phones. Christopher was distributing mugs of coffee. Everybody looked at the returning woman with her young charges and said nothing for several long seconds.

'Gosh, it's an invasion,' she said with a smile.

'Sorry,' said Moxon. 'It's not as bad as it looks.'

'They want to talk to Lily,' said Christopher.

'Better hurry, then. She's off on holiday tomorrow and has a very busy day today because of it. That accounts for all of you except Ben, I suppose.'

'Ben wants to do a bit of quiet googling. I told him he could do it here. He's got an idea, apparently.'

'That's right,' the boy confirmed. 'It came to me while I was eating my sandwich. But it probably isn't important.' He took his laptop into the kitchen without another word. Moxon and Smith took themselves off to find Lily, leaving a relatively peaceful scene.

'Dad phoned,' said Simmy. 'And Bonnie. We've been for a nice walk by the river.'

'Ben and I decided we didn't need to stay and answer the phone, when most people are contacting us via email. They know we'll tell them as soon as we've got a date to resume the sale, anyway. Mrs Deeping came to see me. She had something important to say.' And he reported the salient elements of the conversation. 'It seems a long time ago now. The day's going very slowly.'

'That about Mr Deeping should have moved things along. It confirms a lot of what we were already thinking.' She paused. 'That's good, isn't it? It's all starting to connect up much better than before.'

'The Smith chap was wondering whether Sir John's death was suspicious as well. I think that's what Ben's trying to find out on his computer. Nearly everything is now pointing at the cousin as far as motive is concerned. But there's still a few missing links.'

'Not to mention his very solid alibi.'

'He's got to have paid someone else to do it. Unless he's got a partner with equally urgent reasons for eliminating Jennifer Reade.'

'Surely the police will know if he has by now?'

Christopher snorted. 'They look to me to be all over the

place. Nobody's got the full picture. Two deaths in the same house on different days is too much for the poor things. No witnesses, not much forensic evidence. There's a third thing they need – oh yes, confession.'

'Well, they've nearly got that. Julian Baxter came pretty close to admitting he'd helped to kill Mr Deeping.'

'Which I expect counts as hearsay and is not therefore admissible. But Ben's hoping there's some footage from his photographer friend, which would be extremely helpful, if so.'

'Oh,' said Simmy. 'Do I get some coffee? Robin's going to want a nap. It wasn't easy to stop him dropping off in the buggy. He's done some excellent walking.'

'Good lad!' Christopher applauded. 'You take him up and I'll do the coffee.'

But when he joined Ben in the kitchen, some thought association arrested him. 'I forgot to pay Hughie!' he gasped. 'I never went for the cash, did I?'

'Didn't you?'

'You know I didn't – when would I have had a chance? He's probably there now, waiting for me. I don't remember what he said, exactly. But I think he was coming back for it after lunch.'

'Surely he'd phone you?'

'Why would he have my number? I don't give it out to temps.'

'Oh, right.' Ben was fingering his keyboard and scanning pages on the screen. 'I've got absolutely nowhere,' he complained. 'Nothing we didn't know already.'

'Look, I'll have to go back to Keswick. I would anyway, to take you home, but a bit sooner than planned.

I feel awful – poor Hughie. I owe him about five hundred quid.'

'Serves him right for demanding it in cash.'

'He gave me a good reason. Something about not having a bank account because of all the travelling he'd been doing. Sounded sensible to me. Reminded me of myself twenty years ago.'

Ben looked up. 'How could he actually *do* any travelling without a bank account?'

'Post offices, and those places that transfer money. Western Union. He's probably got a rich daddy who sent it out to him once a week.'

'Hm,' said Ben sceptically. 'We don't know anything about him, do we? Working for us for two weeks or more and he's never said where he's from or what family he's got. Just rabbited on about that precious motorbike.'

'Typical Brit, then. He did the work and I have to pay him for it.'

'It'll be after three by the time you get there. Is he going to wait all this time?'

'Wouldn't you?'

'We locked the gate. He'll have to sit outside doing nothing.'

'I know and it's all my fault. Come on. I'm going in one minute.'

Ben closed his laptop and stood up. 'Ready,' he said, gently slapping his pocket to ensure that his phone was in its rightful place.

Giving Simmy a brief explanation as he rushed through the living room followed by Ben, Christopher was driving up to Patterdale and Dockray in no time.

'This road goes on forever,' he grumbled as they headed north to the A66.

'Why did we come back to Hartsop anyway?' Ben wondered. 'It was a bit silly, really.'

'Moxon,' said Christopher shortly.

'Who's going to wonder where we've gone. He was a long time talking to Lily, wasn't he?'

'They've probably gone back to Penrith by now. I didn't expect them to come back to us – did you?'

'I didn't think about it. Lucky old Lily, off on holiday. Bonnie and I aren't going to get away at all this summer.'

'You live in one of the top holiday destinations in the world, so don't complain.' Christopher had often said this and Ben was never very impressed.

'Why did Jennifer want the sale stopped? Why did she kill Deeping? How far back does all this counterfeiting business go? Who knows who?' Ben was obsessively ticking off the recurring questions. 'Don't you think it feels like one great sprawling network, where they *all* knew each other? Deeping did the fakes, sent them off to Asia, as well as Wiltshire, where Warwick Bennett and Maurice Phillippson disposed of them at a good profit. Bennett being more or less related to Jennifer implies that she was involved. Plus Julian Baxter, of course.'

'Who's the only one any of us has actually met,' Christopher pointed out. 'Except Simmy has seen the Bennett man. And we've all listened to the infernal Steve and his missus.'

'Right. Not that I can see how that matters much. Maybe Deeping was double-crossing Jennifer and Julian somehow. That would explain why they killed him. And,' he held up an excited finger, 'what if old Sir John was in on it? He might have had some originals in the house, for Deeping to copy. They might have been using his cellar to do it in for ages.'

'Doesn't work,' said Christopher. 'You're implying that Jennifer already knew about her wealthy old fourth cousin before he died. She didn't. She was thunderstruck when they found her and told her.'

'Or so she pretended,' said Ben in a melodramatic voice. 'The whole thing might have been staged. In which case they probably did bump the old man off.'

'Lord help us,' Christopher groaned. 'And all this began as such a splendid opportunity. Remember that – how excited we were? Seems ages ago now.'

'It leaves a lot of unanswered questions.'

'Yes – you listed them just now.'

'That was only the half of them.'

They were finally on the main road, rushing westwards to Keswick as fast as the holiday dawdlers would allow.

'What if he isn't there?' Ben asked.

'He will be,' said Christopher.

'Funny how he fits in as well,' Ben mused. 'Not having a bank account, wanting everything in cash. Like Jennifer Reade. How unusual is that?'

'Not very. You've seen how many people pay for their purchases in cash after the auction.'

'Okay, but that's mostly to dodge tax and paper trails.' He did a double take. 'Hey! What if that's what was driving Jennifer Reade as well? What if she was living a perfectly normal life most of the time, but just kept all the counterfeiting business off the grid?'

'Stop it, Ben,' said his boss wearily. 'You're hurting my head – again.'

But Ben couldn't stop. 'Could be *she* was the one doing the double-crossing – cheating the Bennett man out of his rightful inheritance? Once she'd got the proceeds from the sale of the house and contents, there wouldn't have been much he could do about it – probably. She'd make sure the contracts and everything were watertight. I bet she intended to turn the whole lot into cash and hide it somewhere. Like the Wild West when they kept burying hoards of gold. It'd work, I should think, with a bit of judicious money laundering. I must write all this down before I forget. There's so much to keep in mind.'

'We'll be there in a minute. Please stop talking.'

'You were right, look. There's Hughie.'

The unpaid worker was indeed sitting on the ground beside his motorcycle, just outside the saleroom gates.

'Looks as if he's been there a while. Lucky it's not raining,' said Christopher.

'You still haven't got any cash for him,' Ben pointed out.

'Oh, God! Well, there's a machine a couple of minutes away. He can come to it with me.'

'It won't give you five hundred quid. You'll have to go into a bank – if you can find one. There's a Barclays that's closest.'

'No, it has to be Lloyds. This is ridiculous,' Christopher exploded. 'I'll have to put it through the books properly, and get him to sign for it. Look – you go in with him and wait for me. Keep him happy, okay?'

Hughie's expression manifested reproach, martyrdom and impatience in equal measure. Christopher gave a brief and limp explanation and drove off to the centre of Keswick after handing Ben the keys to the saleroom.

'We won't need to go in,' said Ben to Hughie. 'Will we?'

The young man shrugged. 'Up to you,' he said.

'You can't really blame Christopher. The police were here this morning, after you'd all gone. We had to take them all the way back to Hartsop – and then we remembered about you. We came dashing back when we realised you didn't have Christopher's mobile number. And we didn't have yours, obviously.'

'I never give it to anyone anyway.'

'At least you've got one. Not like some people.'

'Why did you need to take the police to Hartsop?'

'Good question. I don't think we did, really. It just seemed good to be helpful and Chris wanted to get home for a bit. He's still pretty wobbly after Friday's fiasco. He doesn't know where things stand with the auction, and people keep clamouring at him. Then all that with Mrs Deeping first thing today. He doesn't know where it's all going to end.'

'They should never have stopped the sale going ahead. That was totally out of order. It wouldn't have made any difference in the long run.'

Ben cocked his head. 'How do you mean?'

'Well, the inheritance wasn't going to change, was it? The three-times-removed-cousin or whatever he is gets it all, regardless. It has to be sold sooner or later – why not make it sooner?'

It was always tricky to keep track of who knew what, and Ben had had a lot to think about, formulating theories as he went. But had anybody other than Moxon known about Jennifer's relative, who wasn't even a cousin? And had Moxon told anybody but the Hendersons? It seemed unlikely. Even the friendly detective inspector had more sense than to reveal details of the investigation to people like Hughie – who had a surprising grasp of the relationship. The police had not actually interviewed any of the saleroom staff other than Christopher, although they had taken the fingerprints of everyone who had collected items from High Gates, as part of the forensic work. That was on Friday afternoon, before they'd all been sent home.

Hughie had only been to Borrowdale a few times on auction house business. Hughie had known where Sir John's pixie had been sitting days earlier. Hughie had a very handy motorbike that could take him down the little lanes without attracting notice, unidentifiable in his helmet. Hughie had been to India, where Warwick Bennett had been living for years.

'Don't know,' Ben said vaguely to Hughie's question. 'I guess they had their reasons.'

He had to act normal, and give no hint of where his thoughts were tending. Clues were flying at him from all directions, coagulating into something stronger than a theory, making him breathless. Then he took a calculated risk.

'Somebody said they'd found an old printing press in the cellar at High Gates,' he said. 'Pity we didn't know about that – could have fetched a pretty penny in the auction.'

There was no reaction other than a shrug. 'Must have been well hidden. Jack swears he scoured every inch of the entire house on that last day.'

Ben wavered. Was *Jack* the person he should be focused

on? Was his thinking completely askew?

Then Christopher came back, with an envelope full of cash. Hughie almost snatched it from him and hurried out to his bike.

'Thanks for the work!' he called over his shoulder. 'Good luck with everything.'

We shouldn't let him go, thought Ben desperately.

Christopher was still looking at the space between his fingers where the envelope had been. 'I was thinking of what you said earlier today, about Hughie.'

'Yes!' shouted Ben. 'Yes! It must have been him. We've got to stop him.'

But Hughie was away on his motorbike before they left the car park. 'We'll never catch him,' said Christopher. 'Besides – we've probably got it all wrong.'

'I don't think so,' said Ben, running through all that he'd been thinking in the past minutes. 'It fits too well. Hadn't he even said something about being in India?'

'We'll never catch him,' repeated Christopher. 'And we'd probably never be able to prove anything.'

Ben had his phone in his hand. 'I'm calling DS Price. You call Simmy or Bonnie or someone. We have to tell them all.' But he paused. 'Where would he go now? You must have an address for him. He doesn't know we've rumbled him. We can still get him if we're clever.'

'Um . . .' said Christopher. 'Let's have a look and see what I've got on the computer. He did give an address, I think.'

It took more minutes than Ben could easily endure for Christopher to locate the right file. 'It says "555 Axminster Street, London N9 9GG". Does that sound right?'

'Of course it doesn't,' snarled Ben. 'He just made something up. He'll be camping out somewhere, or on a caravan park, completely anonymous.'

Christopher snarled back. 'I'm sick of people lying to me. It's not unreasonable, surely, to take them at face value – is it? And yet with every passing day I'm realising I can hardly believe a word anybody has said. It's hopeless.'

'Never mind now. We have to get everyone out there looking for him.'

'Problems, boss?' came a voice from the small lobby outside the office. 'What's all the to-do?'

'Jack?' Christopher spun round. 'I thought you'd gone. The gate was locked.'

The small man brandished a set of keys. 'I told you I'd be staying to do a bit of tidying. But I thought you'd want people kept out, so I locked myself in.'

'Didn't you see Hughie out there?' demanded Ben.

Jack's face changed. 'Had some words with him. Told him it was none of my business whether he got paid or not and he could just wait out there. Should have heard the language.'

He shook his head in disgust. 'He might be clever with his CCTV and so forth, but he's not nice, for all that. None of us is going to miss him.'

'Do you know where he lives?' asked Ben urgently.

Jack shook his head. 'Can't be far, though.'

'Why do you say that?'

'He's always popping back for some reason or other. So quick, you two never even noticed. Strikes me he's got another job on the go, something shifty, shouldn't wonder.'

Christopher's head went up. 'He's not been nicking stuff from here, has he?'

Jack grimaced. 'No chance. He's too clever for that – see how he found that woman who took the vase. It's more like computer stuff, or drones and whatnot. Ask Kitty – she's the one he talks to about it. Too deep for me, it is.' His expression went vague. 'Don't know what the world's coming to.'

'So – what do we do now?' Christopher asked Ben.

'Find him.'

'How?'

'We'll have to persuade the police. They might track his phone if they're convinced he's a killer.'

Jack's eyes bulged. 'Killer? You think it was him? No!'

'Why not?'

'Well – we'd *know*. I mean . . .' He tailed off, remembering earlier episodes where he'd been unknowingly close to a murderer. 'So get onto the police, why don't you,' he finished with a sigh. Then his face lightened. 'If it helps, I've got the number.'

'What number?' asked Ben.

'The bike.' And he recited the registration plate. 'I've got a habit of remembering them.'

'It helps,' said Ben, who repeated it, committing it to memory. 'It helps a lot. Thanks, Jack.'

'What a thing, though. I'm off home now. That's enough for me.'

'Okay, Jack. I'll let you know what happens,' said Christopher, watching his faithful employee shamble off like a much older man.

Ben had his phone to his ear. 'This is Ben Harkness, with

302

reference to the murder of Jennifer Reade. Let me speak to Detective Superintendent Price,' he said, a moment later. 'No – it really does have to be him . . . Thank you.' He addressed Christopher. 'They're trying to put me through . . . Oh! DS Price?' He proceeded to give a concise account of the past ten minutes, repeating the motorbike's make and number plate and concluding, 'We're sure it was him. Everything fits. Do you see? We need to find him quickly. He'll be off and away somewhere any time now.'

He disconnected the call twenty seconds later. 'I'm not sure he believed me,' he said, 'but at least he listened.'

'So what now?' asked Christopher again, sounding annoyingly helpless to Ben.

'We should be out there looking for him. The bike's probably sitting outside wherever it is he's living. It might only be a couple of streets away.'

'Isn't that a bit futile? Shouldn't we try to be cleverer than that?'

'How? We've got nothing concrete to go on. He's the clever one. Did Jack say *drones*? How in the world do they come into it?'

'The police are bound to catch him,' said Christopher. 'I just want to go home.'

'You're as bad as Jack,' scorned Ben. 'Just humour me, and drive round the streets for a bit first, and then take me home. I'm going to need my car.'

Driving round the streets turned out to be as futile as Christopher had predicted. Keswick was thronged with tourists and the resulting traffic, even on the outskirts. Anyone on a motorbike was at a big advantage.

'Where would he *go*?' Ben kept asking. 'We don't know enough about him to make any proper guesses.'

'Back to High Gates?' hazarded Christopher.

Ben's initial instinct was to dismiss this idea, but then he thought again. 'If he really is a wizard with cameras and stuff, he might possibly have left something up there – maybe. If he did kill Jennifer, he might have been watching her movements somehow – and a hidden camera would make the best sense. Since then, there's been a constant police presence, so he wouldn't have been able to get it back. Do you think?'

'Surely he'd have taken it with him after he killed her? Why leave it there?'

'Right. Yes. Of course. Although – maybe he didn't have time to move it.'

'The police would have found it, surely, if it was still there?'

'Not necessarily. They can be pretty small. Easy to hide.' A connection took place in his suddenly active mind. 'That Peter bloke! He might still be there. Anyway, I've got his details. I bet he's involved, after all. Cameras . . . on the spot . . . acting all innocent. We can go and look for him.'

'Not me, Ben. It's all too Keystone Cops for my liking. And your photographer man's sure to have gone by now.'

'If it was Hughie, there'll be some of his DNA on Jennifer's body, I bet you. Or some of her blood on his clothes. If he was confident that he'd never be suspected, he might not have tried too hard to clean everything up after himself.'

'Yes,' said Christopher wearily. 'I expect that's right.'

'Although a defence would argue that he'd been to High

304

Gates as part of his job, so his DNA being there wouldn't come as a surprise and didn't prove anything. Even on her body, they could argue it was from lying on the floor and picking up one of his hairs, or something.'

'Please stop, Ben,' begged Christopher, as everybody had done in their turn. 'Go and say all this to the police. You can walk from here, can't you? I'm going home.'

Chapter Twenty-Five

It was one of DI Moxon's finest hours. He had volunteered to tail Warwick Bennett, in the finest *Spooks* fashion, from early on Monday morning. The man had found himself a small room in a somewhat raffish B&B and given the police the address.

'Just for the record, sir, you understand,' they said to him. He made no objection, claiming to want to stay around for the auction of the High Gates contents, when it finally took place.

'All the same, he's still the one we're most interested in,' said DS Price. 'There's some game going on and it's not over yet.'

Moxon's early-morning offer to engage in active surveillance was received with good humour.

'Go on, then,' said Price. 'See how long it is before he spots you. It'd be better if it was one of the lads he's never met, don't you think?'

'Probably. But I can be very unobtrusive, sir.'

Price smiled. 'I'm sure you can. Just don't go dark on us – keep us posted of all your movements, right?'

It was not yet nine o'clock when Moxon witnessed

the arrival of a small car outside the B&B, containing a single unidentified male who sat and spoke on a phone. Three minutes later, Bennett emerged and got into the car. It did not drive off, but proved to be the scene of an obvious altercation. Arms were waved, and heads jerked angrily back and forth. Then Bennett got out and went back into the house. Moxon experienced a dilemma. It was clearly crucial to identify and question the man in the car, but he could hardly do it right under Bennett's nose. If he followed the car, he might lose his original quarry.

Luckily, the car drove a scant hundred yards away before pulling into the side of another road where there was a single yellow line.

'Better not sit there for long,' muttered Moxon, conscious of the unrelenting parking rules. He pulled up behind it and got out.

'Sir?' he began. 'Could I speak to you for a moment?'

The man – youngish, handsome in an ordinary sort of way – gave him a horrified look. 'Good God – are you police?' he blurted.

'Actually, yes,' Moxon admitted. 'It's about Mr Bennett.'

'I *know* it was him. I just don't understand *how*. I shouldn't have tackled him, but I thought I'd be safe out in the street. He wanted to hit me, but he had more sense.'

'We should go somewhere and talk properly. Could I have your name, sir?'

'I'm Julian Baxter. Jennifer Reade was my friend. My very *close* friend.'

'Ah!' said DI Moxon.

'And I fully realise that I'm wanted for questioning and

am a person of interest and all that guff. That's why I've been keeping out of your way.'

'I need to keep Mr Bennett under surveillance. Could we use this car?'

'Don't worry. He's not going anywhere for an hour or so. He was just starting a full English breakfast and wanted to get back to it. He's keeping the landlady sweet for another few days, apparently.'

'Did he tell you that?'

'More or less. Said I was rocking his boat for no good reason, and to get the hell out of his face, and shut my mouth and get lost. That sort of thing. So now you'll have to arrest me, I suppose.'

'Will I? Why?'

'I figured you'd got me down as Suspect Number One, seeing that Cousin Bennett has an alibi and there's not really anybody else.'

'Mrs Henderson rather liked you,' said Moxon slowly. 'For the moment, that's good enough for me.'

Baxter smiled. 'She's a nice lady, isn't she? So – what, then?'

'You can help me. Give me your phone number and I'll give you mine. And give me your assurance that you won't go missing again. Essentially, there's only one credible theory and it involves Mr Bennett to the point where we don't want to lose sight of him.'

'Sounds a bit flimsy.'

'It is *extremely* flimsy,' Moxon agreed. 'But it's all we've got.'

The *Spooks* paradigm turned out to be impossible to emulate. Moxon was diverted to the auction house and

308

then Hartsop, but was back with Baxter by mid-afternoon. The two of them spent the next hour making a surprisingly successful job of maintaining contact with Warwick Bennett. They followed him, in their two cars, from the B&B to the main car park in Keswick, which only had two spaces left. Moxon pulled rank and left his in the street with a discreet police badge that traffic wardens were trained to recognise. Just as the two of them were trailing Bennett into the main street, Moxon's phone jingled.

It was Ben Harkness. Moxon answered it, because he judged that he would appear less conspicuous if he was engaged in a phone conversation. Ben explained, with some difficulty, that the identity of the killer had been established with little room for doubt, and now there was a search underway for a certain Hugh Jamieson, riding a motorcycle. DS Price was aware and was examining evidence.

'We have to catch him,' urged Ben.

At the end of the Keswick street was an open area, close to the river and the pencil museum. Bennett was hurrying towards it, with Baxter close behind. Moxon had slowed down, as he tried to make sense of Ben's outpouring, and he watched events unfolding from a distance of twenty yards.

'Is it a big bike, with a lot of red on it? Registration looks like CV55 something something.' He added the location for good measure. Never before had his training kicked in so automatically. He hadn't even had to think.

'My God!' choked Ben. 'Is it there, right in front of you?'

'Ridden by a young man, by the look of him. Broad shoulders. Blue jeans.'

'Catch him!' yelled Ben. 'Whatever you do, don't let him go.'

'He's speaking to Warwick Bennett, on the corner of the pavement. I've got Mr Baxter with me. I can't just apprehend him – them. And we've left the cars three minutes away. Where are you?'

'Get backup, man,' screamed Ben. 'Those are your killers, right in front of you. *Do* something.'

'I will,' said Moxon stoutly. 'But you can help – get onto Price for me. I'll call him as well in a minute, but every second's going to make a difference.' He ended the call, feeling both brave and foolish, and immediately rang Baxter, clearly hearing the ring tone over the short distance between them. 'That's the likely killer,' he said softly. 'On the motorbike. We've got to try and catch them both. Or keep them there until backup arrives. It could be a while.'

'Oh joy!' breathed Baxter. 'Just you watch me.'

'Wait!' Moxon cried. His training definitely included something about not allowing members of the public to put themselves in danger's way.

'I'll take the biker; you grab Bennett.'

Bennett had perhaps heard Moxon's cry, but his attention was entirely on Hughie. When Julian Baxter calmly walked up and climbed onto the pillion seat of the bike, everyone was paralysed for fifteen seconds. Hughie then turned and tried to push him off. Baxter wrapped his arms around Hughie and held on tight. The bike wobbled.

'Mr Bennett, I have to tell you you're under arrest,' said Moxon, equally calmly. His tone was almost friendly. Inside he was wondering just how the thing could possibly be achieved. Where was he going to take his man? And how long could Baxter hang onto Hughie? He had no handcuffs or taser with him. He was not a fast runner.

'What's happening here?' came a voice. Four heads turned to look at a large man with a beautiful Alsatian dog, standing three feet away.

'I'm a police officer,' gasped Moxon, wondering if he'd slipped into another reality without noticing. 'These men are under arrest.'

'All of them?'

'Not me,' said Julian Baxter.

'Is that dog trained in police work?' asked Moxon optimistically.

'No, but she's always up for a good game. I wouldn't advise anybody trying to outrun her, for a start.'

Hughie was behaving oddly, letting the heavy bike slide sideways, and cringing away from the dog.

'Watch out,' warned Baxter. 'It'll fall on your leg.' He was leaning the other way, trying to correct the balance.

'Keep hold of that animal,' choked Hughie. 'Don't let it get me.'

Encouraged by this obvious phobia, the dog's owner moved forward, slackening his hold on the lead. The Alsatian willingly co-operated, moving to within inches of the terrified Hughie, who screamed.

Bennett had every opportunity to make a dash for freedom, but did not avail himself. Moxon remembered his role and took firm hold of the man's arm.

'Thanks,' he said to the owner of the dog. 'This is very helpful.'

Hughie's bike finally capitulated to gravity and fell onto his ankle with a crash. A second scream emerged. Baxter jumped clear and gave a little dance of triumph. A small crowd was gathering to watch the entertainment.

'I'm supposed to be calling my senior officer,' Moxon remembered.

'No need, by the looks of it,' said the man with the dog, ducking his chin at an oncoming police car, sirens blaring.

And it was all over in moments after that. Moxon and Baxter returned to their vehicles and the whole assemblage returned to Penrith. It took the rest of the day for the story to be completed, understood and acted upon.

Epilogue

Simmy and Christopher had firmly rejected Ben's request that he and Bonnie come over for a debriefing, later that week.

'There really isn't any more to be said,' insisted Christopher. 'All we want now is a bit of peace and quiet.'

But he knew this wasn't true. Simmy wanted answers and explanations, as did Russell. Moxon himself was sufficiently unprofessional to demand an admiring audience, too. They listened to him as he described the conclusions reached by the police investigation.

'Jamieson knew Bennett in India, and was hired by him to establish the facts about Jennifer Reade regarding her inheritance and intentions for the house. No notion of killing her at that point. The counterfeiting business had been going on for years – Sir John and Deeping were in it together and had been using Bennett as one of several outlets for their product across the world. When Sir John died – of natural causes – Deeping insisted he could carry on, with Bennett the new owner of the house. But they had reckoned without Jennifer Reade. They had no idea she existed. She and Baxter were simple folk, living an old-fashioned life in Swindon – they were fiercely opposed to the digital age, and had engaged in a few fights over it.'

'But if Bennett assumed he was the only heir, wouldn't he have presented himself right away, when the old man died?' asked Christopher. 'Instead, he sat quietly and let Jennifer think she was the one.'

'He had to tread very carefully, because of the counterfeiting,' explained Moxon. 'He got Hughie to track the whole thing in minute detail. Getting him onto your payroll was a stroke of genius. He had access to absolutely everything. He had a natural gift for making himself useful, as you'll have discovered.'

'Making a real patsy out of me,' moaned Christopher. 'Just as Jennifer Reade did.'

'It's no crime to be trusting,' Moxon consoled him.

'More like gullible, naive and brainless. I can't believe I was such a fool.'

Simmy patted his hand. 'Anyone else would have been the same,' she assured him.

Moxon went on. 'So, when Jennifer and Julian decided they ought to go for one quick look at the house, that's when it all went wrong. They walked in on Deeping churning out his fakes in the sealed-off corner of the cellar, and he tried to put up a fight. Baxter says it was self-defence when Jennifer pushed him down the steps – but then she bashed him on the head to finish him off, which really can't be justified.'

'No,' said Simmy and Christopher in unison. Christopher then added, 'But it must have been incredibly well hidden. We'd just spent two weeks clearing the place. What did Deeping do during that time?'

'Stayed clear, presumably. Baxter thinks he was madly

catching up on lost time when they caught him, which made him careless. That was the Monday, before you showed up on the Wednesday. And yes, it was very well hidden. A false wall with a door you'd never dream was there unless you were really looking for it.'

'So why didn't they hide his body in there?' asked Simmy. 'It might never have been found.'

'We wondered about that, but we think they meant to remove the press and sell it. It's worth thousands, apparently. It looks as if they thought it best just to leave the body where it was for a day or two, and go back at night and dispose of it in the river. The house and contents would be sold and the proceeds safely in the bank. The new people might not start work for ages.'

'But she deliberately drew my attention to it,' Christopher reminded him.

'Yes, because Julian had been losing his nerve in the meantime and told her he'd have to report it. It was too much for him to cope with. He says he was on the brink of persuading her by the Wednesday, and she'd gone back to the house to try and make it look more like a total accident. You being there wrecked the plan, so she quickly invented another one.'

'A very silly one,' said Simmy.

'Maybe. The thing is, the auction had to carry on. Julian had agreed to that. And he thinks Jennifer panicked at the thought that some of your people might yet find reasons to go back to the house. She had to get rid of Deeping's body, but it was too big and heavy to move.'

'So they dumped him in the river.'

'Exactly.'

'Did you find that photographer? Did he have it on film?'

Moxon shook his head. 'No need, with Baxter's testimony. He's come clean about the whole thing. He'll get five years for it, in all likelihood.'

'That's a shame,' said Simmy.

'Nothing to what the others are going to have to serve.'

'Did Hughie confess everything as well?' asked Christopher.

'He did not. He denies the whole thing. But Bennett's not so tough. We've got them connected in India, with some highly incriminating text messages on their phones. We've got that motorbike on cameras, luckily enough. And we've got Jennifer's words.'

'"Stop the sale",' said Christopher.

'Right. The only reason she would say that is to prevent Bennett from profiting. Which strongly implies that Hughie told her who he was and why he'd been sent to kill her. She most likely wasn't asleep at all when he bashed her. That's what a prosecutor would assert, anyway.'

'And a defence would challenge it as supposition, or whatever,' said Christopher.

'But *why* kill her?' asked Simmy. 'Am I being very dim, not being able to understand that?'

'Simply to remove her from the inheritance, surely?' said Christopher. 'That's what we assumed all along.'

Moxon beamed an all-knowing smile at them. 'That, yes. But also because Bennett and Hughie Jamieson had a lot else to lose.' His pause was intended to be dramatic, but his listeners were past being impressed. 'Well, you'd be amazed what can be learnt from reading unguarded texts. It turns out that the two of them were planning to get married – and no way could they do that in India at the moment.'

'Ah!' sighed Simmy. 'I suppose that explains it all, then.'

'It does when you think about it,' Christopher agreed.

The auction was resumed two weeks later. 'At least I got a good watering can out of it,' said Russell.

'And we all learnt the definition of "incunabula",' added Angie.

'And I won't believe a word anybody tells me ever again,' sighed Christopher.

'But poor Jennifer Reade,' said Simmy. 'Poor, poor Jennifer Reade.'